The Lion Lover

Doctor Mathilde Valentine and Baron Olensky walked away from the compound and along the palm-fringed white-sand beach. 'Doctor Valentine. I must warn you,' he said, 'you are in danger. I believe there is a white slave trade operating out of Mombasa. The missionary is involved. Women have disappeared.'

'But that's absurd,' she replied. 'This is the twentieth century. Things like that don't happen any more. Do they?'

The Lion Lover
Mercedes Kelly

BLACK LACE

Black Lace books contain sexual fantasies.
In real life, always practise safe sex.

This edition published in 2003 by
Black Lace
Thames Wharf Studios
Rainville Road
London W6 9HA

Originally published 1997

Copyright © Mercedes Kelly 1997

The right of Mercedes Kelly to be identified as the Author of
the Work has been asserted in accordance with the Copyright,
Designs and Patents Act 1988.

Printed and bound by Mackays of Chatham PLC

ISBN 0 352 33162 3

Prologue

Canaries sang sweetly in the gilded cages hanging from tiled balconies overlooking the central hall. The floor was an intricate pattern of copper, lapis and ivory. Flowers grew in hanging baskets, throwing their strong perfume over the women below. Ferns grew in copper pots and waved in the cool breeze that filtered through the trellised walls.

The women were in various states of undress. Mostly they lounged on low silk-covered couches, or combed each other's hair and oiled their rounded limbs. Black-skinned, turbaned men stood by marble pillars, their voluminous trousers hiding their eunuch status. Modestly attired girls, in short silk togas, strummed stringed instruments that made delicate music similar to the soothing sound of the many small fountains that decorated the massive hall.

There were around a hundred girls and women in this harem, ranging in age from twelve to 40 and in colour from white, yellow or amber to roast coffee brown and blue-black. Some had never seen their master, the Sultan of Abizir. These virgins were dressed in diaphanous silk shifts in every hue, which were draped around their lissom bodies, exposing their breasts or hip bones and accentuating their erogenous zones. One lovely creature, perhaps eighteen years old and of Caribbean origin, wore a white garment which covered her completely, from her square, athletic shoulders to her narrow, brown ankles. Only her belly and sex were exposed, her shaved sex shining through the hole carefully cut into the diaphanous stuff. Her face was hidden behind a veil of white. Her eyes, black and velvety, glinted above the white.

Some of the concubines had only seen the sultan once in their period of servitude. These lucky creatures wore gold collars, and their ankles were encircled with gold chains. Their bodies were unencumbered by clothes. They still talked excitedly and proudly of the one night they had spent with the sultan.

Some saw him regularly. These women kept apart from the others, like a freemasonry of concubines. They were naked except for gold and diamond collars and gold anklets. They did not talk or laugh together; they were subdued, their quiet eyes lowered.

Within this group were two white women sitting together. One was a dark-haired Scottish beauty, with very fair skin, narrow hips and small breasts. The other was older, large breasted and pretty in a very English way, with light brown wavy hair tied back in an elaborate knot. They both looked weary and low spirited. They sat apart from all the others on a leather couch.

At that moment two young slave-girls approached them. Pulling them to their feet, they took the two women to the cleaning pool and bathed them. Then they placed them on low couches where they massaged their bodies with herbal oils and dried them with silk.

'I am so tired. Please hurry with my toilet so I may go to sleep,' said Janet McKinnon.

'My bottom is still sore. Can't you do something for

me?' asked the dark-haired woman, who was called Rosemary.

Her slave-girl, a Nubian adolescent with black hair fashioned in tiny plaits close to her head and her neck encircled by a series of thin silver rings which stretched her neck and made her head stand proud, clicked her teeth and looked again at the sorely whipped buttocks.

'I can give you more salve, if you like,' she said.

'Please do. It hurts,' said Rosemary McKinnon.

The slave-girl moved away silently, her slender hips swaying above her long, slim legs, the silver chains on her ankles tinkling like bells. Her only other garment was a thin piece of silk hanging from a silver hip chain to hide her pubis.

'What a pretty creature!' said Janet, watching the slave-girl and admiring her natural grace. 'The sultan certainly has good taste.'

Her handmaiden – a good-natured, plump West African – laughed loudly and massaged the tired shoulders of the English concubine.

'It is said that the sultan has a taste for white women now,' she said.

'Well, it is nice to be appreciated, I suppose,' said the Englishwoman philosophically.

Janet was still tender from the thorough fucking she had been subjected to at the hands of the demanding Sultan of Abizir. She was not allowed to be seen enjoying the procedure – she had to pretend to hate his sexual attentions. He had had so many women, he needed the extra thrill of a scenario of enforced sex. So Janet, a skilful lover with years of experience in the art of seduction, gave him what he wanted, knowing that she would continue to be a favourite while she did.

'How long have we been here?' asked Rosemary suddenly, whose slave-girl had returned with the salve and was gently applying it to her red buttocks.

'Well, I've been here for two years. You are the new girl, really, darling,' said Janet.

'Will we ever get away?' demanded the sorrowful Rosemary.

Janet slipped away from the administrations of her slave-girl and sat next to Rosemary.

'You poor darling! You will get used to it, I assure you. And there are compensations, after all. Just think! Never again will you have to clean or cook; never again will you have to shop for food or wash a man's socks. We have total freedom within these walls to play, enjoy ourselves and gossip, and to have sex with the sultan – who, after all, is not unattractive – and each other. It is a lot better than what I had to put up with from Charles, I can tell you. He was such a peculiar man. I don't think I would go back to him even if I could.'

'Well, I want to be free. I hate it here. It's so boring! And I loathe that gross brother of the sultan's. I wish he would leave me alone,' the younger woman sobbed.

'Poor darling, don't cry.' Janet put an arm around Rosemary and stroked her thick, dark hair. Her hand strayed to her narrow hips and the gentle rise of her sorely beaten buttocks. She caressed the rounded curves and slipped a hand between the slender thighs.

'You are so lovely, my dear, like a pretty boy, really. Perhaps we should cut your hair short and disguise you as a lad – then maybe you could escape.' Rosemary moved her legs apart to allow Janet further access.

'That isn't such a bad idea, you know,' Rosemary said. She rested her heavy head of hair on her arms and gave in to the voluptuous feelings that overtook her as Janet's fingers probed and stroked between her legs. 'Oh, that's so nice, just there. Mmm! Mmm!'

Janet lay down next to the younger woman on the leather couch, her head close to Rosemary's feet, her feet next to Rosemary's head. She gently manoeuvred Rosemary over on to her side so she could reach down and

4

press on her shaved pubis with the palm of her hand. Their two slave-girls sat together on the other couch, watching the white concubines. The Nubian girl idly stroked the plump breasts of the other.

Janet McKinnon had indeed been incarcerated in the harem of the Sultan of Abizir for nearly 24 months. She was a favourite with the sultan, who was getting on in years and needed more and more novelty to keep him satisfied. He was still a handsome man, tall and straight backed, with a big hooked nose, fleshy lips and a long, lascivious tongue. His cock was rather battered from many battles of love and lust, but it was long and thick and gave much satisfaction to his favourites. He usually enjoyed masturbation, administered by his concubines, above all else, which was sometimes rather frustrating for the healthy females who serviced him. So more often than not, they were driven to pleasure each other. Unfortunately, he had an older half-brother, who had been staying with him for a year, and the harem was also at his command. The Sultan of Jerah's girth was enormous. His fat belly was like a mountain of flabby flesh, under which his small penis poked like a puppy's, pink and wet. He had not seen his sexual organs, except in a mirror, for many years. Indeed, he had had specially distorted mirrors installed in his bedchamber so his organ looked bigger than it actually was.

The concubines had to please him or they were punished. If a concubine did not achieve ejaculation for him, she was beaten severely.

The Sultan of Abizir was a generous man, and what was his was his brother's. Therefore, he found it necessary to allow his obese relative the use of even his favourites – the two white concubines. Both women had serviced Jerry, as they called him, in recent days, but he preferred the younger, fair-skinned beauty, Rosemary. Her weals and bruises had been caused by his less than

5

tender attentions, and she was not experienced enough to turn his mind to other pleasures.

Janet continued caressing the slender Rosemary, feeling inside her folds of pink flesh, deep into her secret places. The young woman sighed with pleasure. Janet thought meanwhile of how she had been tricked and trapped into this harem. Her husband, a missionary, had insisted that she go off on safari without him, to have a 'well-deserved rest from her arduous duties as minister's wife at the beach mission'. She had agreed at once. She had wanted to go with Baron Olensky, the handsome Polish hunter who was enamoured of her already, but her husband had forbidden it. He had instead found another hunter – a German, Heinlich, to take her into the bush. She sighed as she thought how stupid she had been to trust her husband. She knew he was jealous of her innocent flirtations with the bourgeoisie of Mombasa, but he had already shown her that he was not really interested in her sexually. She had caught him once with a servant-boy, a muscular lad of about seventeen, in the servants' quarters. He hadn't even stopped when she entered the room, but looked disdainfully at her and said, 'You see how firm his buttocks are!' She had run away in disgust. Now she knew why he had only made love to her from behind.

Rosemary suddenly woke her from her reverie. 'Oh, that is really very nice, my dear. Do go a little further in, please, will you? Mmm!'

'You really are shaped like a boy, you know, Rosemary. Turn over so I may look at your little bottom.' Janet pushed the young woman over gently, and Rosemary let her indulge her fantasies, wriggling her buttocks and allowing Janet's fingers to slide between her bottom cleft and stroke the dark, puckered hole.

'What does he do to you?' asked Rosemary.

'Who?'

'Jerry,' said Rosemary.

'Masturbates over my buttocks, usually. Or gets another slave to do it for him. Yours are very pretty little buttocks.' Janet slapped them playfully with one hand while her other was otherwise occupied.

'Oh, I prefer your delicate touch to Jerry's any day.' Rosemary squirmed on her friend's fingers. She breathed heavily and her buttocks quivered and the muscles tightened suddenly as her whole body gave itself to the exquisite pleasure she was experiencing. 'Thank you, darling, that was lovely. Shall I do the same for you now?' She turned over, half sitting to kiss Janet.

'Not just yet, my dear, thank you. I did reach several climaxes with the Sultan of Abizir earlier. He does know how to give a woman satisfaction, I'll say that for him.'

'Unlike his fat slob of a brother! At least Charles gave us *some* pleasure!' said Rosemary, lying now on her own couch while her slave-girl rubbed her legs and buttocks with scented oils.

'Oh God, what a man! He sold us both.' said Janet. 'Charles liked other men, did you realise that?'

'Yes, I did know that,' said Rosemary.

'How did you find out?'

'Well, it was common knowledge, apparently. Of course, I was the last to know, being his wife. His second wife, that is. Someone told me, I can't remember who, and I didn't believe it. He had always seemed so manly, so Scottish, so ordinary in his demands.' Rosemary rearranged her pretty limbs and allowed the slave-girl to shave her already smooth pubis. 'He did always say I should have been a boy – he liked my flat hips and stomach and my tiny breasts.' She moved her hands to cover her breasts completely and she rubbed them gently, moulding the tender flesh under her palms. 'Of course, I was a complete innocent. I didn't know what was normal and what wasn't.'

'So what he do to you, exactly?'

'Oh, he always wanted me to bend over something so he could get at my bottom.'

'Do you mean he – '

'Oh yes, he always buggered me. Never anything else. But he liked to watch me masturbate. Said it was more fun than anything. I had to masturbate him too, of course, and suck his cock. Did you do that?'

'I did,' said the bemused Janet McKinnon. 'But he used to whip me quite severely on the breasts and belly if I tried to get him to penetrate my vagina. Did he do that to you?'

'No, I never even thought of it. He was the only man I had ever slept with. I didn't know what to expect, you see. I thought that buggery was the only way of having sex.'

They laughed.

'What fools we women are, when we love,' said Janet.

'Yes, and I suppose I wasn't even married to him legally. He was still married to you.'

'How did he explain my "demise"?' asked Janet.

'Oh, he was the darling of Edinburgh that season. His suntanned face was so tragic and wonderful! He said you had been eaten by a lion.'

'Huh!' Janet exploded with mirth. 'What a man!'

The slave-girl massaged more firmly between the thighs of Rosemary McKinnon, who opened her legs wider. Her voice got slower and quieter. 'Scottish society did nothing to prepare me for this sort of thing,' she said in her superior Edinburgh whisper.

Janet turned over for her special massage and said, 'If there were two more Mrs McKinnons here we could play bridge.'

They both giggled.

Later, the Sultan of Jerah called for several concubines – he had need of quantity rather than quality tonight. His choice was for five seventeen-year-old Abyssinnian girls.

One he had tied down naked; her legs and arms wide apart, her belly pressed over a narrow leather bench and her private parts painted red. Her buttocks jutted up obscenely so that her decorated sex was exposed beneath. The sultan stood with a whip a few feet from the bound concubine. He wore a female garment – a voluminous dress of finest silk. Under this he had a tightly fastened corset, laced behind and in front, so his enormous stomach was held in. His flesh was compressed and pushed upward, so he looked like he had breasts, bulging up in two moons over his dress. To complete the obscene travesty he wore red lipstick and black eye make-up. His fat cheeks were rouged and his eyes were like a pig's. His naked balls hung low and his little cock sat on them like a plum on two old leather cushions.

Two girls then approached him and stood on either side, lifting the skirt of his dress and fondling his balls and the base of his penis. Another girl lay beneath him on the floor, her head propped on silk pillows, and put her mouth around his cock. He flicked the long thin whip, trying it for size. As he moved, his immense buttocks shivered and his cock grew. The concubines sucked and played with his private parts. The fifth slave-girl stood behind the obese sultan, her tongue inside his anus. He whipped the upturned bottom, and the concubine cried out. Red stripes appeared on the dark skin and he whipped harder. The concubine's sex parts, raised and exposed to the gaze of all the others, grew fat and soft. As the bare flesh pulsated, juices flowed and glistened around her sex lips. Her anus was oiled by one of the standing slaves. The whip came down harder and harder on the bare buttocks and flicked her pink and swollen orifices. The sultan whipped more furiously, and the concubines pulled and pummelled, stroked and licked, sucked and fondled. The massive mound of flesh that was the Sultan of Jerah shuddered and trembled like a small earthquake. He cried out and came, his arc of sperm hitting the bound concubine's bottom and thighs.

Afterwards, the concubines played with each other in the pool. They stroked each other's little breasts and kissed lightly. They held each other's shaved pouches in the palms of their hands and rubbed hard. They inserted fingers into each other's hot vaginas and gave each other satisfying climaxes. Dildos were not allowed in the harem, but the inventive concubines found ways and means of satisfying themselves, hiding fruit and vegetables from their rations each day. Two of the concubines played with a large yellow courgette. They had washed and oiled it and one girl was pushing it into the open folds of the other's sex lips.

'Yes, that's it, push it right in, right the way, deeper, deeper,' the lucky concubine begged. She lifted her hips and buttocks and pressed her legs around her concubine lover, drawing her closer. Soon the yellow vegetable had almost disappeared inside the girl's soft flesh. Her eyes glazed and she clung to her lover's thighs, pressing her fingers inside her. The lover manipulated the courgette with admirable expertise, drawing it out slowly and pushing it in again, noting the blush of red on the other's chest and neck and the softness of her lips. Their orgasms were strong and they fell into each other's arms gratefully.

The bell tolled in the high tower. The Sultan of Jerah slept alone, his bottom raised high and naked on swan's down pillows, a long dildo inserted into his anus. As every hour struck, a different concubine appeared to twist the dildo and push it in and out of the sultan's anus 100 times. He slept soundly, only stirring if the dildo was not manipulated firmly enough or long enough as every hour struck. One second late and he would wake, and Allah help the concubine who caused the sultan to lose his beauty sleep!

Unlike the Sultan of Jerah, the Sultan of Abizir's cruelty was not inventive. He had simple needs. He liked to see female flesh redden. He liked to hear the cries of the women he whipped. It made him feel strong and powerful, like a sultan ought to feel. At the moment he had a preference for forced intercourse.

The white-robed beauty in his chamber still wore her veil. Her doe-shaped eyes, black and proud, stared at him insolently. She was held by chains to the marble pillar, her arms out wide, her legs apart. The gap in her garment showed her triangle of thighs and pubis. The pubic area had been shaved, as was the tradition. He gazed at this dark shadow of enticing flesh, her little round belly and Mount of Venus. He took out his cock from the folds of white cotton that draped his 50-year-old body. He was still proud of his manhood. It grew in his brown hand and the concubine's eyes watched it. He stroked her belly and pressed a firm thumb between her labia. She flinched. Then he tore her garment from her so that her belly and thighs were exposed completely. She cried out but he hissed a command and a turbaned eunuch tied a cloth around her face, covering her mouth tightly. He left her eyes uncovered, so she could watch her own violation.

He tore the gown from her small breasts and squeezed them tight in his cruel hands. He held his cock high and beat her belly and thighs with it before pushing into her. She was tight. A virgin. She cried out. At a sign, the eunuch once more moved forward and rubbed a scented oil on the girl's private parts. He did this quickly, his eyes averted from her body. The sultan made the eunuch smooth some of the oil on his swollen organ too. His cock stretched, like the neck of a strange beast, with one squinting eye on its helmet-shaped head.

The concubine was whimpering now, her eyes still open though hypnotised by the dark purple-red cock which threatened her. She tried to draw her sex lips

11

together by clenching her buttocks, but to no avail. The sultan liked this show of fear. He slapped her breasts lightly to see the nipples, pale as pink rosebuds, rise and harden. He bit them. Her eyes grew huge, the blacks of her pupils taking over the violet iris. The sultan smiled a cruel smile, his fleshy, red lips parting to reveal a set of white, even teeth. His black hair was swept back from his high forehead. He shoved into the young flesh, between the dark, silky thighs. She turned away her proud head as he slammed into her virgin sheath. Her forehead furrowed in a frown of pain. He came as soon as he saw the anguish on her face, then left her, panting and frightened, but knowing that she had missed out on something.

The introduction of white slaves to the harem was a relatively new innovation for the Sultan of Abizir. He particularly liked the smell of these European women. They smelt of butter and apples. Their hair was fragrant. He particularly liked blonde hair. He had had so many dark-haired beauties in his life.

Next morning, he called for his favourite – Janet of the pale breasts. She was indisposed, the eunuch told him. He bellowed in rage and frustration. 'Then bring me the new one – the skinny one.'

'I cannot, sir, I beg your pardon.' The eunuch knelt on the floor, his head on the floor.

'Cannot? Why, cannot?'

'She is with your brother, my lord.'

'Ugh! But I need a white woman,' he cried. He thought for a moment. 'Send the slave trader to me,' he said. The eunuch nodded and left the room.

Moments later, the slave trader appeared.

'I want more blondes,' he commanded.

'Yes, your excellency,' said the slave trader. 'I will see what I can do.'

'Quickly!' the sultan shouted.

12

The Arab bowed low and withdrew from the sultan's presence, backing out of the throne room on his knees, his head on the floor.

'Bring me a voluptuous blonde!' the sultan shouted at the closed door.

Chapter One

Mathilde Valentine stood under the canvas bucket and pulled the rope. The cool flood drenched her head and she threw back her hair and let the water flow down her neck and shoulders, between the crease of her full breasts, down her white flanks and between her legs. She felt the heat in her head lessen and her pain floated away with the liquid on to the dirt floor of the shower tent. It had been an arduous journey and she was exhausted.

'*Memsahib*, your dinner will be served in half an hour, at sunset.'

'Thank you ... er, thank you!' Mathilde spoke cheerfully to the disembodied voice.

Half an hour later, she was refreshed and ready to eat.

'For what the good Lord has given us, we are truly thankful. Do sit down, Doctor Valentine, we are not on formal terms here in the African bush.' The missionary laughed and beckoned her to sit on the canvas chair.

He was, she saw, much younger than she had imagined. She had envisaged the missionary as an elderly man. Why would a virile, handsome Scot want to bury himself in the African wilds? Still, *she* had wanted to see this exciting country, and she was not without physical charm herself. But she had good enough reasons for leaving England. She sighed and turned her mind to the present.

The missionary poured them both a whisky.

'My one weakness, I am afraid. I have it sent over whenever a boat comes out here.'

'Well, I won't say no, Mr McKinnon. It has been an exhausting journey.'

'Good health, Doctor Valentine. And I welcome you to Ndizi Mission.'

'Mr McKinnon, I am delighted to be here at last. I do hope you will be able to make use of my few talents.'

'Yes, yes, to be sure, Doctor Valentine. I have heard so much about your skills, I know you will fit in well in our little community. The sisters are away until tomorrow, up in the hills, visiting a settlement. They will be grateful for your help. They are good souls, but have little nursing experience, and I am afraid things get rather too much for them sometimes.'

Charles McKinnon brushed back his rather long, dark hair from his high forehead and took another draught of his whisky.

'Have another wee drop, will you, and tell me all about yersel'.' He had slipped into Scottish vernacular, Mathilde noticed, probably because his tongue had been loosened by the spirit.

'Are we eating, or is this our only refreshment?' She could smell meat cooking and knew that there would be food, but she wanted to change the subject. She had not expected such open questioning from him, and was unprepared.

He laughed and threw back his head again as a lock of hair fell forward over his dark brown eyes. He had rather severe, chiselled features, with lines that came from his nose to the edges of his mouth. His black moustache was clipped to just above his red lips.

Between them, his teeth looked very even and white. His brows met in the middle above his long, straight nose, giving him a rather intimidating look. But when he smiled he was transformed. His 36 years slipped from him and he became the adventurous youth, eager and jovial, as he had been when he had first arrived in this humid, colourful, heathen country, ten years before.

As if on cue, a native appeared out of the dark night carrying bowls of steaming food. He wore a length of checked cotton cloth around his slender loins, and his muscular chest and arms shone with perspiration. His feet were bare.

'*Jambo, memsahib, abari?*'

'*Jambo, msuri.*' Mathilde was delighted to remember the Swahili greeting and response. She had taken Swahili lessons in London before she left. Her teacher had been an elderly, retired doctor, who knew the area she was coming to and had lots of good advice to give her.

'This is Joseph. Joseph, this is Doctor Valentine, our new administering angel.'

The young black man smiled and put down the hot food on the rickety table. Then he bowed and stood a few feet away.

'Ah, beef stew!' Mr McKinnon tucked in with relish, and Mathilde watched in amusement as the Scot shovelled the very untropical food into his mouth.

'Do you have any clinics set up for me?' she asked later, as they sat on low wooden chairs on the veranda of his small, neat house. He smoked a homemade cigarette – 'to keep away the mosquitoes,' he said. She watched the blue lizards on the whitewashed wall as they darted for insects. The sound of the African night was all around them: a high-pitched hum of some insect or other; the ear-piercing screech of cicadas; other sounds, mysterious and exciting.

'Oh, yes, there is a clinic every day! You'll see! The people walk from miles away to taste our medicines and try out our brand of magic. Every day is clinic day at Ndizi Mission. And they'll all come tomorrow, just to see the new *memsahib*.'

Not long after, Mr McKinnon walked Mathilde to her hut. It was a simple Swahili structure made of palm leaves and thatched *makuti* roof, with two windows in the living room and one window in the small bedroom. The lavatory and washing facilities were out the back in a separate hut.

'I apologise for your primitive abode, Doctor Valentine. We had no time to prepare anything more fitting. Your room will be ready in a week or two, when they send more materials. We are building it on to the mission house. The sisters sleep there, in a room at the back.'

'Please, do not apologise, Mr McKinnon. I find the vernacular architecture charming. I like everything I see about this country.' She meant every word. She was already enamoured of the people and the landscape. She found the very idea of Africa exciting. She had looked forward to this for months.

Chapter Two

Mathilda woke to the sound of high-pitched laughter – a woman's laughter, uninhibited and full bodied. She stretched her arms above her head and opened her eyes. She was surrounded by white mosquito netting and the lingering smell of citronella. A young woman stood by her bed, holding a length of red cotton material in both hands.

'*Jambo, memsahib*. My name it is Grace.'

Mathilde greeted the woman, climbed out of her bed, and slipped the cloth around her body, tucking it around her breasts and under her armpits.

'Thank you, Grace. I am sure there is no need for you to wait on me.' She smiled kindly and walked past the young native girl to the door of the hut.

'But, *memsahib*, I am you maid. I look after you every need.' The girl could only have been fifteen or so, Mathilde thought. She was nicely built, with strong, round limbs and a small but firm bust. Her broad face was creased in smiles. Her hair was braided in tight plaits close to her head.

'Well, all right then, that sounds very good. Is there water for a shower this morning?'

19

'Yes, *memsahib,* there is water. Then there is breakfast. I have made porridge for you.'

Mathilde laughed out loud and made her way to the primitive bathroom.

The sun had just risen over the grotesque upside-down tree – the baobab. A flock of small yellow birds flew from its root-like branches. She stood and gazed at the exotic landscape. Ndizi Mission was on the edge of the Indian Ocean in an area which until very recently had been known as the white man's grave. The malarial swampland had been sprayed with a new chemical which hopefully had eradicated the killer mosquitoes. The sea glistened between the palms, in a turquoise and pink glimmer. Flame-coloured flowers bloomed above her head on tall, feathery branches. She saw Joseph climbing the tallest palm.

'What is he doing, Grace?'

' He is doing coconut, *memsahib.*'

'Oh, I should love some coconut with my breakfast!'

'Yes, *memsahib.*' The lithe girl ran towards the coconut palm and yelled shrilly to Joseph. He yelled back at her and laughed.

On the veranda sat the missionary, eating his breakfast. It smelt wonderful.

'Good morning, Doctor Valentine, did you sleep well?'

'Yes, thank you, Mr McKinnon, I did. What are you eating?'

'It's cranachan – or an African substitute for my native dish. Porridge with cream and honey and whisky.'

'Smells lovely,' said Mathilde.

'Do you want some?'

'No, thank you.' She sat down to eat her porridge with grated coconut and cream.

'So are you feeling ready to perform your duties, Dr Valentine?' asked the missionary as they ate.

'Yes, I am ready.'

Half an hour later, Mathilde followed Mr McKinnon

to the mission room, and found her patients waiting for her by the veranda. There were about twenty of them – barefoot natives, mothers with small babies strapped to their backs or fronts, toddlers clinging to their skirts. There were old men, with sad, wise faces, and a young man with a bad cut on his arm. It bled through the dirty cloth he had wrapped around it.

'This is your clinic. They have been waiting since before sun-up. I don't suppose there's anything wrong with half of them.'

There was a table on the veranda, in the shade. Two chairs and a camp bed were the only other furniture. On the table was a bowl of water, clean sterile dressings, an antiseptic lotion and a notebook and pencil. Joseph stood by the chair and barked at the first patient to come and sit.

'No, Joseph, let the man with the cut arm come first.'

The man gratefully stepped forward and Dr Valentine examined the wound. Then she cleaned it and sewed it up.

'How did you do this?' she asked him as she worked.

'*Panga, memsahib*. My friend he *panga* me when he find me with his wife.' He laughed, and Joseph laughed too. '*Panga* is a big knife, *memsahib*.'

'Well, I hope it was worth it.' Mathilde laughed in spite of herself and washed her hands before attending to the next case.

After lunch, Mathilde lay on her narrow, hard bed, with the white cotton sheet drawn back away from her overheated body. The room was unbearably hot. Her flesh burned and her head pounded. She took a long draught of the drinking water and thought how foul it tasted. She dipped her fingers in the jug and sprinkled her face with a few drops. She dipped her fingers again and scattered the liquid over her breasts. The nipples contracted and puckered. She pinched them lightly in

21

both hands and caressed herself, then she moistened her fingers again and traced a line down between her breasts, across her flat belly, around the little crater of her navel and down between her open legs. She opened herself with wet fingers and felt inside. She felt the swelling lips and the oily surface of her sex. She smelt musk on her fingers. This time she moistened them with her mouth and placed a finger just inside herself. She stroked her inner thighs and raised her hips. She moaned quietly as she came almost immediately. Her little climax was brief but it was enough to relax her and she slept.

When she woke it was mid-afternoon. The mission was quiet. She pulled on a bathing costume and straw hat and took a towel with her to the beach. She remembered to put on her sandals in case of worm infection. There were so many dangers, she thought, but it looked like paradise to her. She loved the sway of the palms, the leaning, diamond-patterned trunks with the fringed heads, swishing in the breeze. She walked the few yards to the white-sand beach, over the sharp, fallen fruits of the casuarinas, watching lizards scatter before her. The sun was hot. Tiny transparent crabs ran to their holes in the sand. She looked and saw that the whole beach was alive with the little creatures. She squatted for a moment to watch as a confused crab was booted out of another's hole. She laughed delightedly.

The sea was turquoise and emerald and half a mile out white breakers traced a lacy ribbon where the reef was. She took off her straw hat, threw it on to the sand and ran into the low, languorous surf. She was surprised that the sea was so warm – almost the temperature of a bath. She swam strongly, arrowing through the water with powerful arms, her legs splashing behind her. When she emerged, it was to an empty curved beach, a veritable paradise, with palms and casuarinas fringing the edge, bending over like exotic swans.

She strode up the beach and between flowering shrubs

to her shower tent, where she washed away the saltiness and sighed in contentment.

There is no slow, voluptuous dusk in East Africa. The blood-red ball hangs in the sky and the metal sea swallows it quickly. With night comes the sounds of Africa. Mysterious screeches pierce the blindness; spine-tingling yells, howls, and grunts. The hunted and the hunting, the quick and the dying. The day's beauty and munificence is displaced by blood and the crunching of small bones; creeping creatures alert to death in the darkness.

The darkness was gently pushed aside by the yellow glow of the hurricane lamps in the mission compound. The mission consisted of a small mud-brick church, big enough to hold the small congregation in cramped, sticky discomfort, and with a small room at the back where the nuns slept; the missionary's mud-brick house with its veranda, where one could relax in the lounge chairs and drink whisky; the servant's blockhouse – a depressing cement block building, dark and airless; a kitchen hut – roofed in makuti and with no walls, with a clay oven, and a charcoal-burning stove; the latrines and showers – separate ones for the missionary, the doctor, the nuns, and the native staff. Mathilde's accommodation was more picturesque, she thought, than the basic, rather austere structures that comprised the rest of the compound. She liked the earthy smell, the peppery scent, of the thatched coconut palm roof and the woven walls.

Later, as she dressed for dinner – she knew it would be stew again because she could smell it – she thought about what she had left behind. Her London friends had thrown up their hands in horror when she told them of her plans. How could she contemplate two years in the primitive African bush? However, her mother had backed her daughter's right to work at what she desired.

Her surgeon father was dead, but her married sister would keep an eye on their mother while Mathilde was in Africa. Deidre was jealous, Mathilde knew, of her independence, but she was fairly happily married, with two small children. What had really decided things for Mathilde was the breakdown of her relationship with Professor Arthur Jenet. He had belatedly decided that he could not, after all, leave his wife of twenty years. Their affair had been secret and passionate, and Mathilde had believed him when he said he loved her. She later learnt that he made a habit of seducing his female medical students, and she had suffered a terrible humiliation as a result. Her reputation was soiled. She felt so stupid; so naive.

Leaving all that seediness behind her for the wilds of a new country was exactly what she needed – a new challenge and an opportunity to redeem herself. Her father's old friend and family doctor, Dr Albert Witherspoon, had suggested it to her, and he had also taught her the rudiments of Swahili. His enthusiasm for East Africa was catching and she lapped up the stories of his adventures there.

'I wish I could go back with you, my dear,' he said. 'I still miss the sounds of the bush. You will love it, I assure you, and the mission needs you.'

Mathilde was still thinking about her life in London when she sat down for dinner. However, she was suddenly brought back into the present when Charles McKinnon arrived with the nuns he had spoken of the evening before.

'So, Dr Valentine, this is Sister Angela, and this is Sister Prudence.' He stood to introduce the three women to each other, then he sprawled on the low wicker lounger, his tumbler of whisky at his elbow. The eversmiling Joseph appeared with the bottle and filled Mathilda's glass without asking her.

'Well, my dear Dr Valentine, are you settling in?' The

nun who spoke was Sister Angela, a pale, wan creature, thin under her veils and the folds of white cloth.

'Don't be stupid, sister, the poor child has only been here five minutes.' Sister Prudence was a stronger looking woman, ageless in the ways that nuns often are. Her face was flushed. She had a round face with high cheekbones, almost like an Eskimo, thought Mathilde.

'Thank you, sisters, I feel as if I have been here for ever. It feels like home.'

The meal was lively, even if the food was not exotic. The sisters related tales of their many adversities in the hill country. They had been to oversee the building of a new church – a mud hut with a crucifix – and they were looking forward to going back to have the place consecrated by the priest when he visited from Nairobi next month.

'So, you are of different religions, you and Mr McKinnon?' Mathilde was puzzled.

'Oh yes, my dear, but we worship the same God.' McKinnon laughed mirthlessly and emptied his fourth glass.

Mathilde was suddenly tired and excused herself. There was more going on here than met the eye, she decided, but she was too weary to be bothered by it.

'Sleep well, my dear,' the sisters chorused.

McKinnon rose belatedly to offer to accompany her to her quarters, but she refused politely.

'I am perfectly capable of finding my own way, thank you, Mr McKinnon.' She disappeared into the dark.

'Have you told her anything?' Sister Prudence barked at McKinnon.

He grunted and wiped a hand across his sweaty forehead.

Mathilde was woken by strange sounds. Her senses were alive to new sounds in this exotic location, and she wasn't yet used to the animal noises. Large monitor lizards marched through the undergrowth; tree frogs barked; a heavy coconut palm leaf scraped across the roof convincing her that there was an intruder. The sounds that woke her this time were animal – a moaning in the quiet night. She was immediately alert, confused and alarmed. Was someone hurt? She wrapped a cotton *kitenge* around her and opened the door. The moon lit the compound through the fronds of palm trees, sending white stripes of light on to the mission post. The scene looked unfamiliar in the broken shadows, with blue lightness shimmering. Her eyes soon became used to the dark and she stood silently, listening for the sounds that had woken her. Cicadas hissed incessantly. There was no wind. She heard the cries again, coming from the direction of the missionary's bungalow. Curious, she walked quietly along the sandy path, taking care not to step off into the darkness. She had not seen a snake yet, but she had a fear of them and was naturally cautious.

She approached the veranda, making no noise, and stood in the shadow of the bougainvillaea, hidden from the house. Then she gazed at a strange scene, which she could not fully make out. On the veranda of McKinnon's bungalow, a trio of bodies were interlinked. Slowly, things became clear. Joseph, Grace and Charles McKinnon were indulging in troilism. The servant-girl was standing against the wall, facing the upright, naked form of Joseph, who was obviously fucking her. His hands were on her small breasts, his face raised to the sky, and his features, almost black in this light, were contorted. Behind him, McKinnon's taller frame was moving in an unmistakable manner, his pale loins thrusting, his arms around the naked Joseph. He was buggering Joseph. Mathilde was mesmerised. This was unbelievable. How could the missionary use his servants in this way? Surely they were not willing partners in this bizarre arrangement?

She watched the three lunging shapes, heard the

moans of passion and witnessed the climax. Then she slunk back to her hut, ashamed and aroused.

When she got there, she threw drinking water over her breasts and face and lay, uncovered, on her bed. She could not bear even the mosquito net between her and the air. She tried to breathe deeply and relax. Had she really seen what she thought she had seen? This *ménage à trois*? Her mind rebelled at the idea. Was McKinnon a homosexual? Or did he also like women? He had a natural power over his servants. Perhaps he had forced them to do his will? Her mind whirled. She had to live here in harmony with these people – did she have any right to question their behaviour?

She saw again the shapes – the naked form of Grace pinned to the wall by the massive dark snake that penetrated her and the beautiful male strength of Joseph, a pumping machine for his huge cock. And then the Scot – slim hipped, naked and reckless in his lust. They had hung together like a line of paper dolls. The sight would be fixed in Mathilde's mind for ever.

She was idly touching herself; stroking the thick bush of her pubic hair, inserting a little finger down the narrow channel into her fleshy lips. She moistened her lips with her tongue and dipped a finger into her mouth to make her touch even silkier. She liked her own body. In spite of what her professor lover had told her – that she needed to lose weight – she knew now that he had only been trying to undermine her self-confidence for his own warped reasons. His love-making had sometimes been sadistic. He had slapped her breasts and said they were too big, but his cock had grown as he did it. He had tied her down and abused her verbally – telling her she was a slut – while fucking her. She had thrilled at his words. Their sex life was so apart from the cleanliness of her everyday life. He would leave her, still tied up after he had come inside her. He liked to see her soiled, he said. She was too clean, he said. He smeared his semen over her and masturbated over her while she was tied to the bed, her arms and legs apart. He had been a strange lover, she knew now, but at the time she had been so infatuated with the idea of him – a medical professor, so much older and so important. She had not only enjoyed the violence of his love-making, but she had accepted his abuse, being too young to fight back verbally and too much in awe of him. She had been so innocent – such a fool! But the memory of his formal brutality still had the power to excite her. She thought now of his prick growing inside her. She imagined Charles McKinnon on one side of her, fondling her. Then she thought of Grace kissing her, and the peppery scent of her skin, and a naked Joseph forcing himself on her. She was surrounded by eager cocks, all snaking their way into her. She imagined Grace's high little breasts bobbing against hers, her bruised lips on hers. Mathilde's knowing hands rubbed her own bud, pulled at the sex lips and churned inside her. She breathed heavily, the perspiration running down her thighs, mingling with the love juices that flowed from her. She climaxed quickly, then breathed a deep sigh of relief. Moments later she fell asleep, as sticky as if she had been left tied to the bed by her professor after he had had his way with her.

Chapter Three

*F*or Mathilde the sultry days started with a shower
and breakfast, prepared by Grace. (Mathilde still
couldn't quite believe that this innocent-looking native
girl had really been involved in such a sensual display
as the one she had seen.) She soon persuaded her
servant-girl to give her pawpaw and coconut instead of
the porridge she had been used to preparing for the
missionary. The building materials for Mathilde's room
had not arrived yet, but Mathilde was content in her
Swahili hut. She loved the simplicity of life there. The
animals intrigued her. The surrounding trees and bushes
were kept cut back to allow no hiding place for predators
or other possible attackers, but still there was plenty of
wildlife to be seen. Vervet monkeys peered at her from
the loofah trees and threw themselves into the bushes
with wild abandon. Butterflies as big as birds fluttered
slowly through the dappled gloom. Each day, Joseph
dragged away any fallen palm leaves to the bonfire area
behind the servants' block. Grace swept the paths clean,
pushing back the windblown sand. When Mathilde saw
them at their menial tasks, she could not believe the love
triangle she had witnessed – that they could service their

missionary master sexually! She tried to forget it and treat them as she had before, but it was difficult. She saw, when she looked at the smiling face of Joseph, his enormous penis shoving in and out of the girl's slight body. Her knickers felt wet and warm at the very thought.

The clinic lasted for three hours every morning, then Mathilde was free to read, swim or walk and discover her new country. She loved to stroll along the white-sand beach as far she could in the heat of the day. The crescent beach stretched for miles, with the waving palms and shady casuarinas leaning over it. Cowrie shells and pink coral littered the sand and she soon gathered a lovely collection. About a mile north of the mission was a small beach guest house – the Casuarina. It was a *shenzi* sort of place – scruffy and uncared for, with a moulding piano rotting sadly and framed prints of Cadgwith and St Ives in Cornwall hanging incongruously on the wall.

The owner was an Englishman, who had arrived ten years before from South Africa. The small dining room was only ever occupied by cockroaches as far as Mathilde could see, and she could not imagine how he made a living. There were never any customers around when she was there.

One lunchtime she called in there for a beer before walking back. She was surprised to see McKinnon propping up the bar.

'Welcome, Dr Valentine! Join me for a snifter. What is your poison?' said the missionary.

'A cold beer would be good,' said Mathilde, sitting on the bar stool next to McKinnon and taking her hat off. 'Thank you!'

She wore a floral cotton dress, buttoned all the way down the front. Her legs felt sticky and she pulled the dress away from her skin, exposing her tanned limbs.

The missionary's eyes were on her, and she blushed in spite of herself.

They chatted amiably, and the beer went to Mathilde's head immediately. She foolishly had another, as she felt she had to buy McKinnon one in return for his generosity. Several men walked in together and ordered drinks. McKinnon knew them all.

'This is the chief of police – Inspector Jacklin. Inspector, meet our new administrating angel – Dr Mathilde Valentine.'

She shook hands, noting the man's lack of eye contact with her. She did not like the way he held her hand rather too long.

He introduced the others. There was a fat, balding importer-exporter who worked for the East African Trading Company and an arrogant young man wearing khaki shorts and a short-sleeved white shirt.

'This is Tim Strong – he's a mining engineer.'

'How do you do.' said Mathilde. 'Well, I must leave you to your business, Mr McKinnon.'

'No, I have no pressing business – I'm going into Mombasa. Would you like to come, Dr Valentine?' asked McKinnon, standing and reaching for his bush jacket.

'I . . . er, well, yes, that would be very nice, thank you,' she replied.

She noticed that Tim Strong scowled at McKinnon and suddenly turned away, petulantly. He walked over to the piano, lifted the lid and thumped away at the keys.

'My God, Stallybrass, why don't you do something about this bloody piano!' He slammed down the lid and walked outside, lighting a cigarette and ignoring everyone.

The proprietor, Stallybrass, scruffy in a sweat-stained shirt with rolled-up sleeves, sniggered and stubbed out a cigarette in a scallop shell.

Mathilde and McKinnon left quickly.

'He didn't seem too happy, that young man,' murmured Mathilde as her companion held open the car door.

'He's a pain in the arse, sometimes, that young fellow,' laughed the missionary.

They drove with the car windows open wide to let the air pass through. The smells of Africa filled the air. Mathilde loved the peppery scent of sweet potato and the honey perfume of thorn-tree flowers.

This was her first trip into town since she had arrived a month ago. She felt hot and untidy and wished she had been able to go back to the mission to wash and change her clothes. She combed her fingers through her hair and tried to pin it back under her straw hat.

'Leave it, Mathilde – may I call you Mathilde? It suits you, the tousled look.' He turned to smile at her, and as always his rather stern features were transformed by the white teeth gleaming under the black moustache and red lips.

She smiled. 'Yes, of course, call me Mathilde.'

'And you must call me Charles,' he said quietly.

She felt light-headed and free of all the old inhibitions of England. She was happy to be in this exciting country. She was a free woman and a qualified doctor, and she knew, from the eyes of men she met, that she was attractive. They always looked at the roundness of her breasts through her dress, her long slender legs, and the curves of her hips and buttocks. She felt suddenly powerful. Here, she could do as she wished.

'This is wonderful, Charles,' she said genuinely, and smiled her devastating smile at him. He touched her knee gently and patted it in an almost brotherly way, so that she could not possibly take offence.

After all, he is a missionary, isn't he? A man of God, she thought. And then she saw him again – his belly pressed to Joseph's muscular buttocks.

'What are you going to be doing in Mombasa, Charles?' she asked.

32

'Oh, not much. I have to go to the bank, that's all. Then how about a drink at the Britannia Coffee House? We'll be dehydrated again by then.'

'Whatever you like – I am your prisoner,' she said. 'I have no money with me, and I am hardly dressed for grand society.'

'Mathilde, you are fishing for compliments. You know you are a most attractive young woman, and your dress is charming. Do not worry. The cafe society in Mombasa does not compare with the Happy Valley set of Nairobi.'

As they approached the town they had to cross the Nyali pontoon bridge. It was packed with people coming back from market. Beautiful coastal Kenyans carried huge bunches of bananas on their tight-curled heads. Men rode bicycles with packs of coconut shell piled high on their backs. Women dressed in bright-patterned cottons carried babies on their backs and firewood on their heads. Children waved to Mathilde and McKinnon.

'Everyone is so friendly.' Mathilde smiled and waved. 'I feel like royalty.'

'You are as pretty as a princess, that's for sure.' He began to sing a Scottish air – a love song – and she blushed. She felt ridiculously young and carefree, and she had to admit she was enjoying the attentions of the good-looking man next to her. She was aware of his tall body close to her, his clean, lemony scent, his red lips and the clipped moustache.

Later, they sat in Lloyd Loom chairs on a wooden veranda with palms in pots casting cool shade over them. Charles poured black tea into porcelain cups and squeezed lemon into hers.

'How long have you been in East Africa, Charles?'

'Oh, not long – ten years or so. I'm not an old colonial hand yet. There are people who've been here since the First World War, you know.'

'And were you always a missionary?'

'Oh no, not always. But I think you have misconceptions about me, Mathilde. I am not a priest, you know. I have taken no vow of chastity.'

She blushed again. 'Oh, I didn't mean – '

'Come, let me take you home. You must be tired,' interrupted McKinnon, taking her arm and lifting her from her seat. She did feel tired, and hot, but the tea had refreshed her. As they rose to go, a large Arab ran up the steps on to the veranda of the coffee house. He bowed briefly to Mathilde, and said something in Arabic to McKinnon. McKinnon's face closed into its Scottish sternness. The Arab glanced at Mathilde, taking in the independent demeanour, the long legs and the firm, full breasts. He smiled at McKinnon and jerked his head at Mathilde. She lowered her gaze and felt hot with disgust and shame.

'How dare he look at me in that way!'

'Come, my dear, let us go.' McKinnon led her away without introducing her.

'Who was that man?' she asked as they drove through the giant, elephant-tusk arch of Kilindini Road.

'No-one; a trader. Tell me more about you, Mathilde. How did a beautiful woman like you find herself in a dump like Mombasa?'

'But it's not a dump, it's wonderful. I love it. I have always wanted to come to Africa. I want to go on safari when I have time – probably at the end of my first six months, when I have leave.'

'Oh, safari – yes, of course, the wildlife. Well, I could accompany you if you like. I know my way around Kenya, you know.'

'Well, that's very kind of you, Charles, but ... we'll have to see.'

'Yes, of course.' He turned his devastating smile on her and she felt her stomach lurch. 'We mustn't rush these things, must we? But, you know, you really are a very attractive woman.' His hand fell on her knee again, and slid inside her dress. She breathed heavily as

34

he stroked her tanned leg, and suddenly realised that she was drunk. Part of her wanted his sexual attentions, but part of her knew this wasn't right. She was not fully in charge of her emotions. Her head started to swim.

'Excuse me,' she said, and pushed his hand away.

'I'm sorry, Mathilde, no offence.' He laughed and smiled in a disarmingly youthful way, and she forgave him immediately.

The morning's clinic was always busy, and Mathilde was glad of Sister Prudence's help. She was a sensible woman, strong willed and physically strong, and Mathilde appreciated her good sense and dry humour.

'Are you aware that Mr McKinnon is married?' the nun asked her one morning after the clinic had finished.

'What? I mean, no, it hadn't occurred to me, Sister,' said the shocked Mathilde.

'Yes, there is a mystery, I'm afraid, about what happened to the woman.'

'What do you mean?'

'She disappeared.'

'Disappeared?'

'Well, she went to town one day and didn't return. The police – if you can call them police! – investigated, or so they said, but she was never found.'

'When was this?' asked Mathilde.

'Six months ago. The poor man has been out of his mind with worry, as you can imagine.'

Mathilde was shocked and intrigued. It explained the missionary's heavy drinking, at least. But why on earth hadn't he told her?

'Why didn't anyone mention this before?' she asked.

The nun threw back her muslin hood impatiently. 'Well, now, I suppose he didn't want to frighten you,' she said.

'Why would it frighten me? Did she run away?'

'Oh no, I don't think it was that, my dear, not at all. They were newly married, you see. Though she might have found the life here not to her taste, after Edinburgh society. But they seemed happy enough. No, it was worse than her leaving him. We think she was kidnapped.'

'What!' Mathilde was astonished. 'Kidnapped? By whom? Why?'

'There is a slave trade here, still, it is rumoured.'

'A slave trade! I don't believe a word of it!'

The nun looked offended and Mathilde tried to calm down. 'I'm sorry, Sister, but that sounds so ridiculous. This is the middle of the twentieth century, not the nineteenth. I feel sure there is some rational reason for the woman's disappearance.'

Later, Mathilde thought again about what the nun had said. Why, she wondered, had McKinnon not mentioned his wife, and why did she have an uncomfortable feeling that he did know where his wife was? He did not seem like a tortured man – more a weak man, caught up in something that he could not control.

But she didn't want to get involved. She had almost forgotten her own unhappiness. London, and her impressionable, naive student days, seemed a million years ago. She no longer felt any residual affection for the professor who had, she now admitted to herself, seduced her. Her life was now simple, as she wanted it, and a foolish flirtation would spoil it. She treated the sick and injured natives who came to the mission clinic each morning. She practised her Swahili on them and on the servants. She swam in the warm sea and watched the wildlife around her. Life was peaceful. She didn't really want to know about mysteries and disappearances. And how Charles McKinnon behaved was no concern of hers.

One evening, Joseph served Mathilde and her companions a spicy fish and coconut curry.

'This is delicious, Joseph. What fish is it?' asked Mathilde.

'Parrot fish, *memsahib*, very good eating.' He smiled his devastating smile at her, looking straight into her eyes.

'Yes, indeed it is.' Mathilde lowered her eyes from his admiring gaze.

The nuns excused themselves early, as they usually did, and the young doctor and the missionary sat together on his veranda. Mathilde drank coffee. McKinnon was on his third whisky.

'We have a visitor tomorrow.' McKinnon was smoking a cigar and the acrid smell hung in the still, humid night air, whirling in the yellow light of the hurricane lamp that hung over them. 'Horace Heinlich, German chap, tea planter up-country. He often pops in for a break, you know, when he needs a bit of company. He does a spot of safari work, too. Interesting chap!'

Mathilde had not asked him about his missing wife. If he wanted her to know, he would tell her, she reasoned.

'I look forward to meeting him. And now I must get to my bed. Goodnight, Mr McKinnon . . . Charles.' In her new determination not to be over-friendly, she stood and nodded curtly at the man, who lounged lazily in the easy chair, his head thrown back, the smoke puffing from his rather cruel mouth. He nodded back, and waved his cigar at her.

She headed back to her hut, but heard a noise and turned towards the beach instead. There was quiet laughter, and splashing. Then she saw, in the light of the new moon, two figures in the shallows. They were cleaved together, joined at the waist and hips, like one person with two heads. She recognised the neat head of her maid bobbing up and down. She knew the strong shoulders and back of Joseph. She saw him support the small girl in his muscled arms, and saw the girl's legs wrapped around his back. She stood on the sand, hypnotised by the erotic sight of his cock rising and falling, disappearing into the slender girl. The shadows fell between them, turning the water purple and silver, like their bodies. Mathilde had never seen anything so beautiful. The girl's high breasts jabbed his face and he bit them playfully. His hands held her buttocks tight and pushed her on to his cock again and again. They cried out loud, like some strange sea creature, and fell together under the water. Mathilde held her breath and watched for many seconds before they rose out of the water, spluttering and laughing. She fled to her hut and got ready for bed.

Mathilde Valentine was not the only voyeur at Ndizi Mission. As she undressed for bed, Charles McKinnon was looking through a specially made tiny hole in the woven plantain leaf wall of her bedroom. He crouched outside, in the dark night, hidden from sight. He watched as she drew her dress over her head, revealing her strong body, her white limbs and her firm buttocks. He saw the triangle of fair hair between her legs. She bent and he saw her heavy breasts dip and sway. She stood, unknowing, while he narrowed his eyes and breathed faster. He watched as she lay on her low camp bed, naked, and placed her hands between her legs. He saw the delicate movements of her fingers as they disappeared into her sex. He heard her small moans and her fast breathing. Her hips and belly rose as her fingers stroked slowly and then faster. He watched as she reached her climax – her head thrown back, her long white neck curved – and then sank back on to the white sheet, the perspiration shining on her breasts.

Chapter Four

*M*cKinnon and the tea planter were not to be disturbed, according to Sister Angela. The two men were ensconced on the veranda, whisky flowing freely – Heinlich had brought several bottles with him – and they were whispering together. Heinlich had thinning hair the colour of apricots and a puffy, pale complexion. Mathilde had been introduced earlier, at luncheon. She did not like him. She did not trust him, though she could not have said why. His watery blue eyes moved over her body, devouring her, as if she was meat. She felt as if she was being regarded by a cattle merchant or a greedy butcher. His gaze made her feel dirty. And hadn't McKinnon said he was a part-time hunter? He did not look fit enough.

'Don't bother yourself with the likes of him. The man's an animal!' was Sister Prudence's proclamation, as she and Mathilde walked together under the bougainvillaea and palms.

'But why does McKinnon put up with him?'

'They are a pair. They bring out the worst in each other.' Prudence shook her head in disapproval.

'Tell me more about Mrs McKinnon.'

'What do you want to know? I didn't know the woman very well. She was a flighty piece, if you ask me, but a good-looking woman, and too young for this life.'

'Was she unhappy?' Mathilde asked thoughtfully.

'I don't think she liked being the *second* Mrs McKinnon.'

'The second? I didn't realise there was *another* wife.'

'Oh yes. She was killed on a trip up-country. Tragic! A lion, you know! Or so we were told. *He* wasn't with her when it happened. She was on safari. He was here, working. Can you imagine? We didn't meet her, of course. We arrived here only a year ago, when the new wife had just been installed. He met her on leave, back in Scotland, married her only six months after the death of his first wife and brought her back to East Africa with him. Rosemary. A pretty little thing, but totally unsuited to the life of a missionary's wife. I felt sorry for her, actually.'

Mathilde felt she had discovered more about the missionary today than she had learnt in her four weeks at the mission. He was a mystery to her. At first she had been attracted to him – physically, anyway – but now, strangely, she found him rather repulsive. She didn't like weak men, and his drinking was a sure sign of lack of moral strength, as was his friendship with that charlatan the tea planter. What a shame about his first wife, though, she thought, and then to lose another! It was not surprising that he drank to excess. She must try to be more Christian in her judgement. But then, he was a strange sort of Christian. His services were conducted in a perfunctory way, on Sunday morning and evening, to a small congregation including herself and the nuns. She had no religious convictions, but thought she had to attend out of politeness. The missionary read from a tattered copy of the Bible, and stuttered and laboured over the words as if they were unfamiliar.

Later that night, Mathilde, dressed in a cotton *kitenge*

wrapped around her like a native woman, kept her eyes on the moonlit water and walked the few yards from her hut to the beach. She had heard whimpers and shrill cries and felt the magnet of eroticism draw her to the two lovers in the water. They were rolling in the surf, the white of their teeth gleaming in the silver road laid by the moon across the water. She could see quite clearly what they were doing. Naked, their bodies were perfectly in tune, moving together as if dancing where they lay. She stood still on the shore, the wind whisking the palm fronds behind her.

The lovers' climactic cries were drowned by the sound of the waves and the wind in the trees. Mathilde shrank back into the shadows.

Back in her room she shivered with a sudden longing. She touched herself between her legs, feeling the moist lips swell. She cupped her breasts and squeezed her nipples, feeling the little erections. Her hands went between her legs again and stroked firmly, parting the hair to gently pat and smack the sex lips, then letting her fingers penetrate the soft, fleshy tunnel. She imagined Joseph pushing her to the sand, roughly penetrating her with his hard purple column of flesh. She felt his big hands holding her down, parting her, opening her and pushing himself into her. She thought of him pumping his cock into her and spurting his white eruptions into her womb. She came quietly, secretly; her 'little death' known only to her – or so she thought.

Outside, in the dark African night, the wind blew the palms into a tender curve over her and the waves crashed on to the white-sand beach in thunderous applause. And Charles McKinnon crept away, back to his bungalow.

Several days later, on a Sunday, Mathilde took her walk early in the morning before the sun became too hot. She paddled in the shallows, watching the transparent little

41

crabs run bravely into the approaching waves. She picked up juicy sea slugs, squeezing their black bodies gently until they squirted water. She avoided the spikes of a puffer fish, dead on the beach, like a fat man winded.

She reached the edge of the compound that made up the Casuarina Guest House. There were several cottages for guests, all facing the beach, with brick walls and iron roofs. They were not attractive. The guest house main room and bar was decorated on the outside to look like a half-timbered English cottage. Mathilde despised the whole idea – trying to bring a little piece of England to this exotic beach.

She was thinking of turning back when she heard voices raised in anger. It was McKinnon, she was sure. She recognised the other man too.

'You absolute bastard, Charles. You don't give a damn about me.' It was Tim Strong. He was crying.

'Sorry, kiddo, but you are not as young as you used to be, you know. You want to watch it – you're losing your boyish charm.'

Charles McKinnon sounded so cruel and unmanly, Mathilde thought. She stood for a moment, hypnotised and astonished. What was McKinnon doing here so early in the day in a hotel guest room with Tim Strong? She didn't understand. She could not help but look through the mosquito-screened window half-covered with a faded blue curtain hanging from a wire, and she could see clearly the two men inside. Tim Strong was on his knees, naked, while the older man stood behind him in the gloom. McKinnon wore his dashing jodhpurs, a white shirt and riding boots. He carried a heavy riding crop, and as she stood, mesmerised by the scene, he raised the crop and lashed at the young man's upturned buttocks. She saw Tim's cock, erect, bouncing at each blow.

'You need to watch it, young Tim. You're not as pretty as you were a year ago,' said the missionary. 'Your buttocks do not hold as much pleasure for me as they used to. And the same goes for your arse.' He lashed again and again at the flesh, and Tim cried out in agony at every blow. But he was not tied up or restrained in any way, she saw. He could have stood up and walked away if he had so chosen.

She pressed herself close to the wall and saw a small lizard, blue with yellow spots, next to her face, clinging to the cement wall. It flicked a forked tongue out at her. McKinnon, she suddenly noticed, had his swollen cock in one hand, poking through the fly of his riding breeches. It stood stiff and full, dark red, the swollen head visible between his moving fingers. He pushed the looped end of the crop between the youth's arse cheeks and rubbed it hard. He squirmed on it, his buttocks moving sensually.

'Stop that, you little slut!' said McKinnon. He threw the crop to one side and knelt behind his 'victim', pressing his cock into the boy's anus. Mathilde could not tear her eyes away. McKinnon's hands were on the young man's cock, pumping in time to his own thrusts. Tim's circumcised cock was obscenely swollen, and the head was a dark ruby red. McKinnon's balls banged against the boy's buttocks and she distinctly heard the moist sounds of his cock sliding inside Tim's dark orifice. They came almost immediately, with moans and muffled cries.

43

Chapter Five

Sister Angela ran a small school in the mission compound in the mornings, starting at seven o'clock. She was surprisingly good at it, being a gentle soul and patient with the children. She was less intelligent than Sister Prudence, but the work suited her because she had the innocent mind of a child and so related well to the class. She was involved in their pastoral care, too, making sure that they were well fed before they left the mission compound to go back to their home duties of tending cattle, planting crops, driving the oxen or fetching water with their mothers.

Sister Prudence helped with the clinic duties, acting as Dr Valentine's assistant, and she was already delighted at how Mathilde was getting on at the mission. Prudence had not been altogether happy with her lot before the young doctor had arrived. She was always disagreeing with the missionary, and she disapproved of his dissolute lifestyle. He drank too much and sometimes smoked an odd-smelling herbal tobacco which he said helped to keep biting insects away. She had noticed that if he ran out of this tobacco he became belligerent and nervy, but

44

when he smoked it he relaxed and looked as if he might fall asleep.

Mathilde was settling in to the life of the compound. She loved the vivid colours and sounds of the surrounding bush and the sight of monkeys and exotic birds, and she got on well with the nuns. The only problem was the missionary, but she had kept him at a distance since witnessing the decadent scene at the Casuarina.

However, one night, after a dinner where the proximity of the almost naked Joseph disturbed her equanimity more than usual and she had had a lot to drink, she sat on afterwards with the missionary, talking.

'I believe you have been twice married, Mr McKinnon?'

'Yes, I am sure you have heard of the disappearance of my wife, Dr Valentine. Don't pretend you haven't!'

'Well, yes, I have been told she disappeared. I hope you don't mind me knowing?'

'Of course not, though I suspect she has left me. There is no real mystery.'

'Why do you think that?'

'Because she was young and beautiful and not suited to this austere life.'

'Was? Mr McKinnon, you speak of her in the past tense.'

'Yes, well, I have given up hope of seeing her again, Dr Valentine,' he said.

'I'm sorry.' Mathilde poured herself another drink.

'Don't be. It was a mistake, that's all. We all make mistakes.' He leant towards her across the table and his dark eyes glistened. The lines around his mouth tightened and she felt suddenly afraid.

'And what about you, Doctor? What is a beautiful, intelligent woman like you doing in a mission clinic in the middle of nowhere? Have you no relatives to worry about you? No lover?'

She bristled at his forwardness.

'No, no-one at the moment. And what happened to your first wife, Mr McKinnon? As Oscar Wilde would have said, "To lose one wife may be regarded as a misfortune; to lose both looks like carelessness."'

McKinnon laughed loudly and clinked her glass with his.

'Be careful, Doctor Valentine. Do not look too closely into matters that do not concern you.' He touched her hand and she withdrew it immediately. There was an electricity between them, but she suspected it may have a lot to do with their mutual inebriation.

'Goodnight, Mr McKinnon.' She stood and walked unsteadily to her hut.

'You used to call me Charles,' he called after her.

Charles McKinnon had need of the servants to help him to bed. He called for them both and they half-carried him to his room. Then he roused from his semi-stupor, grabbed Grace and started fondling her, running his hands up inside her *kitenge* to feel the warm flesh of her firm thigh. He was aroused and pressed himself to her belly. She laughed and kissed him, teasing him. She put her hand over his crotch and felt the hardness. Joseph undressed his master and Grace played with the exposed penis, which was still semi-flaccid. She knelt to suck it and stroke the pale stem. Joseph grew excited at the sight of Grace's dark mouth enveloping the white man's cock, and he took out his own large penis and fondled it, bringing it to a greater length and width than McKinnon's. Joseph's rod was dark purple-brown, and when he slid back the foreskin he revealed the brighter red of the mushroom head. Grace was enjoying the white master's cock in her mouth. She sucked and dug her sharp little teeth into his almost numb flesh, causing him to groan and move his hips slowly, churning his loins in her moon-like face. Joseph needed the same treatment. He pushed forward and offered himself to

McKinnon, standing close to his face and waving the swaying erection enticingly. McKinnon took the offered fruit into his mouth, and Joseph groaned as his lips slid down the shaft to the base. His penis disappeared into the white man's throat and slid out again. McKinnon swayed, his cock in the girl's mouth, his mouth around his man-servant's wondrous erection. Grace put McKinnon's hands on to her breasts and he obediently caressed them harshly. Joseph's fingers were inside the wetness of her sex, rubbing and thrusting their firmness on her soft parts, providing her with the friction she wanted. Their climax was swift and noisy, though McKinnon's yells were muffled by the thick rod of flesh in his mouth.

Grace and Joseph put the missionary to bed and covered him with the mosquito net.

Mathilde had a bad headache in the morning, and wished she had not been so weak-minded. However, she had not given in to her lustful urges. She was determined that Charles McKinnon would not be misled by her and think that she was interested in sleeping with him. Something had instinctively made her hold back from intimacy with the man. He was a challenge, he was good-looking in a devilish way, and he seemed to be attracted to her, but he lived this other secret life, with men as lovers. She smiled to herself, though her head pounded and throbbed. She drank lots of water and ate some salt to help repair the dehydrating effects of the whisky. Breakfast was toasted muffins, which she ate hungrily.

The missionary had gone off somewhere, and no-one seemed to know why or where. He had also taken the old car.

Five days later he had not reappeared and Sister Prudence could not contain her anger.

'We are stuck without the Austin. We need urgent

stores from Mombasa. Where is the stupid man? This isn't the first time, you know!'

'I can drive, if you can find us another vehicle,' said Mathilde.

'Can you really, my dear? How very enterprising and modern of you! I'll get Joseph to find one. He's a wonder, that young man!'

Life continued without McKinnon. Clinics were held every morning except on Sunday. The nuns ran the school and the Sunday services, almost glad that the missionary had gone and that they were in charge.

Joseph and Grace performed their erotic poem every evening, often observed by Doctor Valentine. She felt sure that Joseph knew she watched them, but that he had not told Grace. Surely her sinuous movements would not have been so uninhibited had Grace known she was being watched? Mathilde stood in the shadows of the casuarinas, her flesh hot under her thin cotton *kitenge*, which she wore in the evenings as a matter of course now. It was so comfortable, so loose, and she liked the feel of being naked under the thin fabric. Her nipples pressed on the rough cotton. She pressed her hands between her legs to touch her slit, and her pubic lips swelled as she watched the lovers. On one occasion, Grace knelt in the shallows and took the enormous penis in her mouth. She looked as if she would swallow it in her wide mouth. Joseph stood, his legs apart, the moonlight glinting on his ebony skin. His hands were on the neat, small head between his legs. Grace relinquished her hold on his member as he raised her in his strong arms so that she was lifted and pressed against him, his cock curved against her belly. She moaned and kissed his lips, spreading the scent and flavour of his sex into his mouth. He laughed loudly and lifted her higher, so her legs were around his shoulders and her sex was pressed against his mouth. She held on around his neck and head with her legs as he licked her and sucked at the pink, swollen flesh. She cried out like a dying animal, but she was not in pain. She was not in pain.

After these evenings of voyeurism, Mathilde was in a dreadful state of heat and desire. She slept badly, and then only after long and violent masturbation. She kept a garrison of weapons to penetrate her swollen flesh – short, curved bananas in red and yellow and hard, green fruit. She helped herself to pawpaw from the kitchen, washed it thoroughly and abused herself with the blushed fruit, often bruising herself. Her passions were inflamed. The heat and humidity did nothing to calm her emotions. She took to drinking a large whisky half an hour before her usual time.

Her dreams became violent and sexual. She dreamt of Joseph. He held her down and tied her arms and legs apart. He put his huge cock in her mouth. It grew too big and she could only suck the tip. He placed it between her legs and drummed it on her vagina. He held her sex lips open, wide apart, and thrummed his penis on her clitoris. He licked her face. He became a big black dog. His long tail thrashed against her clitoris. He put his long, wet tongue inside her and moved it fast. Its wet roughness penetrated her. He became a lion, his teeth around her throat, and his long, slender cock, as red as the evening sun, deep inside her; burning her, killing her.

She woke, her throat contracting with thirst, her thighs tingling and throbbing. She drank water, lots of water, and sank back into uneasy sleep. She woke again to relieve her bladder, not bothering to dress. Her movements were seen by the watchful Joseph. She did not see the crescent of his smile in the dark.

One day Joseph had the good news that a truck was for sale. The owner, a Dutch tea planter, had had a new American car shipped in to Mombasa, and he would sell his ex-army truck to the mission – at a price. He and a native servant drove both vehicles into the compound early one morning. Mathilde went up to the tea planter, who was talking to the nuns.

'We will pay your price,' Sister Prudence was saying to him. 'We'll have to believe and trust you that it won't break down on us.'

'It's more trustworthy than that bogus missionary of yours, at any rate.' The moustached man, a blond giant in his forties, laughed and wheezed loudly.

'What do you mean?' Mathilde was curious.

'Everyone in Mombasa knows he is a fraud. The coffee shops are full of talk of his goings on.'

'What goings on?' Sister Prudence bristled.

'He's no man of God, that's for sure. And his wife, the second one, went the same way as the first.'

'What! Was she eaten by lions too?' The nun crossed herself.

'Ha! Lions! No, it is not lions that have devoured them. They have been taken as white slaves. That is what has happened. And McKinnon was involved in selling them.'

'You cannot be right!' exclaimed Mathilde. 'Do you have proof of these accusations?'

'Everyone knows, that is my proof. He is always with that hound Heinlich. I hate the man. They say he had dealings with the Arab traders, out of Mombasa. Huh! It wasn't only tea he was exporting.' He spat a gob of brown sputum into the dirt and took the money from Sister Prudence. 'Good luck to you, ladies. You'll need it.' He bowed and left with his servant in the shiny new car.

The battered truck became a liberating influence on Mathilde. She took Joseph with her into the town to get the stores for the mission. They drove past palm groves and sisal plantations, the smell of sweet potato and pepper filling the air. They stopped to let a family of baboons cross the road. The patriarch stood in the middle of the tarmac hustling the females and young ones across like a fussy policeman. Tiny dic-dic leapt prettily on the yellow grassy verge. As they got closer to Mombasa they saw busy villages, bare-breasted women with bundles of fresh-cut grass balanced on their heads, and men on bikes, carrying beds or bundles of cloth to market. Children laughed and waved at Mathilde and ran beside the car.

They could smell the meat market long before they reached there. Mathilde always dropped Joseph off with instructions to meet her later. She drove through the busy, dusty streets, excited by the number of people and the noise of the town. Bicycles wove in and out of the traffic. She hadn't realised how much she missed the bustle and excitement of town life.

One afternoon, she stopped at the police station and reported the missionary as missing. The policeman, in his khaki uniform, wrote slowly and painstakingly and only grunted when she asked him to let her know if there was any news. As she was leaving the station the tall figure of Inspector Jacklin rose from the doorway of a police jeep.

'Inspector Jacklin!' Mathilde approached him.

'Doctor Valentine?' He stopped and looked down at her.

'Have you any idea where Charles McKinnon might be?' she asked quickly.

'McKinnon? No. Has he gone missing?' The inspector didn't appear to be overly concerned.

'Yes, I have just reported it. He's been gone for two weeks.'

'Perhaps he is on business somewhere.'

'What business could a missionary have, Inspector?' Mathilde asked, hoping for some kind of explanation.

He shrugged his shoulders, bowed his head slightly and walked past her into the police station..

Mathilde ran back to the truck, pulled away, and then parked it in the centre of town and found the coffee shop. She was moist with perspiration already. The town was an oven. She realised how lucky they were with their beachside mission location, where the afternoon breezes kept them cool. She sat at a wicker table on the shady veranda, under a huge, slow-moving ceiling fan, and ordered black coffee and a glass of water. The uniformed waiter bowed and took her order.

'Good morning, ma'am. I wish to introduce myself.' A tall white man, wearing a neatly pressed safari jacket, a broad-brimmed bush hat with skin from a leopard's tail around it, and loose cotton trousers tucked into jungle boots, stood in front of her. She looked up into amber-brown eyes, which regarded her unflinchingly. He removed his hat to expose a head of blond hair and gave a small, nodding bow.

'Baron Jorge Olensky, at your service.' His voice was low and quiet. The light brown eyes smiled, revealing laughter lines which were etched into his tanned skin.

'Yes, Baron? What can I do for you?'

'May I sit for a moment?'

'Certainly. I'm sorry, do sit down.'

The waiter arrived with her coffee and the baron ordered one too.

'I'm sorry to intrude like this, but I heard of the missionary's disappearance.'

'Do you know anything about it?' Mathilde sipped her tiny cup of coffee, realising she should have asked for English-style coffee. The Arabian mixture was thick as toffee, chalky and bitterly strong. She drank it down with iced water.

'Well, no, not really, but I have an idea of what might be going on. I wanted to warn you.'

'Warn me of what?'

'I must explain and introduce myself properly. I have an interest in the Tsavo big game. I am a hunter and game warden. I have reason to believe that the first Mrs McKinnon was not killed by a lion.'

'I am interested to hear it, but what has it got to do with me?' Mathilde asked.

'Be careful, Doctor, you have no male to protect you.'

'There is a male-servant – Joseph. He is strong enough.'

'But is he to be trusted?'

'Why shouldn't he be?' Mathilde could not believe that the smiling Joseph was a threat.

The baron observed that the young woman was blonde, pretty and young. Therefore she was probably stupid, he surmised.

'Doctor, I must go now, but please believe me when I say that I am sure you are in danger, and I would like you to know that I am at your service if you need me.'

'Well, thank you, Baron Olensky, but I really don't think that will be necessary. We are quite able to look after ourselves. And why should there be any danger?'

'Forgive me, Doctor, I cannot explain at this moment. There are reasons. May I see you again and we can talk further of this serious matter?' He stood, took her hand and shook it, bowing again and clicking his heels together in a rather military fashion.

'Of course, Baron, if you insist. Come to the mission.'

'Thank you, I will. I will come tomorrow, if that is convenient.'

'You know where we are?'

'Yes, I know where it is. Good day, Doctor . . .? I'm sorry, I don't know your name.'

'Valentine. Mathilde Valentine.'

'Be careful, Doctor Valentine. Make sure your quarters are secure.' This was his parting shot.

53

Chapter Six

Mathilde watched the ranger walk quickly down the steps of the coffee house and step into a jeep, the door of which was held open by his native driver. Other people watched him too, she noticed. The tea planter, Heinlich, was drinking whisky with an obese Arab character, whose belly bulged and distorted his spotless white djellaba. They had both turned to watch as Baron Olensky left. Mathilde paid her bill and went, pointedly ignoring Heinlich as she walked past their table. She heard them whisper and then laugh loudly. She bristled with anger, but did not look back.

After picking up the medical supplies they had run out of, Mathilde stopped to collect Joseph, who was loaded down with fresh produce. He had two live chickens hanging by their feet from a string, a bundle of sweet-smelling herbs and a sack of rice, as well as unspecified vegetables in another sack, all of which he put in the back. Mathilde opened the passenger door for him.

His face was shining with sweat. His body odour was strong but not displeasing. In fact, his proximity unnerved her. She was aware of his naked shoulders, his muscled arms, and the size of his hands. She drove through the town's outskirts, concentrating on not colliding with the throng of cyclists and laden pedestrians. When they got further away from Mombasa, she spoke to him.

'Joseph, do you know where the *bwana* is?'

'No, *memsahib*.'

'We must manage without him.'

'Yes, *memsahib*.'

'Are you happy at the mission, Joseph?'

'Yes, *memsahib*, I am happy. But the *bwana*, he paid me. Who will pay me now?'

'You will be paid, Joseph – and Grace. Do not fear.'

'Yes, *memsahib*.'

The missionary's dusty Austin was the first thing they saw as they drove into the compound.

Sister Prudence was standing next to the car with McKinnon. As Mathilde and Joesph jumped out of the truck, they heard the nun's sharp voice.

'So, you have returned. Are you going to tell us where you have been, Mr McKinnon?' Arms akimbo, she was a formidable sight. She reminded Mathilde of a large, white, angry bird, and she felt quite sorry for the man.

'I had business in Lamu, Sister. I was unfortunately delayed. I'm sorry I did not let you know where I was going. I didn't realise you would be so put out by my absence.'

'Hmm!' The nun folded her wings and turned her back on the missionary.

'And we have been put to the expense of a new vehicle, Mr McKinnon,' added Mathilde.

'My apologies, Doctor.' His smile was arrogant and his eyes flew over her warm, perspiring body, noting the sweat marks between her breasts and on her belly, where her cotton dress was stuck to her.

* * *

It was late when Mathilde bathed in the sea. The sun had set and the African night was about to enfold the quiet compound, the white-sand beach and the warm sea with its dark blue velvet. She bathed naked. She saw Joseph come alone to the edge of the sea and drop his cotton wrap on to the sand. His soft penis, hanging low between his legs, reached almost halfway down his long thigh. He started to walk into the sea but stopped as he noticed her a few yards away. He turned his small, neat head and she saw his wide smile catch the blue light from the stars. He had seen her but pretended he had not. His hands went to his sex and casually stroked the flaccid stem. Mathilde's eyes were glued to the growing thing in his hands. She stood up to her thighs in the bath-warm, salty water, which still had the heat of the day in it, only twenty feet from him. Still he pretended he did not see her. The penis grew and curved towards her, a dark snake of power. His hands moved up and down the shaft, stretching the skin to the tip and gathering the loose foreskin in a bunch, then holding it there for a moment before drawing it back down the long gleaming pole into his groin. Her hands went automatically to her own sex, and she echoed his strokes with pelvic thrusts, aching to meet his sex but knowing she would not. He looked through the darkness at her and pierced the night air with his gleaming eyes. There were taboos they could not break, but they could desire each other from a distance. She played with her clitoris, rolling the little ball of silk in her salty fingers. The waves lapped at her pubic mound and licked her thighs and buttocks. One finger found her anus and stroked it. The warm water sucked in and out of her sex and anus. She rolled her belly and hips, making love to the gentle lapping waves, all the time watching the black youth at his exhibition of masturbation. His penis was at least ten inches long and she wondered if it would ever stop growing. Her fingers pinched her bulging vulva, by now swollen and tingling. Her breasts pouted provocatively at him, the nipples grown hard and large. She fondled them with her sex-juicy fingers and pressed her breasts together, imagining his enormous cock trapped between them. Her tongue licked around her entire mouth and flicked in and out like a snake about to strike. She wanted that other dark snake that was forbidden to her. She groaned and strained against her fingers, pushing inside her sex and feeling the juicy walls close. Twenty feet away, Joseph moaned and shook, his teeth formed into a white grimace. His hands moved fast and rhythmically over his entire shaft, which now pointed up to the sky. She imagined the huge, silky black cock pressed into her yielding flesh, breaking through the bars of her fingers and into her sex ... and they came together, twenty feet apart.

'Will you take a whisky with me, Dr Valentine?'

It was that after-dinner hour when Mathilde liked to sit on the veranda of McKinnon's bungalow and watch the lizards catch insects on the wall where the hurricane lamp hung.

'All right. Thank you.' She was intrigued by this man. The stories that went round about him could not be true. He threw back a lock of floppy, dark hair and smoothed it over his scalp.

'Your good health, Doctor!'

'And yours, Mr McKinnon.'

His mood was lighter than it had been before he had left the mission. He seemed highly amused. More energetic. He fidgeted and sniffed. He kept laughing to himself. It was, she thought, as if he was under the influence of a chemical stimulant.

'The good nuns do not approve of me, you know,' he said, lifting his dark head and looking at her. His pupils were dilated.

'Yes, well, I'm not sure that I do either. But what you do is your own affair, Mr McKinnon.'

Mathilde left the man to his whisky and whatever else he was indulging in, and went to bed.

Chapter Seven

S ister Prudence and Sister Angela held the morning service in the cool gloom of the mission room. The congregation, consisting of about two dozen local villagers, sang the hymn 'Abide With Me'. Towards the end of the short service, Mathilde noticed that Olensky had entered the room and was standing at the back near the door.

The people dispersed and Mathilde introduced the baron to the nuns.

'Are you managing without a priest, Sisters?'

'Mr McKinnon has returned, you know, but is feeling too tired to give the service this morning,' Sister Prudence said, with her lips pursed in annoyance and disapproval. 'And yes indeed, Baron, we have managed, with God's help.'

'You'll maybe need more than God's help,' he said, his voice deep with emotion.

At that moment, the missionary appeared, looking decadent and dishevelled. He looked as if he had not slept for a week. His shirt was unbuttoned and his breeches were dirty.

'Good day, sir!' The missionary bowed ironically at the baron.

'I am pleased to see you have returned to your flock, sir.' Olensky's face was like thunder. 'I must leave now.'

He began to walk towards his vehicle. 'Moosa!' he called out to his servant.

'Oh please, Baron Olensky, please stay to lunch. We have roast chicken. There's plenty!' Sister Angela held his arm.

'Yes, please stay,' said Mathilde, smiling calmly.

Baron Olensky looked unsure, but was eventually persuaded to stay, to the obvious displeasure of McKinnon. However, half an hour later they all sat down to an English Sunday roast of chicken and vegetables.

'You keep a good kitchen staff, I see. This is a fine meal.' The baron wiped his clean-shaven face and smiled at the three women. The missionary sat at the opposite end of the table, eating in silence.

'There's only Joseph and Grace. They are good souls,' said Sister Angela.

Olensky was not as tall as Mathilde had thought, but his stocky frame was pleasing, as was his almost Teutonic blondness. Her eyes were drawn to his; he had the strangest eyes she had ever seen. They seemed to see far into the distance, like a sailor's eyes, always on the far horizon.

As soon as the meal was over, the nuns stood up.

'You must excuse us, Doctor Valentine, Baron Olensky, Mr McKinnon. We have our duties to attend to.' They took their leave, the white, soft drapes of their habits sweeping the dusty earth as they walked.

Joseph appeared and began clearing away the dirty dishes.

'Let us walk along the shore, Doctor.' The baron rose and, taking her arm, steered Mathilde away from the compound and along the palm-fringed white-sand beach. The missionary sat on at the empty table, drinking his whisky and smoking.

Mathilde was wearing a blue cotton dress which came to just below her knees and a pale straw hat. Her legs were bare. She removed her shoes and threw them back towards the veranda.

'There, now I have gone native,' she joked.

'You have adapted well to the climate?' The baron was leaning close to her, and she could smell his faint lemony scent.

'Indeed, I feel very much at home here. I love it!' She ran a little way along the sand, noting the shortness of their shadows.

'Wait, Doctor Valentine. May I call you Mathilde?' He grabbed her arm and turned her towards him. They looked into each other's eyes, both feeling the spasm of lust.

'I . . . I must tell you, you are in danger. I believe that there is a slave trade out of Mombasa. Heinlich is involved – and McKinnon. Women have disappeared. Not just McKinnon's wives.'

'But that's absurd! This is the twentieth century! Things like that don't happen any more.'

'Here they do,' the Baron told her. 'Believe me, you are not safe. Close the clinic and go home. Why take the risk?' He held her tanned arms by the wrists.

'But it is ridiculous. I have only just arrived,' Mathilde argued. She shrugged and he let go of her.

'You are a stubborn, stupid young woman,' he shouted. And then he walked away, back towards the compound.

The next few days were busy, with many more sick people than usual needing attention from the new doctor. There was an elderly witch doctor a few miles up the road towards Mombasa, and he had always dealt with ailments such as ulcers, cholic, bronchitis or malaria, but now the locals were fascinated by the young white woman doctor, and wanted her medicine, too. Of course, they had not abandoned the witch doctor, they were just curious. Not many white women came to this coastal area – Nairobi was the place the colonials usually headed for. Mathilde was becoming a minor celebrity – and her medicine worked. The natives loved to be prodded with stethoscopes, painted with red antiseptic lotion and bandaged with clean dressings. They had never seen such modern procedures, and were astounded at how quickly their wounds and injuries healed.

In the afternoons, Mathilde read books she had borrowed from the library. One was a history of East Africa, and she read with horror the accounts of Portuguese governors and their part in the 'black ivory' trade – the buying and selling of human beings. The Arab merchants transported the slaves in large dhows to Arabia and beyond, but it was Portuguese and half-caste soldiers who captured them, deep in the African interior, and led them in their thousands to the East African coast where the survivors – for many died on the way – were chained to the decks and taken from their homeland, sold for only a few pounds. The Portuguese had kept domestic slaves of their own, long after slavery was condemned by the British. It all sounded like ancient history to Mathilde, and she refused to believe that such trade was still in operation in the early twentieth century. And if the baron *was* to be believed, it was white women that were the most precious cargo now. What could they call that? Not 'white ivory' but 'white meat', perhaps? She shuddered at the thought of what might have happened to the two wives of Charles McKinnon, and she remembered with distaste the undisguised lustful looks that the tea planter, Heinlich, had inflicted on her.

Baron Jorge Olensky did not wholly approve of the young Englishwoman. She was too good looking and had too much fair hair to be taken seriously. She was probably a spoilt, rich woman, out in Africa for fun and excitement, like the dissolute women he had met in Nairobi. She would end up marrying a planter, playing bridge, drinking too much and being unfaithful, as they all were. His initial instinct was to stay away from her and let her be – allow McKinnon to have his way with her and probably dispose of her in the same way as he had his wives. Olensky hadn't trusted a woman since his affair with the wife of a nobleman in Silesia. She had humiliated him and led him on, and he had left Silesia because of her. She was seventeen years older than him and he had believed her when she had said she loved him. He had even killed her husband in a duel. And then she had stroked his golden head and laughed and left with another.

At the coffee house in Mombasa one morning, the baron heard some disturbing news. McKinnon was planning to take Dr Valentine on safari, and was buying stores for a long trip to Ngorogoro. He had been heard bragging that the young doctor was in his thrall and would do what he asked.

Despite telling himself to leave well alone, Olensky called at the mission that afternoon. He learnt that the Mathilde was unwell and unable to see him.

'Where is McKinnon?' he then asked.

'Gone to buy food with Joseph,' Grace told him.

'Where are the sisters?' He was becoming impatient. The servant shrugged. 'I insist on seeing Doctor Valentine,' Olensky then said.

The hut where Mathilde lay was hot and the still air was full of incense and mosquito coil smoke. Mathilde stirred and turned towards him as she heard him enter.

'I'm all right, really. Just a touch of fever,' she croaked when she saw his worried face. Her pupils were tiny and her skin dry and flushed.

'You look terrible,' the baron told her.

'Yes,' she replied weakly.

'This isn't fever. Have you eaten anything strange?' Olensky looked at her closely.

'Look here, I'm the medic!' she whispered.

'You have been poisoned. He is poisoning you, drugging you, as he did his wives. Then he will take you away and sell you.'

'Oh, don't be ridiculous.' But as she spoke the words, Mathilde saw the logic of what the baron was saying. She had noticed a strange deposit in the bottom of her whisky glass a few days ago, and she had felt rather odd all that night. She had walked around as if in a dream, and McKinnon had fed her more whisky, saying it would lift her spirits and keep the fever away. And the water that Grace put in her room did not taste right either.

'I am taking you away, now. I am getting you out of here.'

Before she realised what was happening, Olensky had taken her in his arms and wrapped the sheet around her hot, naked body. He carried her out into the bright sunlight, where Grace stood, amazed. He placed her gently in the back of his car, and ordered the servant to pack her mistress's clothes and belongings.

Chapter Eight

The baron took the sick woman to a house in Mombasa, his base while he was in town. His male servants found a woman to take care of her, who bathed Mathilde's inert body and gave her herbal drinks. Mathilde slept fitfully, calling out in her dreams, and she sweated heavily.

She soon began to recover, however, and after two days the baron decided that she was well enough to travel. She was still weak and had lost a lot of weight, but he was annoyed that he had been obliged to rescue the young woman and that he was now saddled with her. Besides, he had work to do. What was he to do with her? Could he send her back to England?

'You are fit to travel now. You must go home,' he told her.

'Go home! No! I will not go home. I am not going to be frightened out of my job. Why can't I go to the police? If I was poisoned or drugged, surely they will do something?'

'You do not know what you are dealing with here. You cannot trust anyone. Go home, Doctor Valentine. Forget your little clinic.' The baron was determined. He had his suspicions about the involvement of the local police department with McKinnon's shady dealings. They probably took a cut of whatever gold passed hands in return for their silence.

'I thank you for your help and advice, Baron, but I will not leave Africa. I have work to do here.'

'And I have work to do elsewhere,' the baron said. 'You are not safe here in Mombasa. You have no choice. You will have to accompany me.'

The next day, the baron dragged a very weak, confused Mathilde to her feet and carried her into his truck.

They drove through Mombasa and headed north into the wilderness. Dirt tracks threaded their way through low scrubland. After a couple of hours, Mathilde began to feel better and watched the wildlife in amazement. The baron pointed out a family of wart-hogs running from the sound of their vehicle and the one driven by his servants. Giraffes lunged between the thorn trees and shiny zebras, round bellied and whinnying, fought and mated. A small herd of elephants, matriarchs and babies, rolled like ships; a slow, beautiful ballet in the morning mist.

Their tents and stores were carried in one truck and the baron and Mathilde travelled in the other. Suddenly the landscape opened up into a broad veldt where the sky was huge and bleached and the land was red and scarred with the giant claw marks of time.

'This is only the edge of the wilderness. There are thousands of miles of nothing but land and wild animals,' explained the baron. He spoke with love in his voice – love for this arid land.

'How many years have you lived in Africa?' Mathilde was exhilarated by the atmosphere. She had removed her hat and her hair flew free. She felt better than she had for days, and she felt like she was a girl again. She wondered how old Olensky was. He looked about thirty-five, but it was hard to tell. The sun had etched deep lines around his amber eyes.

'I have been here twenty years,' Olensky told her. 'I come originally from Silesia, or Poland as it is called now. Great powers have always fought for our country.'

'Ah, that is where your accent comes from!'

He laughed. 'Yes! Look!' He stopped the truck and pointed into the distance. 'There! Rhino!'

Mathilde took the binoculars from him and saw two white rhinos lumbering through the thorn trees in the valley below, about half a mile away.

'Could you really see them without binoculars?' She was amazed at his visual powers.

'Yes, I was taught by a Masai hunter how to use my eyes.'

'Will I meet the Masai?' Mathilde asked with interest.

'Maybe. Come, we will camp here for the night.' The baron stopped the truck as he spoke.

They unloaded equipment and made camp. By sunset, they were seated on folding canvas stools, drinking a sun-downer of whisky.

'You are chilly?' Jorge Olensky took off his bush jacket and wrapped it around Mathilde's shoulders. 'It gets cold here at night. Moosa! *Lete chakula tupate kula*. Bring food that we may eat.'

They sat close together, listening to the sounds of the African night. Jackals howled and strange nocturnal birds screeched, but Mathilde felt perfectly safe with this man. True, there were two armed native servants and a good fire burning to keep away curious wild animals, but she felt as if she was in his care – this exotic baron whose eyes burned like orange flames. He was part of the landscape and he knew its ways. For once she was content to be a helpless female and let him be the protector. Her work made her self-sufficient and empowered her, but this interlude in the wilds of the bush was like a massage. It soothed her and made her feel whole and well. She was willing to let him show her his world.

They slept in separate tents.

At dawn they breakfasted on strong coffee and hot flatbread. Afterwards, Moosa and William struck camp while Olensky and Mathilde walked into the bush. They reached a high rock which commanded a view over the plateau.

'See over there – bison!' Olensky gave Mathilde the binoculars so that she could see hundreds of ambling animals, heading towards them.

'They look like ants! How far away are they?' asked Mathilde, transfixed.

'About five miles. The air is so clear here, everything is visible,' he explained patiently.

Suddenly, behind them, came a low growl.

'Behind me, quick! Don't make a sound.'

Mathilde did as she was bid. Olensky cocked his rifle and stood absolutely still. Mathilde held her breath and she peered from behind his broad body. A large male lion, its mane golden in the glinting sun, crouched on a high rock above them. It rolled its huge head to one side and growled, long and low. Olensky stood absolutely still, the gun pointing at the beast. It growled again, a long, grumbling moan of disapproval at the presence of man in his territory. Then it slowly rose and stood, a magnificent silhouette against the swollen sun. It roared once, loud and thunderously, then turned its back and leapt away from them.

'Has it gone?' Mathilde was as breathless as if she had run a mile.

'Yes, he was just looking. Don't worry. The lions won't attack unless their young are threatened, or they are hungry.'

'How do you tell if they are hungry?' she asked nervously, not knowing whether to laugh or cry.

'We'll know!' Olensky looked at her with amused eyes.

Later that day, having resumed their drive, the couple came to a slow-moving river where hippos lay, wallowing in the mud. There were also crocodiles, hidden in the water with just their nostrils and eyes above it. Mathilde had never known such exhilaration – every moment was an adventure. She also enjoyed being with Olensky. Here, in his adopted land, he had strength and confidence. He was at once the hunter and the protector. His expertise in tracking and finding the wild animals was obvious. She saw in his golden eyes – almost like the lion's eyes – the need he had for the wilderness. His veneer of civilisation was inbuilt, and he was still the perfect gentleman, but she saw the natural animal underneath his tanned skin. Her admiration for him grew, and she watched his every move; his sturdy, muscled body, his sure feet and his broad-palmed, practical hands. She saw the respect his men had for him, and she knew she could trust him. She noted the smile that opened his face like sunshine on a flower. She wanted to touch the laughter lines around his extraordinary eyes.

They drove over dirt tracks that he had used before, and went over the dry red earth of virgin territory, slowly and carefully. He wanted to show her his Kenya. That evening, an hour before sunset, they stopped by a small stream which had cut a deep channel between the rounded slopes of its banks. The bush was sparse but there were flat-topped mimosa trees here and there. The banks were green with maidenhair, wild asparagus and numerous swaying grasses. The rock was red granite and along the length of the stream were bowls, smoothed and hollowed by time. Where they had chosen to camp there was a hollow place about ten feet by fifteen, flanked by flat slabs of granite which sloped slightly to the clear pool of water.

'Oh! How lovely! May I bathe here? Is it safe?' Mathilde asked Olensky.

'Yes, it is quite safe,' he told her protectively.

While the two servants made the camp and lit a fire, Olensky took off into the bush to catch dinner. He reached a little ridge and waited. Sure enough, as the sun sank, a large buck – an eland – came into view, on its way to a drinking place. Olensky lay on his stomach, the gun between his shoulders, watching the creature's beautiful head, with its twisted horns, standing out clearly against the mauve sky. He shot it cleanly and carried it back to the camp, and after handing it over to his servants William and Moosa, he went down to bathe himself in the pond, assuming that the young doctor was in her tent, dressing. His clothes were blood-soaked and he stripped them off on the flat rock before standing up to dive into the dark pool. As he stood there, naked and straight, his strong limbs gleaming in the disappearing light, he saw Mathilde swimming towards the adjacent slab of granite. She drew herself slowly out of the water and stood, yards away, unaware of his presence, her hair flat and sleek on her back and drawn away from her temple. Her strong, round limbs dripped with teardrops of water, like diamonds falling from a goddess. Olensky was hypnotised; stunned by her beauty. He saw the dark triangle between her legs, her swinging breasts, the nipples hard and sharp in the cool breeze of evening. She covered herself and moved silently away. He stood, the hunter, still and tense. He became aware of his cock, arcing upward towards his belly, and then he plunged into the pool and swam furiously up and down for half an hour at least, until he had exhausted himself and his blood had cooled.

On the fifth day one of the vehicles sustained a puncture in a front tyre and damage to the axle as they were ascending a rocky incline, and they had to make camp where they were and see to the damage. Moosa and William cranked up the vehicle and Moosa crawled underneath to get a better look. The chassis shifted on the steep slope and fell. Moosa was trapped underneath. He screamed and was then quiet.

'*Njoo! Njoni utazame!* Come and see, *bwana!*'

Olensky and Mathilde ran from where they were making camp to find William standing petrified and the feet of Moosa sticking out from under the badly listing vehicle.

'*Amekufa!* He is dead!' William was sobbing.

'William, hold that jack under the car. Push hard, man! Lift the car!' shouted Olensky. As soon as the vehicle was moved, Mathilde and Olensky carefully dragged out the injured – but not dead – Moosa.

'Let me see him,' said Mathilde.

Within minutes, Mathilde had established that Moosa had a broken leg and a badly crushed hand. She gave orders to the two men to find something with which to make a splint, and as she had no painkillers she reset his leg before he regained consciousness. They used planks torn from the floor of the vehicle to strap him to, and Mathilde cleaned and covered the damaged hand.

'Come, we must get him to a hospital, quickly,' Mathilde said.

'That isn't possible, I'm afraid,' Olensky told her. 'The nearest hospital is in Nairobi, two hundred miles away over rough terrain. We'll take him to my *shamba*. He can mend there. Come, we'll make camp here tonight, and leave at first light. We'll abandon the damaged vehicle. There's nothing else to be done.' Olensky and William carried the injured man-servant to a tent and made him comfortable.

'He must stay quiet and not move. Get drinking water, William,' ordered Mathilde. She stayed with him, bathing his sweating brow with cool water to keep his temperature down and changing his blood-soaked ban-

71

dages. Olensky brought her hot tea with whisky at intervals throughout the long night.

Eventually she fell asleep, slumped on the floor beside the injured man, and the baron watched over both of them.

On the seventh evening, as the sun was setting and the first star bloomed in the sky, they arrived at Olensky's bungalow. It stood at the top of a rocky ridge, backed by lacy trees, with a view over the river. It was made of stone, with a surrounding wooden veranda overhung by the corrugated metal roof.

'It's so beautiful!' Mathilde said, as they rounded the bend and got their first view of it.

'*Nyumba ya Simba*. It means "House of the Lion",' the baron said, smiling proudly.

A servant, one of two who lived there all the time and kept it ready for the irregular visits of the *bwana*, ran out to help with Moosa. The injured man was taken into the main house and Mathilde changed his soiled dressings again. He was better already, smiling and talking to Mathilde and the houseboy, Samuel, in rapid Swahili.

Mathilde patted him on the shoulder and left him to rest, while she had her first proper bath and shampoo for a week, and put on a clean dress with a warm sweater on top. Later, Samuel lit a log fire and Mathilde and Olensky sat in front of it on large leopard-skin cushions on a lion-skin rug, drinking their after-dinner whisky.

'Here's to Africa!' said an exhausted Mathilde.

'Yes, and to you. I have never shown anyone my home before.'

'Really? I can't believe that,' she laughed, embarrassed but secretly pleased.

'No, really, I mean it. I haven't ever brought anyone out here. This is my refuge: my lair.'

'The lion's lair. You look like a lion, you know, with your yellow hair and your golden eyes!'

He leant towards her, kissed her lips and took her in his arms. They cleaved to each other, as if they had both come home after a long time apart. His kisses tore at her, taking away her breath. His hands were removing her jumper, pulling it impatiently over her head, and then his palms pressed her full breasts through the thin dress and traced her nipples. She felt them harden at his touch. He undid several buttons and freed the ripe fruit, kissing them passionately, before pushing her back on to the fur rug. Her loose-legged cami-knickers were lifted aside by his sure fingers and he stroked her upper thighs, that fine, silken skin that is as sensitive to touch as is the sex. She shivered as his hard hands stroked firmly up and down her legs, now into the folds of her knickers, now down to her ankles. He kissed her feet, licking the underneath of them before putting his tongue between each toe. He nuzzled his way up her legs, stroking the backs of her knees as she lifted her legs. He turned her over on to her stomach and lifted her to remove her knickers. She sank back on to the rug, sighing and moaning.

Olensky removed his own clothes, then knelt over her and stroked her loosened hair. His teeth scraped lightly over her back and he kissed her full, round buttocks. He traced the hollow of her waist and the curve of her flaring hips. His hands pushed firmly between her legs and she spread her thighs to his touch. Her moisture was flowing and he stroked the soft fur of her sex and rubbed the juices over her sex lips. He bent to kiss her there, and she caught her breath in pleasure and bit her lip. She knelt, so he was between her legs and she was on her elbows and knees, her hair flung across her face. She saw the flames through her hair, and held tight to the rug as he kissed her and sucked her. Her orgasm was sudden and violent. She sank to the floor and threw out

73

her arms and legs in total surrender. He turned her over again and she saw his stocky torso, golden and tawny in the firelight. His sex was stiff and she took it in her hands. He was swollen hard, a solid stem of flesh. She pressed her fingers into her vagina to moisten them and then took his cock into her palms and rubbed it up and down, firmly to the base and up to the swollen bulb of the head. He moaned and squirmed, rolling his hips forward to meet her grip. His hands were on her again, rubbing her warm, furry sex. She felt beneath his cock to the thick root and held that as she rubbed with the other hand. His cock grew and she felt the throbbing of his imminent orgasm, so she stopped the tender caress and drew him towards her. He lifted her legs over his shoulders and held her buttocks, drawing her closer to him. His cock pierced her and found its home in her. They were joined together at the thighs, writhing as he pressed himself into her and filled her completely. She felt she had become all sex organ: her body had melted into him and become him. They groaned and panted and fought for their orgasms. They came together, shouting into each other's mouths.

'How do you say "You have killed me" in Swahili?' she whispered in his ear.

Chapter Nine

*T*hey slept fitfully, waking every now and again to throw logs on to the fire and to make love. They lay on and were covered by furs. Mathilde had never felt so beautiful. Her skin felt like silk, shimmering in the glow from the fire. Olensky kissed her cheeks and lips and eyes and she smiled. Her fingertips drew the lines around his eyes, memorising their contours like a Braille map. His breath warmed her ears and his tongue wet her neck. He was all passion and fire again, his cock hard and wanting her. Her legs opened to him, and he slipped into her easily. They lay under the animal skins, wrapped together, their lips pressed together. He whispered love words in Swahili, so she could not understand. But she did. She slept at last, her head on his chest, his arms wrapped around her.

Moosa grew stronger each day. His hand was healing and his leg, though sore, was mending. The baron took Mathilde out riding or trekking each afternoon and made love to her each night. She bloomed like a desert rose in the wilderness. Her eyes shone with enthusiasm for the life he led.

'What do you do exactly? Do you get paid?' she asked on one of their excursions.

'Occasionally! My main job is to count the big cats and elephants that roam through Tsavo and prevent poachers taking the ivory. And I am supposed to take visiting dignitaries hunting.'

'Ah yes, hunting! Do you enjoy killing the beasts?' She looked into his eyes.

'No, I cannot enjoy the destruction of these beautiful creatures. But the numbers are great, and it is work that enables me to be where I want to be, here in the heart of East Africa.'

'Yes, I see. Jorge, tell me more about the McKinnon wives. You never did properly explain why you thought they were kidnapped by slavers.'

'I knew the first Mrs McKinnon quite well ... very well. Her husband treated her with disdain and led her a hell of a life. He doesn't particularly ... like women.'

'You mean he is homosexual?' Mathilde suddenly remembered the decadent scene she had witnessed between McKinnon and the young man, Tim Strong.

'He is bisexual. And he owed money, lots of money.'

'What did *he* – a missionary – spend money on?' she asked. She knew he liked whisky, but not *that* much.

'He has a weakness for hallucinatory drugs,' Olensky told her, matter of factly.

'I see,' said Mathilde, trying to remain calm.

'The story was that Janet McKinnon was killed by a lion. It wasn't true. I was in the area where McKinnon said she was on safari. There was no indication of an animal attack. He got rid of her. Then suddenly he had a large amount of money. Began throwing it around at Mount Kenya Social Club. Bought himself an Arab boy, who didn't stay with him long. He was badly beaten apparently.' The baron sighed, his mouth set in a hard straight line.

'And the second Mrs McKinnon?'

'She was a silly young woman, by all accounts. I never met her – he didn't put up with her for long. My Kikuyu servants knew what happened to her and told me. She was sold into slavery. There is no doubt about it.'

'It doesn't seem possible. Where do you think the women are?' She leant against him.

'Who knows? They could be anywhere by now. But they were taken out of Mombasa by Arab dhow, first to Lamu or Zanzibar, then onward to Arabia, according to my Kikuyus.'

They both fell silent, watching the unfolding drama of a lion kill. A herd of zebras were drinking at the water hole. Hidden in the long white grass, the lions waited. As the zebras jostled for position, their black and white stripes merging and camouflaging them in the landscape, the lions made their attack, turning a zebra foal away from its mother. The end was quick. The family of lions crouched over the dead animal, tearing it apart. The zebra herd fled. A funereal group of vultures jostled for a good position at the deathbed.

'Come, it is getting late. We must get back to the *shamba*,' said the baron, taking Mathilde's hand and helping her to her feet.

Later, they made love. Their love-making was still exploratory. They had to learn about each other's bodies.

'Show me what you like,' she said.

'I like everything you do,' he said.

'What do you like particularly?'

'I like it when you hold my cock tight and rub it hard,' Olensky told her quietly.

'Right to the base, like this?' Mathilde held his thick rod.

'Yes, like that, and then to the crown, firmly.'

'Like this?'

'Mm, like that . . .'

'And do you like it when I suck your cock?'

'Naturally, you hussy!'

She moved to take him in her mouth, but he stopped her, holding her firmly. 'No! Let me do what you like,' he said. 'I will come too quickly if you do that.' She kissed him, marvelling at the softness of his lips. 'Let me suck you,' he said.

They were entwined, each head next to the other's groin. He held her hips, pressing his lips on her belly. His tongue travelled down the valley to her slit, nuzzling the dark blonde curly hair that hid her sex and quickly finding the folds of soft flesh. Her legs slid open and his face was hidden in her groin. His gold hair swept over her thighs while his nose prodded her sex.

She held his cock against her breasts and rubbed it up and down, while her other hand caressed his balls. She put her lips to the straining penis and opened them, so that it slid in and hit the roof of her mouth. Her tongue wrapped around his cock and sucked. His fingers were inside her and on her bottom, squeezing and caressing, pummelling and pressing. His teeth grazed her sex, his mouth sucking the swollen, soft lips. She raised her hips and stretched her sex towards his mouth. His cock grew and stiffened more in her mouth. She felt herself lose control. The spasms gripped her and her legs clenched as he lapped her juices. She groaned and sucked and her orgasm sent him over the edge of control. He came too and she swallowed silently.

In the morning, she found herself alone. She smelt the aromatic scent of coffee in the air, then heard footsteps. Olensky entered the room.

'I must go back to the mission soon, you know,' Mathilde said to him, stretching her long white arms over her head and closing her eyes. The sheets rustled, clean and crisp and cool. 'You cannot go back...' whispered Olensky, panic rising in his throat.

The breeze blew through the wooden shutters, making them clatter impatiently, and the muslin mosquito net rose and fell around them in the wide bed.

'There is my work at the mission,' Mathilde insisted.

'I won't let you go just yet.' Olensky held her wrists with his strong hands and pressed down on to her once more.

Later, he took her out into the bush and they made camp under the shade of a thorn tree. After a simple meal and a glass or two of whisky, they washed and crept under the muslin canopy. A hurricane lamp hung from a hook and lit their eyes, revealing the curves of her body and the hard muscles of his. He clasped her to him, pressing himself to her breasts. He kissed her passionately, pulling her head back so he could kiss her white throat. She gave herself to him absolutely. His body fitted into hers so perfectly, she felt like a velvet glove which he wore. His hands knew her body now; knew the hollow of her groin, the gentle curve of her belly and the tiny cave of her navel. He breathed in the scent of her fragrant hair and between her legs. Their teeth clashed in passion. His arms pinned her down, hurting her, but she loved his passion and the ferocity of his love-making. He kissed the dimples on her buttocks and nuzzled her as if he was a dog. His cock was always hard for her; he could not get enough of her. He wrapped her legs around him and carried her, attached to her by his cock. They made love all night long, and only slept in the early dawn, the ruby sun like a heavy egg yolk hanging above the rosy veldt. Mathilde was wild in her love-making. She felt she could orgasm just by being kissed by Olensky. His touch on her was fire.

One evening, as the night covered the ridges and crept into the hollows, they watched for lions. Olensky had seen their spoor and knew they would be back to drink at the water-hole. They could hear the gentle rumble of their love-calls in the distance. Suddenly, Olensky made the same sound. She froze, thinking it was a lion close by.

She laughed softly and he held her tight. The lions

came – a mother and her two young cubs. They drank carefully, the mother keeping watch while the cubs took their fill. Olensky and Mathilde held their breath. The family of big yellow cats slipped away into the shadows and became part of the velvet night.

Chapter Ten

*I*t was an interlude of great beauty in their lives. They spent their days riding through the baron's beloved bush country, watching the wildlife. The sight of elephants moved Mathilde more than the other big game. There was something incredibly sad about the sight of the great beasts, lumbering around in slow motion. Their time was short, the baron said. Soon the so-called civilised world would take over their territory. Already, settlers from the south were moving in. The East African protectorate was being sold off, piecemeal, to outsiders who did not care what happened to the wild animals. The elephants were being thwarted already in their annual pilgrimage to fresh territories by fencing and new settlements. Once, Mathilde and Olensky sat on their small, hardy horses and watched as a family of elephants moved along the track, helping the babies negotiate a fallen tree trunk. The matrons gathered juicy leaves and gave them to the little ones. A recalcitrant junior who kept snatching leaves from the babies was punished by an elderly matron, who used her trunk to thrash the bully's behind. The lessons of cherishing and caring for one another were being taught by the old to the young.

Everything was fascinating to Mathilde, and she learnt so much from Olensky.

She was falling in love with this lion-like lover. She herself had completely recovered and she attended to Moosa's leg and hand each day. News of her expertise began to spread. Matabele men, women and children queued each day for her to look at their diseased limbs, take their temperatures or bandage their cuts.

'Ah, well, as long as I am of some use, somewhere,' she said, shrugging, secretly pleased that she was working once more.

One day a group of Masai headed towards the baron and Mathilde while they were out riding. The Masai, tall, thin and elegant as mannequins, ran straight at them from a great distance. Olensky reined in his horse and bade Mathilde stop too. She held her breath as the men raced past them, not even looking in their direction. They wore nothing but small loincloths and high collars of black feathers, with necklaces and earrings of small beads.

'Why didn't they stop?' she asked, breathing fast.

'They are running to somewhere they must go and cannot stop. They are like the bison.'

He said enigmatic things that intrigued her all the time. His nature was to be reticent. He announced, one morning, that he had to go to Nairobi to collect two German would-be hunters and take them to Serengeti.

'Can't I come too?' she asked.

'No, you'd better not,' he answered, without hesitation.

'All right,' she agreed reluctantly.

'Will you be all right here?'

'Of course.'

While he was gone, she stayed at *Nyumba ya Simba* with only the convalescing Moosa and the kitchen *toto* to keep her company. William and Samuel had accompanied the baron on the journey. The second truck had been hauled back to the *shamba* and mended, so she had transport in case of an emergency.

She wrote letters home, telling her family that she was enjoying Africa more than she could have imagined. She still hadn't mentioned to them the missionary's drug addiction or the hints of white slavery – there was no point in worrying them, she thought. She taught the little kitchen *toto*, Zamwa, to read and write, and he helped her with the clinic, noting the names and conditions of her patients. Mostly they wanted strong, evil-tasting medicines or the soothing sting of iodine, so painful they knew it must work.

One morning, she rose to find the usual small dribble of the halt and lame waiting by the veranda for the clinic to start. She quickly dealt with several minor injuries and a case of hives, and then examined a young woman who was six months pregnant. As she was saying goodbye to the woman, she saw a man running out of the bush.

It was Joseph.

'But what are you doing here, Joseph?' she asked in surprise as he approached her. She couldn't understand how he had got there.

'*Memsahib*, you must come quick. It is Grace, she very sick.'

'Come where? Why?'

'*Memsahib*, I cannot explain. Please come now. Grace is dying, I think.'

'Where is she?'

'In my village. We leave the mission – *bwana* beat me and he beat Grace. We leave and come home. Please, *memsahib*, come now.' Joseph was sweating profusely even in the morning cool.

'How far is it?' Mathilde asked.

'Two hours walk only.'

'Wait! Zamwa! Go to the house and get this man a drink of tea,' she ordered. 'I will prepare for the journey.'

She gathered her drugs and equipment into her medical bag and called Moosa, who was limping around the garden, watering the plants. 'Moosa, I am going with this man to his village, two hours walk away. I will take the truck.'

'Yes, *memsahib*. But *bwana* say you must stay here,' he reminded her.

She bristled slightly. 'I will go with this man. There is a sick girl I must attend to.'

'Yes, *memsahib*.'

Joseph and Mathilde got into the truck and started off down through the green folds of country, over the dry ford of the river and off towards the south. She reckoned they would soon be at Joseph's village – two hours walk could not be very far by truck. Joseph had little to say once they were on their way. She wondered what he thought of her, running out on the missionary.

'You are very quiet, Joseph. Tell me about Grace. What are her symptoms?'

'Symptoms? What is that, *memsahib*?'

'How is she sick, Joseph? Is she vomiting? Does she have fever?'

'Yes, *memsahib*.' He looked ahead, holding the truck roof with a powerful hand. His muscles knotted and twisted and swelled. He looked anxious and sweated heavily. He had changed, she saw. He would not look her in the eye and he pouted his thick lips in an uncharacteristic way, as if he was angry.

'There is my village. Behind these rocks.' He pointed to a ridge about half a mile away.

There was a small dot moving towards them. A vehicle.

Maybe it's Jorge, she thought.

The dot grew bigger. It was another truck, driven by a Matabele. He hooted at them and stopped. The driver got out on to the track .

84

Mathilde put her foot on the brake and said, 'What now?'

Joseph's large hand was on her shoulder suddenly, clasping it firmly. She looked into his face and saw the jubilation on it. Then she understood. Joseph manhandled her out on to the hard red-earth track. She fought him at first, hitting at his hard chest with her fists. He felt nothing. The other man took her legs and bound them together, and then tied her arms to her body and gagged her. She was hit in the face, blindfolded and thrown into the back of the other truck. She smelt and tasted a sick-sweet trace of her own blood.

Chapter Eleven

Mathilde woke several times and slept again, dreaming that she was being carried in a boat. She knew this could not be so – not in the middle of the African bush. She was aware of the strong odour of an animal, and in her semi-conscious state an awesome sound came to her – a screaming groan; a deep grunting. Camels! A camel train carried her and her captors back through the bush and savannah to the coast. She slept again. When she woke, she smelt the strong fragrances of cinnamon and cardamom before drifting back into unconsciousness.

Later, much later, she opened her eyes, but she felt sick and her head hurt. Her clothes stuck to her. Her hands were bound behind her back and her feet were tied to each other. It was dark but she could discern a lantern light above her head and voices rose and fell in a sing-song language. The boards beneath her were damp and sweaty. There were sacks of spice around her. She realised she was in the hold of a boat, probably a dhow. She felt the shift and roll of the boat, and heard the straining sail groan. She tried to loosen the ropes that bound her wrists but to no avail. She was not gagged or blindfolded any more. She heard footfalls on the deck above her. A trapdoor opened and someone descended the ladder. Mathilde instinctively pretended to be unconscious again, lying on her side and closing her eyes. The man came so close she could smell his breath – a mixture of spice, tobacco and fish. Her stomach contracted and she had to control the instinct to retch. He moved away and started shifting sacks. She opened her eyes a little so she could see him. It was an Arab; a dark, small character.

She slept again, vaguely aware of someone giving her water to drink at some point. It was many hours later that she was gagged and blindfolded by the Arab and carried up the ladder to the deck. She could smell the salt breeze and feel the blessed wind in her hair. There were other voices, speaking a language she could not understand. The sound of small waves breaking on a sandy shore told her the dhow had landed.

She was carried over the man's shoulder. He carried her carefully, like precious cargo. The blood ran to her head, which still ached, she suddenly realised. He walked steadily through sand, his feet quiet and his steps laboured. He was a small man and she was a tall, well-built woman. He breathed heavily and coughed often. Soon he let her fall gently on to something soft and silky. She lay there for some time before she sensed that someone was standing over her. She waited, quiet.

Her blindfold was removed and her gag untied. She blinked in the sudden light that assailed her. Her wrists were sore and her legs numb. She rubbed them.

'You must wash.' The young woman who spoke was slender, and her skin was almost black, with an amber gloss. Her face was veiled by a red gauze, but her long, narrow eyes were visible over it. Her dark, oiled hair was coiled in a plait around her head. Her loose tunic-like garment of thin red silk showed her full-breasted figure. She wore nothing under it.

Mathilde followed the Nubian woman through a marble hall with tall pillars. They came to a large pool, open to the sky. There were several women in the pool, naked. They stared at the newcomer.

'Take off your clothes.' The woman in red unbuttoned Mathilde's shirt.

'Thank you, I am quite capable of doing that myself,' said Mathilde, surprised to hear her own voice. She undressed quickly, glad to be rid of her stinking clothes. God knows how long I have worn them! she thought. She plunged into the shallow water.

'No! Not there! You must go into the cleansing pool first.' The Nubian woman pointed imperiously at a small pool adjacent to the main pool.

Two naked, adolescent Nubian girls approached the edge of the pool and helped Mathilde get out. They accompanied her to the cleansing pool and joined her, rubbing her body with scented cloths. She felt as if she was dreaming. This could not be happening!

The girls washed Mathilde's hair with a herbal wash and she gratefully sank on to her back and rinsed it in the warm water. Her limbs felt numb still and her head was pounding. The two girls scrubbed her all over quite thoroughly, as if she were a piece of sculpture rather than a woman. She floated, not daring to think.

The bath over, Mathilde was then depilated by the Nubian girls. She tried to protest, but she felt so weak and sleepy that she could not. They laid her on a high couch of leather, lifted her legs and shaved off the hair from them quickly and expertly. Her underarms were also shaved. This done, they lifted her long legs, pulled them apart, and placed them in slings. They did not speak. Mathilde slipped back into a light slumber, thinking that the most natural thing in the world was to be shaved by girls. They smoothed a herbal cream between her legs and shaved off the fine, fair hair. She was oiled all over with sandalwood and bougainvillaea essence.

Her face was veiled in a blue muslin and her body covered in a blue transparent tunic. A wide collar of gold was placed around her neck and padlocked on with a gold key. A ring hung from the collar. Then she was left in a low-lit chamber, on her own. The soothing sound of running water surrounded her. She slept.

When she woke there was a man standing over her. He was a large black man, wearing an elaborate costume of green and gold and a tall turban with rubies sewn on to it. He gave her a gold goblet and bade her drink. She did so; she was very thirsty. The drink was good – a refreshing herbal tea. She sank back on to the couch.

She dreamt of lions. The shadow of a golden lion touched her and cooled her hot skin. She called the name of Jorge in her sleep. She reached out for him but there was no-one there.

'Where am I?' Mathilde had woken at last with a clear head. The Nubian woman in red stood over her, her narrow eyes accentuated with black lines.

'You are at the crossroad of your life.'

'What are you saying? I don't understand.'

'You are on your way to a new life.'

Mathilde sat up, surprised to find that she was naked under the muslin sheet. 'Yes, but where, exactly?' She was annoyed at the enigmatic answers to her straight-forward questions.

'You do not need to know anything. It no longer concerns you. You are in other hands now. You have no need to make decisions.'

'I insist that you tell me,' shouted Mathilde, angry now. She got out of the bed and stood, naked, before the veiled woman.

The two Nubian girls who had attended her before appeared and wrapped her in a thin cloak of cream raw silk. She found herself allowing them to clothe her, as if she was used to being dressed by other people. They were lovely girls, she noticed. They could have been sisters. Their round faces smiled at her and their hennaed hands stroked her fair skin with admiration. She was embarrassed when she remembered how they had shaved her bodily hair.

The Nubian woman moved close to her. 'My name is Serena. If you need something, you may ask me.'

Mathilde pushed the eager hands from her arms and breasts and walked to the high window in the small white room. She looked up. There was a pocket handkerchief of pale blue sky. A sea-bird hung motionless.

Am I in Arabia or Dar es Salaam? Or Zanzibar? Please God I am still in Africa! she prayed silently.

Moments later, Mathilde was allowed out into the courtyard to walk and breathe the soft air. She could see that escape was not possible. The smooth walls were high and there were no trees to climb. There were no gates; only a heavy wood door in the wall, which was guarded by an armed man. He looked like the man who had given her drink, but his uniform of grey cotton and turban had no rubies adorning it.

There were only women here, as far as she could see. They were all black women; she was the only white woman. She remembered the turbaned man and the gold goblet.

It was as if she had never lived before. All her past life had been taken from her. She felt as if she had always been in the marble halls. Her neck had always had this gold collar around it, holding her head up high.

For the first few days she cried bitterly. She slept badly, waking in tears. The Nubian girls washed and massaged her every day. Serena tried to stroke her breasts and hold her hand, but Mathilde fought her. She could not believe that her freedom had gone for ever. How could this ridiculous thing have happened to her, a qualified doctor? She cried and prayed and screamed loud in the dark. But no-one who would help her heard her cries.

She was shaved daily. The eyes of the two girls on her, their fingers touching her, was a sensual experience. Her clothes were sheer silk, and she was always aware of her nakedness under the shimmering stuff. Her nipples pierced the finely spun material and her hips and buttocks moved sinuously under it. She saw that all the other women were shaved of their body hair too. She found her eyes being drawn to the triangles between their legs, and then to their plump slits. The scent of musk and jasmine surrounded her, a heady mélange of sexuality.

Weeks passed and she began to stop crying. She was not happier, but she realised that there was nothing she could do to improve her position. She knew that it was her duty to remain fit and strong and ready to take advantage of any situation which would enable her to escape.

She was fattened like a favourite calf with sweetmeats, figs, marzipan and sugared almonds. Her arms softened and her breasts swelled. Her belly rounded and her buttocks dimpled, even though she made sure she exercised each day in the pool and courtyard. The other women who were kept there seemed happy enough, though no-one spoke English or even Swahili, except Serena. The other women whispered to each other and kept apart from Mathilde, only touching her as if she was a precious sculpture. One one occasion a woman, jealous of Mathilde's yellow hair, grabbed it and pulled at it, tugging hard. Mathilde found herself in a fight with her assailant, rolling on the marble floor, their limbs entwined. She punched and kicked as her attacker tried to bite her arm. The woman pulled at Mathilde's breasts and bit her neck, while Mathilde put her hands around her neck and tried to strangle her. And afterwards, when they had been separated like two bad-tempered dogs, she sobbed in horror of what she had done, and what was happening to her.

Later, as she was being dried by the two girls with a large, soft towel, Mathilde spoke to Serena, who stood close, in desperate tones.

'How long am I to be kept here?' It had been four weeks, she reckoned, since she had been captured.

'Soon you will go to another place. This is just a resting place for you,' Serena told her.

'Is it . . . is this a *harem*?' Mathilde said the word with distaste.

'No, this is only a stopping place. A place of waiting. The harem is not here. Do not ask questions like this. I cannot tell you.' Serena turned away from her charge and walked quickly from her.

As she reached the edge of the pool she slipped on the wet tiles and fell heavily and awkwardly on to her left arm, rolling into the water. Mathilde threw off the enthusiastic handmaidens and plunged into the pool. Serena was unconscious, floating on her belly. Three other women helped lift the injured woman on to the side of the pool, and Mathilde automatically became the caring doctor. She made sure Serena's air passages were open, then she positioned her on her uninjured arm and carefully pumped the water out of her choking lungs. She sent the girls to fetch towels and pillows and made her as comfortable as she could. She examined the arm and decided it was broken.

Serena was suddenly conscious again, tears streaming from her black, smudged eyes. She coughed and cried in pain.

'Don't try to move,' Mathilde told her. 'You are all right. You've broken your arm. I'll have to set it for you. Have you any painkilling drugs or opiates?'

'Just do it.' The proud woman took a corner of a towel between her teeth and closed her eyes.

Mathilde did what she had to do, amazed at the

stoicism of the woman. One of the handmaidens fainted when she heard the bone click into place, and had to be carried off. Splints were made from sweetly perfumed slats of sandalwood. Bandages were strapped around the arm and shoulder and then Serena was taken into her own bedchamber.

The English doctor, left on her own, took the opportunity to try every door in the place. There were many doors leading off the large hall of the pool area. They were heavy wood, with large nails studding them. Most of the doors led to bedchambers for the women and were open. Each small room was like the next, with a narrow bed, a chair, a bidet and a small, high window looking up to an empty, hopeless sky. One door led to the dining area where the women ate together three times a day. There was a long, low table holding candles and a silver dish of fruit, and silk, tapestry cushions on the tiled floor.

One door was locked. Mathilde hammered on it with her fists, angry at herself for her female helplessness and her physical weakness. This is unbearable, she thought. She fell to her knees, sobbing.

Chapter Twelve

*T*he Germans had hunted badly and with no finesse, and the baron had had to finish off the injured game for them. He was bored with their brutish company and was only too pleased to say goodbye to them in Nairobi, where they were organising the shipping of the skins and ivory they had bagged. But the men had seemed satisfied with their sport – their blood-lust was sated for a while.

As the baron and William drove the long dusty miles back across the huge savannah, Olensky found that he was tense with excitement at the thought of seeing the Englishwoman again. He had dreamt about her several times and had woken to find his sheet sticky with semen.

In his dreams she was bound and blindfolded, completely wrapped in bandage-like ropes so that only her genitals were exposed. Her hair was loose and her mouth was red and wide, as was her gaping vagina. In his dreams he had penetrated her mouth violently and watched his semen drip down her chin. He had held her plump sex in his hands and pushed his fingers deep inside, pulling her apart. He had licked and sucked at her genitals while his cock was deep in her sucking mouth. She had lain, helpless, while he had his way with her. The dreams came back to him now as they came close to *Nyumba ya Simba*. He wanted her.

Moosa stood on the veranda, his head lowered and his shoulders drooping.

'What is the matter? Where is the *memsahib*?' asked Olensky, immediately concerned.

'She went with a man to his village and has not returned, *bwana*,' Moosa told him quietly.

'You let her go, alone?' The baron barked the words.

'*Memsahib* would not allow me to accompany her, *bwana*.'

'When was this?' The baron felt sick to his stomach, not wanting to hear the answer.

'It was many days ago, *bwana*, too many days.'

They found the abandoned truck, still with petrol in the tank. There was no sign of a struggle. Mathilde's bag of medicines and medical equipment had gone, as had the vehicle's tools. A few things were scattered over the stony ground.

The baron searched for a village. There was a settlement about ten miles to the north and he asked if anyone had heard news of her. But it was no use. No-one had heard of the man, Joseph, or seen anything unusual, and no-one had seen the white woman he described.

The baron drove for days without rest. He was out of his mind with worry. He had had a presentiment that this would happen. Why had he left her alone? He went back to the village and asked again, offering a reward for any information.

Several days went by before a woman with a baby strapped to her back walked into the *shamba* and crouched on the earth in front of the main door, waiting. The dogs barked and woke the household, and Samuel found her, nursing her child, in the golden dawn light.

He offered her food and drink, but she waved it aside and asked for the *bwana*.

The baron went outside to see the woman. They talked for a long time and then he gave her a bag of food provisions and bales of cloth. She went away smiling.

Two days later he arrived at the beach mission near Mombasa and demanded to see McKinnon. The nuns were surprised to see him.

'You look awful, Baron Olensky! What ails you, man?' Sister Prudence called for water for him to drink. The man-servant came – it was not Joseph – with a jug of cold water.

'Where is Joseph?' the baron demanded.

'He left a long time ago, with Grace. Soon after you took the sick doctor away. Where is Dr Valentine, Baron? Is she well?' Sister Prudence could see he was upset.

'No, she is not well. She has disappeared – like the others.' The man's proud head bent in sorrow, anger and exhaustion.

'Like McKinnon's wives, do you mean? Oh, God help us!'

'Yes, like the missionary's wives. Where is the blag-gard?' The baron stood and his hand went automatically to his hunting knife, in anticipation of meeting the man he despised.

'Oh, he's off again, somewhere. We were not honoured with information of his business, as usual.' Sister Prudence frowned in sympathy.

At the coffee houses in Mombasa the baron sought news of McKinnon. He at last caught sight of Heinlich, the tea planter, grubby and sweaty as usual, sitting and drinking with a grossly overweight Arab, who was dressed from head to toe in clean, white robes.

The baron stood to attention and gave a slight bow in the Arab's direction.

'Excuse me, I must talk with you, Heinlich.'

'You must wait. I have business to complete.' The loathsome, sweaty planter threw him a satisfied, sneering smile, totally devoid of humour, and waved him away.

Before he knew what he was doing, Olensky had lifted the man up by his arms and punched him in the face. Heinlich looked astonished for a moment, then regained his balance and hit back. The Arab moved quickly to get out of the way of the two opponents and fled from the cafe. Heinlich was no match for the fit, muscular hunter. He collapsed on the tiled floor, winded and with a bloody nose.

'You bastard! Where is Dr Valentine?' With a warning hand the baron stopped the waiters from helping the floored man.

Heinlich sniffed and wiped his nose with his hand, then looked up at the looming form of the baron.

'I know nothing of the dear doctor, Baron. Is this why you attack me? You think I have something to do with her disappearance?'

Olensky grabbed the dishevelled man and drew him up by his lapels. 'How do you know she has disappeared?' He shook the man like a terrier shakes a rabbit, and threw him to the floor again.

By this time a crowd had gathered. Arab traders, black waiters and passers-by stood and watched in interest and excitement.

'You yourself inferred she had gone, you fool!' The angry Heinlich got up, this time watching every move that Olensky made, ready to defend himself if need be.

The baron threw the table aside, pushed the crowds apart and strode off down the steps, where he joined the worried figure of William. Together they walked quickly away.

Heinlich smiled and felt the bulge of his pocket, thankful that the baron had not seen the Arab pass Heinlich the pouch of diamonds and rubies.

'*Bwana*, I have news of the missionary,' William said quietly.

They parked the truck where they could and walked through the narrow streets. They found McKinnon in an opium den, in one of the many dirt alleyways that made up the old town near the docks. William spoke quickly to the toothless old woman who stood guard at the door and pushed money into her hand. She shrugged and let them pass. Once inside, they were met by the strong, pungent odour of men's sweat and the sweet smell of opium. It was surprisingly cool and very dark inside. It took them a moment before their eyes grew accustomed to the gloom after the bright sunlight. A group of Arabs sat or lay on the ground, with pipes next to them. In one corner slumped the unconscious white man, his eyes half open, showing only the whites.

The baron nodded to William, who picked up the decadent missionary and carried him, over his shoulder, outside into the sunlight. The baron strode ahead with the black man carrying the prone McKinnon like a heavy sack.

Back at the baron's Mombasa house, the missionary was left to recover with William guarding him. Twenty-four hours later he came out of the drug-induced slumber to find that he had been washed and his clothes taken away. His hands were bound to the bed and he could not raise himself. William called the baron. Olensky stood glowering at the stupefied missionary.

'You are lucky I have not cut off your prick, you fiend!' he snarled at the man. 'Tell me what you have done with Dr Valentine.'

'I have done nothing with her. Ask Heinlich if you want to know where she is.' He pulled at the ropes which bound him. 'Let me up, you cad, I have done nothing.'

The baron stood, shaking in rage and frustration. 'You

know what has happened to her. Tell me or I'll kill you.'
He drew out his hunting knife, a long, sharp blade with
an ivory handle, from its leather sheath. Then he held it
close to the man's throat and McKinnon's face tightened
in fear. 'I mean it! I could kill you easily and leave your
body for the vultures. No-one cares what happens to
you, you dissipated, disgusting waster.' The missionary
suddenly burst into hysterical tears, sobbing loudly.
'Right, tell me what you know, and I shall free you.'

'Yes! Yes! I'll tell you! I'll tell you!' The missionary
sniffed loudly and calmed down.

Chapter Thirteen

*H*e is pathetic, thought Olensky, his golden eyes narrowed in hate as he saw the missionary cringe from the knife.

'Take the knife away, for God's sake.' McKinnon sobbed like a child.

Olensky pushed the edge of the blade against the white throat and snarled, 'Just tell me what you know of the whereabouts of Dr Valentine, you dog! Tell me now!'

The story the missionary had to tell was punctuated with sobs and sniffs.

He had agreed to take the Englishwoman to Heinlich, who would give him money. But it hadn't happened like that. He, McKinnon, had failed to drug the woman doctor successfully, and the baron had indeed rescued her in time. McKinnon had got an advance payment from Heinlich for the proposed kidnapping of the doctor, and after McKinnon discovered that the baron had taken the woman, he had spent it on opiates. He was in hiding from Heinlich, in fact. Now he owed the tea planter money, his life was not worth living.

'Heinlich knew where you were. He told me,' said

Olensky. He despised this Scottish missionary, who was such a disgrace to his race and creed.

'Perhaps he is saving me for later,' the bound man laughed, without humour.

'So, if you didn't supply Heinlich with the English-woman, who did?'

'Joseph, I suspect. He knew my plan and knew Heinlich's movements. I wouldn't put it past him. He was a cunning little bastard.'

The baron did not think that Joseph could have planned Mathilde's abduction from the bush on his own. More likely he had gone to Heinlich and Heinlich had hired him direct and told him what to do. The baron believed the missionary, in spite of his past. He told William to set him free and throw him out. Heinlich could deal with him.

Olensky's plan was to have Heinlich arrested on suspicion of kidnapping.

The next morning he went to the Mombasa police and told them his fears.

'But you have no evidence that she has been kidnapped, Baron Olensky.' The English policeman took off his pith helmet and scratched his balding head. 'She could have left the country without informing you. She is a grown woman, after all.'

'I might have known you would be of no help,' the baron spat at him. He picked up his bush hat and walked out without another word.

Meanwhile, Mathilde was in the 'waiting house' on the island of Zanzibar, awaiting transport to Arabia where she would become the latest white slave in the harem of the immensely rich Sultan of Abizir.

Her tormentor, the beautiful Serena, was resting from her arduous duties with a broken arm. The two Nubian girls who attended her bodily needs were delighted that Serena was not there. They had just found out that the white woman was a doctor and they planned to play a trick on her.

The two girls had learnt a few words of English in the weeks they had spent in Mathilde's company. She had been friendly to them because she was desperate for companionship. She admired their natural, animal grace, and had come to enjoy the sensual experience of being bathed by them and shaved between the legs.

One morning, after the ritual shaving, Parveneh, the younger of the two girls, clasped her naked stomach and moaned pitifully.

Mathilde sat up.

'What is it, dear child?' She stood on the bare tiled floor, rather sorry that her depilation was over so quickly and she had not had her massage.

She urged the Nubian girl to get on the low couch so that she could examine her. The other girl, Qitura, stood close, her eyes wide and her moist red lips open as the naked doctor felt the firm belly of the black girl and parted her legs. Parveneh moaned and pointed at herself, saying, 'My private parts, they hurt me, inside.'

Mathilde gently pushed the girl on to her side and raised her legs. She washed her hands and slipped a finger into the moist, pink tunnel.

'Oh! Oh!' The pretty girl put her hands over her mouth and face.

'Does that hurt, my dear?'

'Oh! No! It feels good, so good!' Both girls giggled and Parveneh squirmed in pleasure.

Mathilde was annoyed at the trick they had played on her. She clapped her hands loudly.

'Off with you both, you wicked creatures!' They ran from the chamber laughing.

Mathilde was shocked at the pleasure she was beginning to feel at the gentle and delicate handling from these simple girls each day. This last incident was just one in a series of events, unimportant in themselves, but taken together she saw that it was a probably a plot to eroticise her. The girls would hold her hands and casually place them on their small breasts. They would bend over in her presence so that she could see their round buttocks and their plump, developing sex parts. They shaved each other's bodily hairs in her presence, and she would feel herself getting moist between her legs as she watched.

All the women wore gold collars around their necks, but they seemed content. They laughed and played together, splashed and swam, ate prodigious amounts of food, and drank sweet drinks and curds. They had many diaphanous garments to choose from; clothes which drew attention to their naked buttocks and breasts, the bulge between their legs, the crease and slit, their swaying hips. Mathilde watched the languid movements of the slave-women, and imperceptibly became like them. She moved as they did; slowly swaying her hips and placing her feet straight in front of each other, her head held high by the wide collar around her proud throat.

Mathilde was not an unwilling witness to the passionate couplings that took place daily in the steam-filled bathing pool hall. She watched surreptitiously as two African girls, no more than seventeen years old and just reaching the peak of their beauty, made love on a low divan, just within her view. They had fallen into each other's arms after a long soaping in the pool, their long matted hair wet and clinging to their backs and little breasts. They looked like ripe fruit, Mathilde thought, and felt the urge to press their firm, soft flesh. One slender girl kissed the other passionately and twined a leg over the other's lower limbs. Holding her in this erotic embrace she rubbed her belly and pubis against the other naked body, and Mathilde distinctly heard the rasp of flesh on flesh. They touched each other delicately, holding each breast as if it were a precious, fragile egg. One of the girls – the prettier one, who had almond-shaped eyes as black as coal and skin like polished bronze – had breasts whose areolae and nipples were swollen like the top of a pear. The other had high, round apples of breasts with long, taut nipples, almost liquorice brown. The nipples disappeared between bee-stung lips and were trapped between square white teeth. Their eager fingers explored their private places; the newly shaved triangles, the narrow, dark slits. Mathilde saw the peeping red buds, teased out by the delicate fingering. She watched, and as she watched she touched herself softly and delicately, unknowingly matching their movements. They writhed on the divan and held each other in a close embrace, their legs wrapped around each other. They turned so that they could taste each other's love juices. They nibbled at the tender, swollen, fleshy sex lips and they thrust their hips at each other's mouth, their buttocks shaking. Mathilde was overcome by the beauty of the two female lovers, and she came, silently, alone.

Some hours after Qitura and Parveneh had played the naughty trick on Mathilde, she lay in her lonely chamber remembering the time she had spent in the East African bush with Olensky. It was as if she had been dreaming of a perfect place. It no longer existed; it was all in her imagination. She saw again the firelight in his yellow hair, the taut muscles of his loins, his powerful shoulders, his strong arms holding her down. She felt his fingers on her flesh, parting her legs. His lips on her belly. His tongue.

There was a tap at her door.

'Come in,' she said, and dried the self-pitying tears she had been shedding.

It was Serena. The woman still had her arm in a sling. She wore a long orange tunic, slit up the front to her thighs and at the back to her buttocks. Her round breasts almost fell out of the low-cut bodice.

Mathilde sat up. The Nubian woman sat on the low bed next to her.

'I have come to thank you for saving my life,' she said, her voice soft and low.

'It was nothing.'

'Oh yes, it was something.'

Mathilde was aware of the woman's scent, like honeysuckle in the English dusk. The silky thighs shifted in the silk tunic and the material fell apart to expose the triangle that her thighs made with her pubis. The musky perfume of the dark woman filled Mathilde's nostrils and she felt faint.

Mathilde sat with her hands behind her on the bed, her back straight. The gold collar glinted in the moonlight.

'What do you want?' she asked harshly.

'I want to be friends with you.' Serena's voice was softly seductive.

'Go away! Leave me! You are my captor, not my friend.'

'I am not your captor. I too am a slave. It would be good for you to be friendly with me.' Serena caressed Mathilde's breasts with her one free hand.

'No! No!' Mathilde swiftly removed herself from the proximity of the Nubian woman. She found her tunic and wrapped it around her naked shoulders.

Serena stood and silently regarded Mathilde. The Nubian's whole stance was arrogant and powerful. She was used to being obeyed and was angry that the Englishwoman would not give in to her.

'No matter. You will not be here for much longer.' She turned from Mathilde and walked out of the room, slamming the heavy door behind her.

Mathilde lay on her narrow bed. She closed her eyes and tried again to bring back the sensations of being with her lion lover in his African bungalow. She imagined lying by the blazing log fire on the animal skins, her legs and his entwined, his mouth pressing on hers. She suddenly introduced Serena into her fantasy. The slave pressed her naked body between them and kissed Mathilde, and then her hands were on Olensky's thighs. His fingers and Mathilde's met inside the dark petals of the slave's sex. Mathilde's lips sucked the bullet-like purple nipples. She imagined that dark head between Jorge's thighs, and those rich, red lips around his cock.

Mathilde's fingers moved rapidly in and out of her vagina. Her excitement grew with each thrust. She pushed silken cloth into her slit and rubbed it up and down. The gold collar around her neck felt tight as she breathed heavily. Her breasts were heavy and warm, and she brushed the nipples with her fingertips. She needed something bigger than her fingers inside her. She wanted Jorge's cock. She saw in her inner eye the stiff column of shiny flesh grow bigger and bigger. She felt it pressing her flesh and parting her sex lips. She felt him pushing into her, hard and insistent. She raised her hips to meet the thrusts. Her fingers pummelled and sank into her soft, enveloping tunnel. Her hands slapped at the open lips. She felt the soft swelling of her sex and her fleshy tunnel, wet with longing. Her neck stretched back and she closed her eyes and saw Jorge and Serena smothering her with kisses, caressing her arms and legs and feet. She felt his firm grip and the long fingernails of Serena inserted into her sex. She felt his hands part her buttocks and stretch her anus open. She felt Serena's flickering tongue on her sex and Jorge's swollen prick push between her buttocks.

She was overwhelmed. She came, and came again, her body shaking with the tremors of the little earthquake. Her thighs were on fire. Her mouth was dry. She found salt tears running into her mouth. They tasted good.

The air was full of the scent of cloves. Through the high, barred window of Mathilde's small bedchamber it wafted, strongly pungent, reminding her of home and apple pies. She was so frustrated. This time in captivity was so mind dulling. Such a waste of time! She almost looked forward to being moved on, even though she did not know her fate. She felt that if they moved her she would at least have some sort of chance of escape. Meanwhile, she had come to a decision. She would befriend Serena. It might help her situation, after all. She also needed to talk to someone, to be a part of life. As she breathed the exotic scent she suddenly remembered something that her friend and mentor, Dr Witherspoon, had told her when she was having Swahili lessons with him back in London. In 1882, Seyyid Said, the Immam of Muscat, transferred his capital from Muscat to Zanzibar and made it his permanent residence. He was responsible for the introduction of the clove and it was during his reign that Zanzibar became politically and commercially the principal town in East Africa.

'That's it! Cloves!'

Mathilde was convinced now that she was being held in Zanzibar. She was jubilant. She was still in East Africa. Somehow Olensky would find her. She inhaled the spicy smell, and filled her lungs with hope.

Zanzibar, she remembered from her reading, had been the principal market of the great African slave trade, which only ceased in 1873 when, under pressure from Great Britain, Sultan Bargash closed all public slave markets throughout his dominions. She wondered if British residents were aware of the continuing private trade in slaves in the protectorate.

When Mathilde next saw Serena at the bathing pool, she made an effort to be friendly to her.

'I'm sorry I was so rude to you,' she said. 'How is your arm?'

'Better, thank you.' The woman smiled and her haughty demeanour at once changed. Her open smile transformed the usually stern countenance. Her mouth was wide and her lips plump and fleshy. Her teeth gleamed white in her dark-skinned features. Even her slanted eyes smiled in delight.

Mathilde felt warmed within in spite of herself.

'I cannot swim yet; I go round in circles!' Serena laughed.

Mathilde laughed too.

In Mombasa, the baron and his servant, William, scoured the coffee houses and the docks for news of Doctor Valentine. They were walking through a busy street market, the hot sun immediately over their heads, when a Kikuyu man tapped William on the arm and spoke to him. They followed the man through the colourful crowds to a quiet street, where children played in the dirt and women hung clothes out to dry.

A white man stood at the low doorway to a dark, mud dwelling.

'Baron Olensky! May I introduce myself? I am Flor Brunt. I sold my truck to the Englishwoman at the mission – the doctor you are looking for.'

The baron bowed slightly to the man. A young and beautiful black woman, wrapped in a *kitenge* of purple and orange cloth, and with a yellow and blue patterned turban of cloth on her small, neat head, appeared from the gloom and stood with the Dutch planter. She held a small, pale-skinned baby, which smiled and cooed at the strange men. The woman smiled shyly and stared at them.

'Excuse me, I won't ask you inside,' Brunt said. He inclined his head and pointed at the wood bench and table outside the dwelling, and they sat down. The woman brought small cups of black tea and they drank.

'Do you know something?' The baron's flecked brown eyes looked straight at the planter, imploring him to give them useful information.

'I think I can help you. I know of Heinlich's low

dealings. He is like a cur with rabies and should be destroyed. The missionary is no good, but he is simply a weak man with an addiction and has been used by Heinlich.'

'Tell me, man, for God's sake! Tell me what you know of the whereabouts of Doctor Valentine.'

'It's like this . . .'

The tea planter had access to the docks and the shippers, as did Heinlich. He knew the Arab dealers, legitimate and otherwise, and had reason to believe that Heinlich, together with Joseph, was involved in some low deal. He had seen them carrying a long, heavy sack on to an Arab dhow late one evening, as the sun was setting. It was not tea they were carrying, of that he was pretty sure.

'When was this?' the baron asked urgently.

'About five weeks ago. It didn't register at the time. But when I heard through the grapevine about the young woman doctor, it came back to me.'

'Where was the dhow bound for?' The baron was sweating profusely and took off his bush hat to wipe his head with a scarf.

'To Zanzibar. I heard the crew say. They were looking for more men.'

'Thank you, sir, I am very grateful to you.' The baron shook hands with the Dutchman and pressed a silver coin into the palm of the baby.

'One more thing,' said the Dutchman. 'I remember something of the name on the dhow. It was in Arabic, of course, but it looked like *Qita*. I hope that helps. Please God that you are not too late to save her.'

The Dutchman sat on and drank more tea as Olensky and William took their leave and hurried off down the dusty, narrow street.

Chapter Fourteen

The baron went to the docks at Mombasa immediately. He avoided the main docks where the cruise ships spewed the tourists on their grand tour and the merchant ships unloaded the latest trucks from England and Germany, but he went instead to the smaller harbour where the elegant dhows lay in rows like swans on a lake, their white triangular sails billowing as they set sail. Men were hurrying like ants along the duck-board ramps and decking, carrying on their heads bundles wrapped in sacking, wooden chests of fragrant tea, overloaded baskets of fruit or parcels of animal skins. Great curved tusks of ivory were manhandled on to the wooden boats and stored close together, like naked ballerinas. Sandalwood, ebony, pepper and sisal were packed and moved from one place to another by men of every shade of yellow and brown and black, unclothed except for turbans of bright-coloured cloth and short *kitenges* wrapped round their hips. Their feet were flat and strong and their legs muscular and lean. Their bodies were honed to a spareness, built by intense physical activity.

William pointed to a small outrigger with folded sails,

seemingly unmanned. On the side were the painted symbols *QITA*.

'Come with me, William,' said the baron, and strode towards the scruffy outrigger. It was moored at the end of a row of larger dhows, all busy with sweating men loading and lifting, shouting and packing.

William called to the overseer of the dhow moored next to the *QITA*. 'Where is the captain of this boat?'

The man grunted. 'He is resting. He's made enough money with his last load and doesn't need to work this month.'

The crew laughed, grateful for the brief break from their hard work. They stood and watched as the baron and William jumped on to the outrigger and made a cursory examination of the hold. William suddenly called to the baron. The two men stood and looked at something on the deck. The baron bent down and picked it up.

'My God, she *was* here!' he said in amazement. In his hand was a thin gold chain. He had last seen it gleaming on Mathilde's ivory neck by the light of his fire at *Nyumba ya Simba*.

'Tell me the name of the owner of the *QITA*,' the baron said to the overseer.

'He is Obah Qadir of Pemba.' The Arab spat the name. 'May his bones be eaten by sharks.'

'Where can I find this man who deserves your undying hatred?' asked the baron.

'He will be in the boy brothel at Juniper Street,' said the overseer. 'May Allah rot his genitals.'

The baron and William made their way to the mis-named Juniper Street, a crowded dirt alley, narrow and malodorous, full of Arab sailors and dock workers. There was a smell of smoke and cooking, pepper and sweet potato, excrement and drains, and the insistent noise of high-pitched, whining music played on exotic instruments.

111

The brothel had no special name or sign outside, but everyone who needed to know knew which of the dark, mud dwellings it was. In the dark, low doorway hung a curtain of glass beads, red and purple and yellow.

The baron pushed the beads aside and bent his head to enter. William kept watch outside, standing with his arms crossed, his face impassive. Men sat cross-legged on the dirt path, playing cards and wagering. Naked children ran by. The evening was drawing in fast, and candle lamps were lit in the doorways, transforming the hovels and squalid alley into a fairyland of flickering lights with flashing eyes and white moons of mouths shining in the gloom.

'Obah Qadir!' Baron Olensky barked the name into the small dirt-floored room. A tall woman, half clothed and her belly swollen with pregnancy, rose from the earth floor and approached the baron. She stood close to him so he could smell her pungent sweat, and placed her hand on his crotch. He pushed it away gently.

'Rest in peace, woman, I am looking for an Arab – Obah Qadir, is he here?'

She grinned, showing many gaps in her teeth, and inclined her head over her shoulder and moved her eyes to indicate a small doorway hidden in the dark.

The baron opened the door without knocking and dragged out a naked man, who howled in humiliation and shock. On the bed was a scared-looking boy. His eyes were huge in the dark, elfin face.

The baron shoved the Arab on to the floor. 'You disgusting cur, tell me where you took the Englishwoman.'

'Which one?' said the Arab.

'You mean she wasn't the only one? You took them all?' the baron cried.

'Yes, I took them all, all three. Why should I tell you where I took them?' he said defiantly, wiping his brow with a thin hand.

The baron dragged him up by one arm and punched him on his nose, sending blood spattering over the wall.

The woman stood and screamed. William looked in the doorway and hissed at her to stop, then went back to his post.

'Tell me or I'll tear off your filthy balls,' Olensky snarled, his yellow eyes gleaming in the amber light from the lamp. He kicked out at the man's crotch and the Arab cringed and huddled on the floor. The boy had covered his nakedness in a dirty *kitenge* and stood watching, frightened and wary, in the low doorway to the back room.

'Don't hurt me,' the Arab whined in a high-pitched voice. 'I will tell you. But give me *baksheesh*.' He held out a claw-like hand.

Olensky roared and kicked again, this time making contact with the man's folded legs. The Arab screamed and bent his head down low to the floor.

'Do not hurt me. I will tell. I will tell.'

'Tell me!' The baron was dark faced in his anger. He dragged the Arab captain from his ignominious position and pushed him against the wall, his powerful hands on the small man's shoulders.

'I took each white woman to the waiting house at Chukwani on Zanzibar Island,' Obah Qadir said. 'They stay there until passage is arranged to Arabia.'

'The English doctor – when did you take her?'

'I do not know any doctor; she is woman only. I take the last one four weeks ago.'

'And where in Arabia will they be taken?'

'I know nothing more,' the Arab said, bending his head.

Olensky slapped his face hard, causing the skin to redden immediately. The Arab did not move.

'Come, William,' said the baron, and walked out of the sordid hovel, followed by the waiting servant.

They went back to the police station and told the

officer in charge, Inspector Jacklin, what they had heard from Obah Qadir.

'It is all very well for you to hurl accusations at missionaries and Arab merchants and tea planters, but you still have no proof, Baron,' said the arrogant officer, flicking his riding crop against his immaculate khaki trousers. 'It's all hearsay. I cannot help you.'

'But I have a witness.'

'A frightened Arab? Look, Baron, slavery was abolished in Zanzibar in 1873, for God's sake. The high commissioner would be horrified at your inferences. So would the sultan.'

'Bah!' The baron turned away from the Englishman in disgust.

Back at the waiting house, Mathilde was with Serena, determined to make a friend of the slave who was more than a slave.

Serena was dressed in a transparent wrap of cream silk draped across her slender body, her nipples piercing the thin stuff. Mathilde was gently manipulating the slave's arm.

'There, you have far more movement now than you had a week ago,' she said.

'Thank you, Mathilde,' Serena said in honeyed tones.

She touched Mathilde's bare arm gently and stroked with long, sharp nails along the length of it; down to the capable hand, along the trembling fingers, then up again – slowly, slowly – to her elbow, pausing to circle the inner arm with her fingertips, then moving up to her armpit. Mathilde shivered as if she were cold. Serena's touch was knowing and sensual. She moved her fingers subtly under Mathilde's arm to her tingling breast, hidden tantalisingly by the thinnest blue silk. She touched the nipple, and it hardened. Mathilde hissed her breath through clenched teeth. Serena carried on her infinitely slow love-making, using only the one hand.

She stroked the other breast and gently pushed Mathilde back on to the couch. Mathilde allowed herself to be persuaded into this female love act. Part of her said it was only because she needed to gain the confidence of this relatively powerful woman, who would perhaps be able to set her free, and part of her knew she wanted it. She wanted the gentleness, the forbidden, the exotic. Yet before she arrived at the 'prison', she had never thought of other women in this way before.

Serena's long fingers, hennaed with intricate symbols like delicate tattoos, moved slowly across Mathilde's concave belly, and scraped the jutting hip bones.

'You are too thin, still, you must eat more sweetmeats and marzipan,' she laughed quietly. 'The sultan will discard you quickly if you are not plump enough for his taste.'

'The sultan?' Mathilde almost whispered. Her skin felt like the silk of her garment; she was melting into a state of desire. She tried to control her urge to touch the slave's skin.

'Yes, my lord, the Sultan of Abizir. He will be your new master. I must tell you, he is cruel sometimes.' Serena moved away slightly and drew her gown over her shoulders, down to her waist. 'See, it is he who has done this.'

Mathilde saw the white scars and raised pink ridges, the remains of slashes that had not healed completely on the dark, glossy skin. She touched the silky channels. Serena drew in her breath.

'Does it hurt you still?' asked Mathilde.

'No, but your touch is like fire.' She turned and her naked breasts touched Mathilde's. Their faces were close. Serena opened her fleshy lips and Mathilde saw the red tongue, the white, even teeth and the tunnel of her throat, shining and wet. Mathilde lifted her hands to the dark-tipped breasts, inclined her face towards the slave and kissed her.

115

The Englishwoman had not known a woman's touch on her most private parts before, and she dreaded and yearned for it. She let Serena trace her white skin with slim fingers, drawing a pink incision with a fingernail down over her breasts, to the cave of her waist and out to the jut of her fine-skinned hips. The fingernail left its snail-like pink trail in the soft flesh, and Serena watched as it faded and the white skin blossomed and healed. She leant forward to kiss the white belly and leant on her good arm while she parted Mathilde's milky thighs and found the font of her desire. Mathilde laid back, seemingly asleep, quietly and surreptitiously enjoying each new experience, each gentle lick and kiss; the gentle parting of her outer lips, so soft and swollen; the lapping and licking and nibbling of her inner, tighter labia, with the pink, erect bud pouting through. She moaned and sighed quietly, hiding her emotion and her rising passion, as Serena expertly brought her to a mounting climax. Mathilde exploded, her hips thrusting into the slave's face, her juices and Serena's spittle running down her throbbing, aching thighs.

Chapter Fifteen

Olensky had much to do. He asked around the coffee houses about the reliability of various seafarers, but there was no obvious choice of boatman. He did not tell any of the Europeans he knew in Mombasa of his plan. Indeed, he had no clear idea of what he was going to do. He only knew he had to try and rescue Mathilde Valentine. He had not felt this way about anyone since the noblewoman whose husband he had killed in Silesia many years ago. His brief affair with McKinnon's first wife had not touched his heart. Her disappearance had upset him, but he had not realised until much later what had happened to her, and he certainly did not feel this obsession to find her that he now felt for the English doctor. His body yearned for her and his soul cried out for her.

He dreamt of her every night. She was always in some sort of bondage. Her eyes were blindfolded, her legs tied apart. Or her legs were tied together but slung above her head so that her genitals were exposed as she swung from a rope. Or she crouched, legs open wide, sex lips yawning open, her arms strapped behind her, her eyes covered and her breasts bound with ropes. It was a

117

strange sensation he had in the midst of these dreams –
he always felt that he had the power to set her free from
her dream bondage, but he inevitably used her sexually
instead of freeing her. His cock was sometimes outrage-
ously huge in his dreams, like a slippery pole between
his legs. He always penetrated her mouth and the
enormous rod would go straight through her to her
vagina and stick out as if it was her penis, coming from
her groin. He watched the end of his penis moving in
and out of her vagina as he fucked her mouth. He woke
ashamed, his semen and his sweat drying on the sheet.

But his dreams belied his tender feelings towards her.
She was like a beacon in the dark to him. He saw her as
his natural mate. Never before had he wanted to be with
a woman for all his life, but he had no idea if she loved
him in the way he wanted her. He only knew he had to
find her and tell her he loved her. This was his woman.
He was like the lion – he would mate for life. He had to
find her.

He and William scoured the beer shops along the
docks, talking to the seamen and sailors, the dock hands
and traders. One day they were standing at the bar with
a group of men who had just unloaded a boat from Dar
es Salaam. The captain was a coastal East African with a
strong face. His eyes were honest and his chin was
square and firm. The baron liked the look of him and
William knew him.

'What is your name?' asked the baron.

'Sabah Madaan,' said the sailor.

'What is your next job?' the baron asked him.

'Nothing at the moment. We are without work after
today, until next month.'

'How much will you charge to take me to Zanzibar
tomorrow and wait for me while I do business there? I
might need six good fighting men also, if I find what I
am looking for.'

'This sounds interesting,' the African laughed, and his

men looked pleased at the opportunity of a *fracas*, whatever it might involve.

After a long discussion the two men shook hands on the deal and Olensky bought all the crew drinks.

Sabah Madaan and his men had packed the dhow with provisions for the short voyage – water, fresh fruit and dried fruit, maize, pulses, candles and sharpened *pangas*. The craft was ready to go. The baron and his servant, William, went aboard under cover of the dark. The baron did not want any word of his project to be transmitted to those who might try to stop him. He was sure that more people knew of the trade in white women than were admitting to it. The police, for example – why were they so sure that there was no reason to suspect McKinnon? Were they in the slaver's pay? Who was the slaver? He could expect no help from the official bodies.

He had his revolver and his hunting knife, his rifle and his wits, and he had the trusty William and his strength, and the swarthy Sabah Madaan and his faithful and well-paid crew. Olensky was ready for anything. He placed the fine gold chain he had found on the *QITA* around his neck, kissed it as if it were a crucifix, and swore to find Dr Mathilde Valentine.

Mathilde was being bathed by the two young Nubian girls. One girl stood in front of her, the other behind. They pressed themselves against her, rubbing their hands all over her naked body. Their faces shone in the gloom of the dark-tiled bathing chamber. Their small breasts pressed against her. They laughed and chatted all the while, soaping her and splashing the lather away with fresh water, poured over her from shiny copper jugs. Mathilde stood as if in a dream. Her situation was becoming more unreal to her. She felt as if this experience in the waiting place was outside her real life. It was happening on another plane. Time stood still for her in this strange, exotic prison, where women dressed to expose their erogenous zones and her senses were heightened. She was aware of the heady scent of jasmine and spices. She tasted foods and flavours she had not realised existed before. Her flesh tingled at each delicate touch from the other slaves. She heard strange laughter in the night; owls called, night jars and other nocturnal creatures screeched and kept her tense and on edge. She became more aware of her emotions. She had given up weeping. What is the use of weeping? she thought. She asked for paper and pen but they were refused her. Instead she wrote letters in her mind to her mother, her sister and her dead father.

Dear Mummy,
I love you very much. I want to hold you. I want to be a child again with you looking after me. I am alone; I need you. Please help me. Forgive me for the daughterly sin of taking your love for granted.

Dear Daddy,
I am sorry I did not care for you when you were dying. Forgive me. I did not love you enough. I only loved me. You were always a good father. Dear Daddy, I love you.

She did not write love letters in her mind to Olensky. Her heart had closed like a clam. It hurt too much.

She allowed the slave, Serena, to make passionate love to her. But as the slave's lips touched hers she did think of her lion lover, the baron. While Serena moved her hennaed hands between Mathilde's thighs, caressing her delicately, she thought of Olensky's firm touch, his passion and fire, his hardness.

While Serena's soft breasts slid across Mathilde's spread legs and the slave's tongue flicked inside her, the doctor remembered Olensky's muscular chest, and his strong arms holding her safe. While the Nubian gazed at Mathilde with narrow, black eyes, outlined and lengthened with kohl, the English woman thought of the orange-brown eyes of the Silesian baron – the lion's eyes, piercing her, turning her flesh to honey.

She had lost all sense of time. How long had she been there? She did not know. It was weeks. Was it months? Did her parents know she was missing? Did Olensky know she had been kidnapped? Why didn't he come for her? She hated the feeling of helplessness. She was truly enslaved.

She remembered her professor lover. With shame she remembered how she had allowed him to tie her to the bed and place his hands between her legs. He had wanted her to cry out and struggle as if she did not want his caresses. He had gagged her and blindfolded her and pressed his thick cock into her, hurting her. And she had enjoyed it. Was that what made her feel guilty? She had enjoyed the feeling of helplessness.

Now there was this dichotomy in her life. She was really imprisoned, a true captive, and she hated it. But a small, secret part of her enjoyed the inevitability of her situation; her collapse into eroticism, her helplessness and slavery to her sexual and sensual feelings.

She looked forward to the time at the end of each tedious day – when nothing had happened except bathing and massage, perfuming and depilation, idle chatter and games, listening and dreaming, afternoon sleeping, idle caressing and voyeurism – when Serena would come to her and dress her in a fresh garment, stroke her breasts, kiss her thighs, and make long, slow love to her.

On one of these occasions, Serena's tone was suddenly serious. She kissed Mathilde's pink ear.

'It is like a little shell. Your ears are so pretty,' she said, sighing. 'Your time here is nearly over, Mathilde. You must go to the sultan soon.'

Mathilde sat up, pushing the hot body of the slave away from her. 'What do you mean? When must I go?'

'I do not know. But soon. Never has anyone stayed this long here. They must move you soon.'

'How long have I been held here?'

'Ten weeks, my darling.'

'Ten weeks!'

'I do not want you to go,' said Serena, grasping Mathilde's hands.

'Then help me, help me!' Mathilde sobbed, suddenly aware that her fate was sealed. She was to be a slave in a foreign land. She would be abused, beaten, scarred. Never again would she see her mother or sister. Never again would she be free.

'I cannot! How can I? I am a slave also. I will die if I help you.' Serena rose from the low couch and drew her pale silk garment to her breast. She had become the powerful slave overseer again, no longer the gentle lover, and her eyes flashed and narrowed. 'I must preserve my own life.' So saying, she left the chamber.

Mathilde pushed her fists into her eyes and cried bitter tears, angry with herself for having given way to her feelings. She needed Serena on her side if she was to escape. She must calm herself and try again.

It was 155 miles from Mombasa to Zanzibar. The dhow keeled over in the freshening wind. The large white sail filled and billowed. The men sang a Swahili song about the good wind and the kind sea, and pulled on ropes and stays with strong hands, and the captain, Sabah Madaan, steered the tiller and kept his eyes on the rise and fall of the waves. Flying fish gathered in the wake, leaping and diving.

'We will be at Tanga soon,' said the captain to Olensky. 'Perhaps there you will learn more of your English doctor's whereabouts.'

'You are a good man, Madaan. I knew I could trust

you,' said the baron. 'I know one or two men there who might have heard gossip about the slave trader.'

He lit a cigarette for the captain and gave it to him. The wind was fresh and the heavy craft groaned and shook. Soon the Tanganyika port of Tanga came into sight and they changed their tack, drawing in the sail tight and heading almost into the eye of the wind.

The dhow's sail was lowered and stowed and Olensky and his servant stepped ashore, ostensibly to enjoy the delights of the small harbour bars.

Olensky was no longer recognisably European. His face had been darkened with henna. His fair hair was hidden under a cotton turban. He wore a long, white *djellaba*, covering his arms and legs. He had a knife in his waist belt. He looked like an Arab trader.

The baron and William entered the first bar they came to. It was empty. They walked on along the dark stone wharf and came to another bar, the Dolphin. They ordered drinks from the disreputable, toothless barman and drank for a while, talking to each other quietly. The bar filled up. There was a feeling of menace in the small room. Large men, dressed in nothing but short, dirty *kitenges*, jostled and murmured and drank.

Olensky deliberately knocked into the large man next to him, spilling the sailor's drink. The man went as if to hit Olensky, and the baron threw his arms up in supplication.

'A thousand pardons, matey. Let me buy you another. Let me buy your friends drinks too.' He went to the bar and ordered drinks for the motley throng, who were silent now. 'Now, matey,' he said, 'a thousand pardons again. I am after some information, and you look like a man who knows what is what, eh?' He slapped the man on the shoulder – no mean feat as he was at least eight inches taller than Olensky.

The African scowled again and folded his huge arms. Olensky drew a wad of money from his pocket and peeled a few hundred African shillings from the pile, surreptitiously showing the sailor.

'I need to know about the slave trade in Zanzibar. Do you have any idea of where the holding place is – where the slaves go first?'

'Why should I know?' The big man grunted.

'Have another drink,' said the baron, pushing a glass into the man's hand.

The sailor was not averse to a free drink or two. 'I might know something,' he said, throwing his massive head back and pouring the alcohol down his throat.

'Good, good!' The baron smiled ingratiatingly. 'Tell me.' He pushed the notes into the sailor's hands.

Olensky and William left the bar and staggered towards the pier where they had moored. They sang, leaning on each other's shoulders, laughing loudly. Behind them, in the dark African night, there followed five men intent on mischief and theft. Olensky turned first, and yelled instinctively. A heavy blow felled him and he saw only blackness.

The dhow at the pierside was quiet. The crew waited. The baron did not appear. Their eyes stared into the darkness. They grumbled and huddled together and waited. The captain sighed, threw away the toothpick he had been chewing, and stepped ashore, calling nine large crew members to go with him. They were all armed with *pangas*.

They found the injured baron and William lying where they had fallen, and four of the crew carried them back to the dhow, where their wounds were bathed.

The captain, meanwhile, along with the most powerful of his men, went looking in the bars for evidence of the attackers.

Later he returned to his craft.

'How are they?' he asked.

'The baron is conscious,' said one of the sailors. 'He is asking for you.'

'I have good news,' said the captain, as he gazed down at the bloody face of the baron. 'You, my pale Arab friend, are about to have a change of occupation.'

Chapter Sixteen

Mathilde lay in her bedchamber, her eyes wide open, her senses alert. There was a new sound in the night. She heard the sounds of loud love-making – grunting and heavy breathing – and a bed being moved about the floor. She listened to the creaking of springs. This was not the sound of women making love. Serena had not come to her this evening, nor for the last three days. She had waited for her scent to come before her, her sandalwood perfume to waft through the doorway, but she had not come. Now Mathilde lay with her thighs hot and apart, her breasts aching and her nipples taut and tingling. She yearned for Serena's tender touch on her hot flesh. She wanted to trace the scars on Serena's back with her lips.

The sounds were close. She rose and went to her door, trying the handle. It did not budge. She went back to her bed and lay down again.

The noises grew louder. A woman – she felt sure it was Serena – moaned loudly, her voice muffled by – a gag? a pillow? Mathilde held her breath, listening to the animal sounds. Then the sounds changed. She heard a whip lashing on to naked flesh. She heard muffled screams. Mathilde stood again and pressed her perspiring back to the wall where the sounds were loudest. She heard the man drop the whip on the tiled floor. She heard him throw himself on top of the bound slave. He groaned and grunted some more. Serena was silent. The man began to orgasm. He howled like a wolf, and then was silent also.

Next day, at the depilating couch, the two Nubian girls were quiet and subdued.

'Where is Serena?' asked Mathilde.

'Oh, she is resting.' said Parveneh. The girl's swift strokes soon removed the fuzz of hair under Mathilde's raised arms. Mathilde looked up at the underneath of the girl's little breasts, admiring their bobbing prettiness. The other Nubian slave, Qitura, was smoothing lather on Mathilde's private parts. Her fingers slipped inside the older woman's sex lips a little way. Mathilde half-heartedly tried to move away from the delicate touch.

'Please do not touch me there,' said Mathilde.

'Oh, you do not like it? I thought you did,' said Qitura, innocently.

'Yes, I do like it, but not now, please. Tell me, where is Serena? Can I see her?'

Qitura began the shaving between Mathilde's legs. The razor grazed her skin. She flinched as the girl's hand slipped and she felt the blade go too close.

The slave-girl's eyes flickered. She would not look Mathilde in the eye.

She is frightened, thought Mathilde.

'Why are you frightened?' she asked. She touched the girl's arm, reassuringly. 'Tell me!'

'It is the man from Arabia. He has come to fetch you,' the lithe Parveneh whispered into Mathilde's ear when Qitura said nothing.

'Has he hurt Serena?' Mathilde asked.

'Yes, she is hurt,' Parveneh said quietly.

Mathilde sat up and said, 'Take me to her.'

The girls obeyed, and Mathilde was taken to a shaken Serena. She lay on her stomach, her head on one side, her eyes red with silent tears. Her back was badly marked. She lay quietly, suffering stoically.

'Get me hot water and soft cloth – lots of water,' the doctor commanded.

The Nubian sisters ran to fetch the things. Mathilde dropped to her knees by the bed. She stroked the matted, black hair back from the slave's forehead. Serena gazed at her over her shoulder. She sobbed quietly.

'Thank you, my darling Mathilde.'

'Who did this to you?'

'It was just a man. He is nothing. Just a man who has come for you. Oh, Mathilde, I am so sorry. I do not want you to suffer as I have suffered.'

'Shush! Do not tire yourself.'

Mathilde soon bathed the cuts and cleaned them, and then treated them with soothing balms and covered them with clean cloths. She bade the two Nubians to change these dressings every few hours and keep the wounds clean.

'I don't know if your wounds will heal as well this time as before. If Parveneh and Qitura continue with the cleansing and dressing it should be all right,' she told Serena. And then she thought to ask, 'How did you get your original scars? Why did the sultan whip you? Do you want to tell me about it?' Mathilde sat by the low divan and stroked the slave's wet cheeks. 'At least your arm is getting better,' she comforted.

'Yes, I want to tell you. I want you to know of my past life, and why I am here.' Serena sobbed quietly and Mathilde hushed her, pressing her fingers to the sad lips.

'Tell me.'

Serena held both of Mathilde's hands in hers, drawing them to her breast.

'I was a favourite, once. A favourite little concubine of the Sultan of Abizir. But I did not love him or want to

stay with him. I was betrothed to my cousin, Ahmed.'
Here she sobbed again at the memory of her long-lost
beloved, and then recovered herself to continue. 'I was
fifteen. A child. At the market one day with my mother,
I was taken by the slavers. I could hear my mother
howling for me, like a she-wolf for her lost cub. They
had grabbed me from her in the crowded street; plucked
me from my life and all I loved.' Mathilde started to cry,
in total sympathy with the slave.

'I was gagged and tied and carried off, and I never
saw my family again. This was eight years ago.'

'And why did he beat you?'

'I tried to escape. I pretended to be happy there in the
harem, but I hated it. I wanted my freedom. I wanted
Ahmed, not the Sultan of Abizir. He whipped us all,
sometimes; for fun, for his amusement. He likes to hear
women cry out in pain and pleasure. And it is pleasurable, sometimes, believe me, Mathilde, to be chastised
during the act of love.'

'Go on!' said Mathilde quietly.

'I was often spanked, and I enjoyed it, I suppose. Yes,
I did enjoy it, but the whipping was frightening. He
would sometimes lose control and do it too hard. But I
was the favourite, and I had presents of gold and
diamonds which I hid away, keeping them for the time
when I could use them to help me escape.'

'And did you escape?'

'Nearly! I bribed a fisherman to get me off the island
of Abizir in his boat, disguised as a cabin boy.' She
wiped her damp face with Mathilde's hands and smiled
wanly.

'Go on!'

'I was caught. Another fisherman, jealous of the jewels
I had given to my fisherman, told the sultan so he would
get a reward. My fisherman was beheaded.' Mathilde
gasped. 'I had to watch this happen. Then I was whipped
by the sultan in front of the whole harem household. He

did not hold back this time. He whipped me as if he wanted me dead.' She sobbed again and Mathilde held her close. Serena sniffed loudly and stopped her crying. 'Now, Mathilde, you must not get in his clutches. Please! Please go from here. Before it is too late!'

Mathilde bent to kiss the swollen lips.

Then she took the keys that Serena gave her and slipped them under her garment.

'Goodbye, beautiful Serena. Thank you!'

Mathilde went back to the routine of the waiting house, pretending to be as she had been; bored and helpless. Lunch was late in being served in the communal dining room. The other women gossiped and whispered among themselves. Some stared at Mathilde impudently, and laughed loudly to each other. The woman who had been jealous before and fought with her taunted her again and poked at her angrily. Mathilde ignored her. She ignored all of them. She watched and listened.

She heard the sounds of revelry behind the locked door. Men's voices were raised. She did not know the language they spoke. She listened and waited for the dark and quiet. The day passed as slowly as ever, with nothing to do but play games, bathe and shower, apply make-up and henna, paint nails, pluck eyebrows and depilate. She felt she would burst with frustration and impatience. But she had the keys. She readied herself for escape. She gathered as many items of clothing together as she could find – the discarded garments dropped at the poolside and several changes of the loose, flowing gowns they all wore each day. She chose garments which would cover her nakedness and hide her identity, then she put the rest in the laundry room.

Night fell at last. She went to bed and put out her candle early, listening to the night sounds. She could hear soldiers or a group of noisy men, still drinking in the locked chamber. She willed them to get paralytic and fall asleep. She heard the men with the women; the screeches and laughter. She covered her ears and tried to rest.

Chapter Seventeen

*T*he night was warm and fragrant with the scent of almond blossoms. Frogs croaked to their loved ones. The moon was a crescent, hanging in the purple sky like a white, cupped hand waiting to catch a gleaming Venus falling slowly from velvet cloth. It was an African night of promise and fear, of sensuality and blood. There were sharks in the shallows, thrashing in an orgy of killing, and lovers on the sandy shore of the island, lost in each other's arms.

The dhow had cut out all its lights and drifted silently on to the little, steep-sloping beach. The 'Arab trader', limping slightly, led his men on to the dock. The captain had managed to extricate certain information from the brigands who had robbed the baron. It had not been gentle persuasion.

'He was begging me to let him go,' laughed the captain. 'Begging me! I had his balls in my grip and my *panga* was raised. He screamed for mercy.' The big man laughed until he cried.

'Tell me again what he said,' said the baron.

'The waiting place where your doctor is held – it is

close to Zanzibar Town in Chukwani. He said there are many soldiers. We are prepared for anything, Baron.'

They climbed the soft sandy dunes at the top of the beach and hid in the valleys, looking over the parapet of the sand hills to the small fortress whose dark shape they could see beyond the low scrub which grew at the edge of the dunes. Their *pangas* and cutlasses gleamed in the faint light from the waning moon.

Mathilde covered her face and arms and ankles in henna and dressed herself in the long, flowing garments. She covered the bright glow of her blonde hair with a dark scarf, wrapping it around her neck several times. She was ready. The house was quiet at last.

She slipped quietly to her door, unlocked it with one of the keys and moved silently across the communal area to the door which was always locked. She pushed the heavy key into the hole and turned it, holding the door handle firmly to avoid making any noise.

The door opened. She pulled it towards her. It creaked. She moved it suddenly, and the creak stopped. She went through the door into the room where the soldiers had been at their revels. As she suspected, several men lay on the floor in a drunken stupor. She stepped between them, trying to be as quiet as she could. Her feet touched the face of one of the soldiers and he flinched and whimpered, moving his hand to his mouth. She froze. This is like a game of statues, she thought. He was quiet again and none of the others had been disturbed. She tried to see through the unlit gloom to where the last doorway was. Her eyes hurt with the looking. Then she saw the faint gleam where a chink of moonlight slipped under the door. She held her breath and went towards the light.

The baron and his band of men were slipping towards the fortress.

'How do we get in?' William asked the baron.

'Wait and see what happens, William. We'll play it by ear,' he said. He was excited at the thought of the proximity of Mathilde. If she was here, he would find her.

They saw the guard leaning sleepily against the tower, his head slumped forward on his spear. They crept up to the walls, climbed swiftly and surrounded him. His end was quick. Then they moved in all directions, covering the area and searching for a way in.

Mathilde opened the last door with her keys and locked it behind her. She nearly threw the keys into the vast expanse of sand that greeted her. Then she thought better of it and hid them behind a sweet-scented lemon tree in a tub by the door. She stood, not knowing which way to go. She remembered her arrival on this island, and a man carrying her over soft sand. The boat. There must be water nearby. She ran upward and came to a peak of the sand dunes and looked down at the beach. The thin moon glow shimmered on the oily sea. It was freedom. She threw herself down the sandhill, running and tumbling, sand in her hair and eyes.

Olensky and William stood outside a locked doorway and shouted and banged on the thick wood. Inside was a panic of hungover soldiers, sleepily stupid and alarmed. They stood, raggedly, and looked for their weapons.

'We are being attacked!' said a relatively sober man.

The door burst open and the soldiers found themselves fighting for their lives.

Minutes later, Baron Olensky was desolated.

'She is not here,' he said.

They had found many women locked in their chambers. They had found the slave Serena, semi-conscious from her injuries and unable to speak. They could not find the doctor. Then the baron noticed the clean dressings on Serena's back. The Nubian sisters had slept on the floor of Serena's chamber, hiding from the soldiers.

'Tell me, where is the doctor woman?' the baron begged them.

They shook their little heads.

'We do not know, we do not know.'

Serena opened her eyes and moved her head to look at the baron.

'I gave her the keys,' she whispered. 'She is gone, tonight.'

The baron ran from the fortress, followed closely by William and the rest of the crew. They ran in all directions, searching the horizon for the shape of a woman.

Mathilde still ran in the wrong direction, away from the beach where the dhow offered freedom. She was tired. Her flowing garments dragged in the prickly undergrowth and her legs were cut by marram grass spears and cactus needles. She tried to get above or below the line of flora but found herself unable to escape this new prison. She began to sob hysterically. She saw shapes in the sand behind her. A pack of men were following her. She fled from them. She found a sudden dip in the land and a bare sand hollow. Gratefully, she fell into it and dropped to the ground, breathing painfully. She felt sure she was safe for a while. She was hidden by the low scrub all around, and the prevalence of the surrounding cactus would make the soldiers think she had not gone that way. She began to pull out the needles that were embedded in her legs and feet.

Meanwhile the baron was desperate. Where was she? He called her name.

Mathilde listened to the sound of the waves on the distant sandy shore. The wind had risen as the moon waned. It was totally dark now. Olensky's voice was drowned in the wild air. Exhausted, Mathilde slipped into an uneasy slumber.

Chapter Eighteen

*D*awn turned the sand dunes pink and grey with a mist that rose slowly, transforming the hills into sky. The tops of the dunes emerged suddenly from the white mist, a mysterious landscape which was then hidden again in the swirl of milky cloud. The blessed cool dampness kissed the sand flowers with dew and caused them to bloom. The sun burnt off the mist and the dunes rose, orange, brown, golden. Little waders stabbed their long beaks into the shallows and curlews cried. The sea's small mauve waves spluttered and splashed on the sand. Out in the deep, diving birds exploded the water with their arrow bodies. Mathilde woke to see the narrow eyes of a large Arab who loomed over her. She screamed. He dragged at her arm and pulled her up. Her whole body hurt.

'Be quiet, woman!' he said as he slapped her hard across the mouth. She fought him. He was unprepared for this onslaught of fists. She kicked out at his groin and he howled in rage. She tried to run from him. He grabbed at her hair and hit her hard on the face. She tasted blood. He hit her again and this time she slipped into unconsciousness, but not before she recognised him. It was the same man she had seen with Heinlich at the Mombasa coffee house.

She woke to find her hands bound behind her. She was lying on a low couch, in a dark, circular cell. The walls were of cool yellow stone. She must have been taken back to the fortress. This must be the tower room, above the main door. She thought, with a pang of remorse, of the keys left behind the lemon tree. Her head throbbed and her mouth was cut. Her arms and legs were swollen with the cactus needle punctures. Her hands were numb. Her wrists were tightly bound. She still wore the gold collar. It chafed her neck. She was naked.

The obese Arab unlocked the door and entered the room. He stood over her, breathing heavily.

'Who helped you to escape?' he said quietly. His voice was syrupy and sly, with a barely hidden malice.

'I stole the keys after Serena was injured by you, you evil animal,' she lied.

He laughed quietly. He was a big man, gross in every way. His stomach was like a pregnancy. His features were hidden in the fat of his face, and there were rolls of flesh at his wrists, like a plump baby. His small hands went to his face and he sucked his thumb thoughtfully.

Mathilde was suddenly aware of her nakedness. The Arab ate her up, consuming her torn breasts. He raped her with his stare.

'You cannot go to the sultan in that state, my dear,' he said, leaning forward to touch her face. 'We must clean you up and make you presentable again,' he whispered.

He called for Perveneh and Qitura, who carried bowls of rose water and witch hazel. They did not look Mathilde in the eye. A soldier untied her bonds then stood and watched as they bathed her wounds. She rubbed her sore wrists and examined her injuries. There was no lasting damage, she thought, though the cactus needles had turned her flesh into a pin cushion. She was a fit woman, generally speaking, and would recover fast. Her head still hurt whenever she moved it, but she didn't think she had any broken bones or dislocations. Her jaw was swollen.

'Get me a gown, for goodness sake,' said the doctor to the soldier. He only leered and shook his head. She turned away from his intense gaze.

The two sisters were gentle with her and soon she felt more human. Her lacerations were clean, at least.

'Where is Serena?' she asked Parveneh.

'She is being punished for your escape,' whispered the girl.

'Oh God, why didn't I really escape!' She started to cry, suddenly realising that she really had not got away from this awful place. Her fate was sealed, it seemed. There was no one to help her now.

Later, she was fed and given sweet *lassi* to drink. She felt her spirits rise with the food in her stomach.

Parveneh and Qitura bathed her cuts again and gave her clean dressings as she had taught them. She flinched at the Nubian slave-girls' delicate touch. She felt sore and aching still, but her thoughts were of Serena, who had bravely given her the keys to enable her to escape, and now was suffering for her generosity. She thought she could discern the sound of screaming, but it could have been the sound of gulls wheeling and swerving in the blue sky.

'Is there any news of Serena?' she asked.

'No, nothing.' Parveneh lowered her eyes.

Mathilde imagined the awful things that were being done to the slave. She closed her mind to the thoughts. She could do nothing to help for the moment. Perhaps they would let her tend Serena's injuries afterwards.

The Englishwoman tried to rest.

I must get strong and well again. I *will* escape, she told herself.

She slipped into a deep sleep, and she did not hear the

cries of the two Nubian girls in the next chamber, or the grunting of the obscenely fat Arab.

The baron gathered the men together again and made sure he knew the position of the dhow. When dark fell again they made up two camps, one group to cause a disturbance at the rear of the fortress, the other to storm the now heavily guarded waiting-place door. At a given signal the small group of sailors began fighting among themselves and singing loudly. They threw bottles at the high windows and began taunting the guards. The soldiers were alarmed. They had already suffered one ignominious defeat at the hands of these brigands. They were more terrified of their master's henchman, the Arab – Nashif Nadir – who was the most feared man in Zanzibar. He had the sole franchise of white slaves on the island. It was he who the Sultan of Abizir depended on to provide new concubines. He had made the contacts of Heinlich and McKinnon, paying them plenty to keep their mouths shut. He had hired the servant, Joseph, when the miserable missionary had failed to supply him with the latest white woman.

He scratched his belly, looked at his solid gold watch, and thought that this would be the last night the white slave would be held here. It was too dangerous with the band of brigands still on the island. But he had total faith in the invulnerability of the fortress. He was weary after his exertions with the young slaves. He had better sleep.

The sailors began letting off firecrackers. The soldiers were very jumpy and thought they were being attacked. They charged the sailors, chasing them towards the beach. The sailors melted into the velvet night.

The baron crawled on all fours around the base of the small fortress. He opened his throat and gave the call he knew she would recognise. She would know it was him. The soldiers on guard inside the fortress were alarmed at the strange sound. They nervously gripped their old firearms and prayed they would not have to use them.

He came to the last window. Inside, in the little tower room, Mathilde dreamt of being in the bush again with her lover, her lion lover. She felt the night air on her skin and saw a family of elephants moving in a slow ballet across the veldt. She heard the lion's mating call, the growling, throaty grunt. She was suddenly awake. It was him. She knew it was him. He was there.

She cried out loud. 'O-lens-ky! O-lens-ky!'

She kept up the cry, and the lion answered.

She jumped out of bed and wrapped the sheet around her. She heard the sounds of guns firing and men shouting.

She suddenly remembered the key she had hidden behind the lemon tree.

'Behind the lemon tree – the keys are there,' she shouted in Swahili, lifting her head to the high window.

Beneath her the heavy door was being wrenched open. There were shots. She heard the baron calling her. She tried the tower door knowing it was locked, but desperate in her excitement. The door opened as if by magic, and there stood Nashif Nadir, a revolver in his hands. With him were two guards. They grabbed Mathilde, knocking her out with a blow to the back of the neck, and carried her down a few steps, all the while with the clamour of the battle below. Nashif Nadir led the way, opening a hidden stone doorway into a secret tunnel. The door closed behind them as Olensky, looking like a dark-skinned Arab, ran up the steps to the door of the tower room. He threw open the door and cried out in disappointment. She had gone! He could smell her perfume still, on the heavy air.

Chapter Nineteen

When Mathilde Valentine regained consciousness she was bound hand and foot. Her evil kidnapper stood over her, his enormous belly hiding his face. He laughed and said, 'So, you little firebrand, you are back in the land of the living again?'

Her head pounded as if she had the world's worst hangover, and she closed her eyes again to escape from the awful brightness.

Later, there was the sound of tinkling water, lightly falling in thin sprays from a height on to cool alabaster. Songbirds trilled prettily. There wafted many flower scents. A harp played quietly. Her skin felt cool, smooth, silken. Was she in heaven? Mathilde's eyes opened. A young girl was bathing her. She had a fragment of cloth between her thighs, hanging from a gold chain which traversed her hips. This cloth was loose on her, now covering her sex, now exposing it, as she moved. Her sex was shaved. The pouting lips of her sex were pierced with gold rings. Mathilde found herself staring at the pubis of this beautiful slave – for that is what she was – as she leant over to bathe her. She smiled at Mathilde. Mathilde knew she smiled, though she could not see the girl's mouth. She wore a veil over her nose and mouth and chin. Her black hair, oiled and braided, was coiled on top of her small head. Her skin was like new chestnuts just taken from their white blanket. She glowed. Mathilde tried to raise herself, but she was restrained by the slave.

'No, do not move yet, you are too hurt.'

'I am fine, perfectly fine. Let me up, I say. Where am I?' Mathilde realised it was a ridiculous thing to say, but what else *was* there to say?

'You are in the harem of the Sultan of Abizir, of course.' The young girl giggled and stood up, looking down at the prone form of the Englishwoman. 'I like your yellow hair.' She giggled again.

Mathilde blushed and sat up. It all came back to her. Her disappointment was as sudden as a shock.

'Oh! Olensky! My love! I have lost you again!' she sobbed and shook, crying uninhibitedly in front of the slave-girl.

'Shush! You must not cry. You must be pretty for the sultan. He wants you straight away,' said the slave-girl.

Mathilde became aware that her body was shaved smooth and her skin was oiled with a fragrant unguent. Her head was still sore but she had sustained no real damage, she thought.

'That brute, the Arab! I am lost!' She sobbed uncontrollably, and the slave-girl looked very worried. She went away and returned with powders and creams, which she insisted on smoothing on to Mathilde's tear-smeared face.

'You have a red nose,' she said in amazement. 'I cannot imagine that the sultan will enjoy you with a red nose.' She smeared on the coloured cream and repaired the damage Mathilde's emotions had wreaked on her face. She had left in place the gold collar and anklets that Mathilde had worn since her incarceration on Zanzibar. She wrapped the distraught Englishwoman in a silk garment which covered her from shoulders to ankles. The yellow silk gleamed and shimmered and clung to her curves. Her breasts showed their sensuous form through the thin stuff, her nipples pushing the fabric and stretching it tight. She immediately felt transformed by the cloth. It made her feel like a sexual animal. She stood, as requested, and moved slowly and languidly, being careful of her sore head. She swung her hips and moved with small steps, her feet one in front of the other. The silk clung to her bottom, caressed her shaved pubis and fell into the cleft of her slit. She wore it like a second skin.

'You must wear the veil,' said the slave-girl, and arranged the yellow kerchief of silk across Mathilde's cheeks and tied it behind her head. 'There! Now you are ready for the sultan.'

The Sultan of Abizir had paid the slave-trader well. He now wanted to taste the fruit he had bought. He had been prepared by three young concubines, who had licked, caressed and kissed him and rubbed themselves over him. Then they had bathed him and massaged his broad back and his muscular calves and thighs. He was oiled and ready. His cock throbbed in anticipation. He lay on a low couch, with only one of the concubines kept by him, playing a lute, as he supped on a glass of deep red wine. It trickled down his chin and on to his hairy chest. The little concubine, a virgin from the Atlas Mountains, leant forward to lick the delicious stains from his person. At this moment a trumpet called, the door was opened by two huge eunuchs in purple turbans and orange tunics, and the new concubine was pushed into the mighty presence of the Sultan of Abizir.

Dr Mathilde Valentine, her eyes still red and sore and her head pounding, automatically stood upright, her head held proud above the gold collar. She did not flinch from the lascivious gaze of the sultan. Indeed, she knew she had nothing to be ashamed of. Her body was strong, healthy and beautiful. Her haunches were high, her breasts full and firm. Her nipples pierced the yellow silk, turning the colour dark as the desert dunes at night.

'Ah, my dear, come and sit next to me.' He patted the silk-upholstered couch encouragingly.

'I am not a pet dog,' said Mathilde. 'My name is Doctor Valentine, and I demand to be set free. I wish to see the British Consul.' She deliberately removed her veil, and stood defiantly, refusing to move.

He looked for a moment on her exposed face, admiring the bones, the intelligent eyes and the soft, wide mouth, and he laughed indulgently. 'My dear, of course, the British Consul? Yes, yes, in good time! But please consider yourself my honoured guest, meanwhile.' His erection drooped imperceptibly, and the little slaves hurried to attend to it, but he pushed them away. He rose from his low couch and let them drape his shoulders and loins with a white silk *djellaba*. As he stood, Mathilde could not help but admire the man's fine figure, muscles and shape. He looked every inch the horseman; the gentleman. His head stood proud on the column of his neck, and his half-erect cock stood proud on the cushion of his taut balls. He turned away from her momentarily and she admired also his strong, muscled buttocks and sturdy thighs and calves. In spite of her fear and trepidation at her position she was impressed by the quality of manhood she was enslaved by.

'My dear Dr Valentine, please do sit and share a drink with me.' The sultan clicked his fingers and a eunuch appeared carrying a tray of iced wine for her and warmed red wine for the sultan. There were sweetmeats and almonds on silver plates, and a sprig of jasmine in a vase.

'I must object to my incarceration, sir,' said the trembling Mathilde.

'Yes, yes, my dear, of course. We will certainly do

what we can to make your stay here as comfortable as possible.'

'I do not wish to stay here at all!' she said through gritted teeth.

'My, but I like a woman of spirit,' murmured the sultan, smiling.

'Good God, man, you sound like a joke! How dare you! I insist on you setting me free.' Her voice had risen higher and higher, until, with a sob, she collapsed in a heap on the couch, her head throbbing with pain.

'Dear me!' said the sultan, with every appearance of real sympathy for her plight, and he felt her forehead. 'Fetch some oil of cloves and saffron essence,' he ordered the eunuch.

The man returned quickly and the little slave-girls applied the yellow mixture to Mathilde's brow.

'What is this rubbish?' said Mathilde. 'Have you no aspirin?'

'Aspirin? What is that?' asked the sultan.

'It is made from the bark of the willow, an excellent anti-inflammatory and analgaesic,' she explained.

'You are indeed a medic. I see I have made a fine catch here. You are just what I have been looking for – a beautiful woman who is not stupid. How novel!' He laughed loudly, showing his cruel white teeth and curving his fleshy mouth in a crescent which reminded her of the blade of a Turkish sword. He took both of her hands in his and raised them to his lips. She let him kiss her fingers.

'But, my dear, I am afraid your medical expertise and intelligence will not help you neglect your other duties. You are mine to do as I wish, and I wish that you suck my cock.'

So saying, he pressed her head downward between his thighs to the rising rod of flesh which grew to meet her gaze. She fought him then. Fought like her life depended on it. She scratched and bit and hit out at any

145

part of him she could reach, sobbing in rage and impotence, before the eunuchs had her in chains, her wrists bound together, her head held by a leash attached to the gold collar around her white neck.

'What a beauty! What a fighter! Wonderful! Place her over my lap so I may spank her,' he commanded.

The two fat eunuchs did as he said, while she sobbed and struggled in vain. She felt the solid flesh of the sultan's cock under her belly as her head was pushed down and her bottom was raised high over his knees. The garment she wore was raised high over her shoulders so it fell over her eyes and face. Her naked body was exposed to the sultan, the eunuchs, and the slave-girls, who giggled in delight and anticipation. The sultan clapped his hands and the girls brought him a bowl of warm fragrant oil. He rubbed this over Mathilde's full white buttocks with both hands, pressing firmly, and began to spank her as if she was a naughty schoolgirl.

Mathilde felt humiliated and furious, but she was totally at his mercy. Her neck chain had been attached to a metal ring in the marble floor. Her hands were tied. She sobbed under the diaphanous veils that covered her blushes. Her bottom cheeks were reddening under the administrations of the sultan. He spanked loud and hard.

'You are a naughty girl, and you must be punished,' he said, his voice harsh with lust. His organ grew under her and she felt it prod insistently at her belly. He shifted his weight and his cock was suddenly between her thighs, the thick stem sticky and hot. She knew it was wrong to be inflamed but her sex was crying out to be filled with his organ. Her bottom was on fire. His hands slapped her inflamed flesh, now meeting the fleshy anus and her sex lips, that were like a swollen pouch below. She wanted his touch on her. She cried out in longing for his touch on her sex. He rationed his caresses so she felt mostly the hot pain of the spanking, and then just a little gentle stroking or slapping on her genitals. Her bottom was raised high and her waist dipped, and her breasts felt full and heavy and soft as silk. His touch on her sex was as delicate as a girl's, soft as her own fingers. He found her little bud that swelled and pouted towards him. He rubbed hard, then gently, then left her genitals to spank her buttocks hard. His cock throbbed against her naked thighs and sex. She was desperate for it inside her. Suddenly he spurted his ejaculation in little fountains. Seconds apart, they fell on her thighs, leaving their stickiness and whiteness on her sullied flesh.

'Oh! Oooh!' he cried out.

Mathilde lay still and the eunuchs removed her from his presence and carried her out of the chamber, her head hung low in shame. The young slave-girls giggled and bathed their sultan, cleaning off the sperm from his thighs and belly with their tongues. He lay back in total abandon, his hands behind his head.

'Yes, she is a good find, this Doctor Valentine. She will be my valentine for quite a while.'

Chapter Twenty

The two Mrs McKinnons were playing chess. They lay on their stomachs, their bottoms bare, eating Turkish Delight and drinking sweet *lassi*.

'Check!' said the first and real Mrs McKinnon, Janet, lazily.

'Oh, poo!' said the younger Mrs McKinnon, the bigamous second wife of the decadent missionary, and she tipped the chess board upside down, causing the wooden pieces to be thrown to all corners of the marble hall.

'Rosemary, really, how very childish!' Janet said, indolently turning over and allowing her breasts to hang outward to her armpits. She smoked a Turkish cigarette in a long ebony holder.

'Oh God! I'm so bored!' said Rosemary, and rose from the couch and walked up and down like a caged beast.

'How long is it since the sultan – our master – has called for us?' said Janet.

'Ages! Days and days. It's always that pervert of a brother of his who wants us, lately.'

'Yes, he is rather a beast, isn't he! I much prefer the Sultan of Abizir. Such a delicious animal, he is, don't you think?' Janet McKinnon was more than a little annoyed that she had been deposed from her position as favourite concubine. She supposed that he had a new woman, but she had no idea who had taken their place.

'It is the girl from the Caribbean, I think, who is presently his favourite. She has that look of being rather pleased with herself,' said Janet.

But the concubine from the island of Jamaica was pleased because the sultan had abandoned violating her innocence for new pleasures. She now had to wear the traditional gold collar and anklets and no other covering on her coffee-coloured fine-toned body. She wore her nudity with pride. She moved with grace and charm and all who saw her admired her lovely shape. Her breasts rose like two small fruit high on her ribs, the little nipples dark and juicy like apple stems from plucked fruit. Her thighs and loins were silky, her belly flat. Her buttocks were two melons, asking to be held and stroked. Janet's slave-girl, a little beauty herself, had taken a strong fancy to the Jamaican girl, whose name was Bonnita. They spent as much time as possible together, caressing and kissing, and Janet felt quite neglected, both by the sultan and her slave. However, it was a pleasant pastime for the two British concubines to watch the delicate love-making of the two pretty girls.

'Come on, let's find Bonnita and my slave Sissy. I bet they are being naughty somewhere,' said Janet suddenly.

She put out her cigarette and rose, her breasts swaying into place. Her rather plump bottom and hips were set off by a narrow waist and long legs. Her heavy, dark-blonde hair was swept back as usual, in an untidy knot, and tendrils of curls fell on to her round shoulders and down her back.

The other Mrs McKinnon followed, lighter on her feet than Janet, as she had a slight, small figure and was a head shorter.

They slowly circumnavigated the marble hall, gazing

into small chambers that were filled with soft cushions and decorated with hanging plants and little fountains and pools full of golden carp. As they slowly idled past alabaster pillars and copper plant pots with banana trees growing in them, they both looked up simultaneously. Above them, in the mezzanine, three eunuchs padded quietly, carrying the sobbing figure of a woman.

'Did you see that?' said Rosemary to Janet. 'It was a European woman, I am sure.'

'Yes! I do believe it was. Well, well, well! I think that must be our sultan's latest find.'

During her first week, Mathilde had been taken to the sultan every day. She had refused to let him have his way with her, so he had forced himself on her. He had offered her wine and sweetmeats, caresses and soft talk, but she had remained proud and unbroken. She had demanded to be set free.

'I will never give in to you, you brute! How dare you treat me like this!' she had screamed at him that day.

'I dare because I am all powerful here. And I can tell you, if you don't like *me*, you may perhaps be happier with my brother!' He had taken a whip from the eunuch and asked them to tie her to wall chains. They had uncovered her back and buttocks, leaving her head covered with the silk of her dress.

'Yes!' The sultan had sucked his teeth thoughtfully as he whipped Mathilde's back. He had remembered with sudden nostalgia the lovely Serena, whose back he had marked with his over-zealous use of the whip. Ah, she had a lovely mouth, he had thought. Is she still at the waiting place, I wonder?

'Take the good doctor away for now,' he had said to the eunuchs, 'and bring the two other white women.'

It was at this point that the two Mrs McKinnons had seen the sobbing person of Mathilde Valentine being taken from the sultan's room by the eunuchs. They stood for a moment, looking up, then moved off slowly and found what they had been looking for – the slave-girl Sissy and the Jamaican concubine, Bonnita. They were, as they had thought, entwined in each other's arms, their swollen lips bruised from so much kissing.

'There you are, you wretched slave!' said the amused Janet McKinnon. 'Why are you looking after *her* so well, and neglecting me, may I ask?'

The two girls started up, and at that moment two eunuchs appeared and bowed low to the two Mrs McKinnons.

'The Sultan of Abizir begs you to join him, both of you, please.'

'Ah, well, I'll punish you later, my dear,' said the languorous Janet, taking her hand from the round buttock of her slave.

They were ready for the royal presence, as always. Their bodies were worked on each day as if they were precious cars. They were toned and pummelled, pressed and massaged, bathed and shaved, made up and perfumed. Their bodies were to be at all times ready for use by the sultan or his brother.

'Come along, my dear, we are to get some action at last,' said the racy first Mrs McKinnon.

Rosemary demurely followed, black hair flowing down her pale-skinned back. Her ankle chains rattled as she trotted along behind the long-limbed Janet.

The sultan was lying on his couch, as usual, prick ready in his hands. It rose like a purple stalk from an exotic plant. The two women stood and admired it volubly.

'What a beautiful stem it is. Let me hold it for you, my lord,' said Janet, who could not wait to have the swollen flesh between her legs.

He posed, pleased as always by the little flatteries this Englishwoman gave so easily.

'Come here, my sweet, and sit on my cock,' he said, smiling.

Janet complied eagerly, getting astride him and settling herself down on his stem.

'Mmm! Now, Rosemary, my love, come and let me kiss your pretty cunt.'

Rosemary tiptoed over and settled herself on his face so that her back was to Janet, and they rode him as if they were on a horse. Janet held tight to Rosemary's narrow hips and buttocks and slapped them when she showed signs of slowing. The sultan groaned and sucked, lapped and yelled, licked and writhed as the two white concubines did their duty. It was a chore, thought Rosemary, but quite enjoyable really. His long tongue slithered into her private places and she began to shiver and moan. His hands were on her little breasts, squeezing and pressing.

'Oh, that's terribly nice, Sultan,' she said in a very posh Edinburgh accent.

Janet was enjoying the fat cock inside her, and she writhed and twisted so she could feel it touch her everywhere. Her thighs slapped on his balls with sharp smacks. She reached behind her to fondle his balls and this was the last straw. The camel's back was broken.

'Aah! Aah!' he cried, and both his concubines reached their own satisfaction simultaneously.

Afterwards all three lay on a wide bed together. Janet smoked a Turkish cigarette in a long holder, Rosemary read *Tatler* and the sultan looked at a photograph album of all his favourite Arab stallions and mares.

'This reminds me of Sundays at home,' said Rosemary.

'Really?' Janet blew out a long, luxurious ring of smoke. 'I wish my Sundays had been like this.'

'I only mean reading *Tatler*,' said Rosemary, waving a hand to get rid of the perfumed smoke.

'Well, ladies, how would you like to meet another Englishwoman?' said the sultan, throwing down his album and putting his muscular arms around both concubines.

'I am not English, if it will please you to remember, Sultan,' said the proud Scot.

'No, of course not. I beg your pardon,' said the sultan. 'But you might have heard I have a new concubine, and I am sure you will get on famously together. Indeed, I rely on you, my dear – ' He playfully slapped Janet's buttocks – 'to make sure that Dr Valentine is made to feel welcome and happy. She is having a slight problem, settling in, you know.'

'*Dr* Valentine? I see!' said Janet. 'Well, of course, Sultan, your every wish is my command, as you know.'

He clapped his hands three times and two eunuchs appeared with the sorry form of Mathilde between them. She was naked, as was the tradition, but for the gold collar and bonds around her ankles and wrists, and her dark blonde hair was shining and stunningly arranged around her face and shoulders. But her face, so proud and intelligent, was the picture of woe. She had a red nose, visible even through the thin veil, which was her only covering. Her eyes were puffy. She kept her gaze averted from the sultan's bed.

'Turn around so I may see your back, my dear,' he said.

She turned slowly, and he saw that her weals had faded.

'Good, I have not scarred you, my dear. I would not want to hurt you for the world. Now turn around and let me introduce you.' She turned and opened her sad eyes. 'This is Mrs McKinnon, and this is ... Mrs McKinnon.' He smiled and patted his concubines on their bottoms.

Mathilde nodded and smiled unsurely at the two women, who did not look at all unhappy at being enslaved, sexual puppets to an out-of-date, ridiculous, sadistic potentate with no real power but what money gave him.

'It is my pleasure to introduce Dr Valentine; Dr Mathilde Valentine,' he said.

Mathilde looked again at the two women.

'My God, it's Rosie Johnson!' she suddenly said, and Rosemary McKinnon laughed in delight and threw out her arms towards the other woman.

'Matty? Is it you?'

'Yes, oh yes!' The emotional Mathilde practically hurled herself into the arms of her old schoolfriend, who she hadn't seen for over fifteen years. They had not really been friends – more rivals at being best at everything at their grammar school – but in this foreign place and under such odd circumstances, yes, they were definitely old friends.

'My, my! What emotion! How nice!' The Eton-educated sultan had no problem in understanding the coldness of the British, but he had no experience of their warmth and was thrown by it. 'Well, I suppose this calls for a celebration,' he said, and called for champagne.

It was a strange picnic party, with the three naked women and their sexual master all sitting cross-legged on his love bed. Mathilde felt relaxed and ridiculously happy for the first time since she had been kidnapped by Joseph. She drank the sparkling wine – it always went straight to her head – and gave in to the voluptuousness of the situation she found herself in. After all, what else was there to do? She had no power here to change her circumstances – at the moment. It was only sensible to go along with the sultan's wishes and become, for a while at least, his concubine. Here was the slender, pretty Rosie, who had caused her heart to flutter not a little at school, it must be admitted. Here she was, naked and musky, kissing Mathilde tenderly. And here was another lovely woman, only too eager to touch and discover Mathilde's many charms. And here was the powerful and not unattractive sultan – muscular, athletic, and with an enormous erection pointed at her. Why

154

should she not enjoy this interlude of sensuality? Olensky would understand and forgive. It was out of her hands, really. She had to do what the sultan commanded. She had tried to repel his attentions, but to no avail. Now she would give in gracefully.

Chapter Twenty-One

J anet and Rosemary set upon the luscious, voluptuous body of Mathilde with all the enjoyment of a dog with a fresh bone to play with. With the sultan's encouragement they caressed and kissed her and discovered with the enthusiasm of an intrepid explorer in a virgin country all her secret crevices, hilly peaks, sheltered valleys and dark, damp caves.

'Oh, I always knew you would be as beautiful as this,' said Rosemary. 'If only I had not wasted time at school simply loving you from a distance.'

'It was hardly a distance, you little minx! Don't you remember how you used to put your hand up my blouse to feel my breasts?'

'Oh stop now, please, ladies, and see to me!' commanded the sultan. 'Enough schoolday talk. How about some schoolday spanking instead?'

Rosemary and Janet leapt into action, as they had done many times before, but this time with Mathilde as the victim instead of the usual handy slave-girl. They grabbed her arms and legs and, though she struggled at first, she allowed herself to be lowered over the lap of the naked sultan, whose proud cock stood straight and stiff. She felt it squashed against her belly and she squirmed. He spanked her lightly on her bottom, which showed no signs of the beating she had previously endured. She was trapped, held down by the lithe and slender Rosemary at one side and the gorgeous Janet on the other. Her naked bottom was exposed to their appreciative gaze. The sultan showed every sign of enjoying the chastisement he was administering, and soon gave evidence of his appreciation over her belly and thighs.

There followed a gentle caressing between the three women, while the sultan recovered himself, all four lying or sitting on his love bed. Mathilde was enjoyed by all three of the others, and she participated fully, holding back none of her passions.

She was most intrigued by the bodies of the two women, having her recent experience with Serena to compare them with. The wine made her languorous, heavy limbed and sleepy. She allowed them to fondle her breasts, part her legs and lick her sex. Their soft lips caressed her nether lips and their soft fingers wandered to her juicy interior flesh. She pressed against them, meeting their touch with her longing. The sultan watched the women's sexual play, toying all the while with his erect member. He drew closer to them, joining in with their caressing. An arm here, a leg there, a breast, nipples, juices intermingled. Lips clashed and hair tangled and swept across hot flesh. His strong fingers slyly interfered with the women's private parts. He had his thumbs in anuses and his fingers in vaginas, while his teeth grazed erect nipples. Mathilde found her arms held down and her legs held apart by her new companions. She felt the sudden anguished thrust of his penis disappearing deep inside her. She moaned in bliss. She cried out as her spasms came suddenly and lasted for what seemed like a lifetime.

The sultan was soon asleep and the three women talked softly over his prone, snoring body.

'You realise I know your husband?' said Mathilde to both women. 'I worked at the beach mission with him.'

'How is the handsome brute?' asked Janet.

'Still handsome, I suppose, and definitely still a brute. And still up to his old tricks.'

'He didn't marry you, too?' Rosemary's eyebrows arched above her round eyes.

'No, I escaped that, at least. But he tried to drug me for his own evil ends, and at last he did succeed, I suppose, in taking me for his slave trade.'

Mathilde whispered her story to them, telling them a little of Olensky and the trap that had been set for her in the bush.

'Did you know what went on between McKinnon, Joseph and Grace?' she asked.

'Oh, yes, I was aware of what went on, but what could I do about it?' said Janet, the first Mrs McKinnon.

'Well I had no idea, actually, I was such an innocent. Just think of it!' said Rosemary petulantly. 'Janet has of course filled me in with all the sordid details.'

'Joseph was a dish,' murmured Janet, thoughtfully.

'Well, I would love to get my hands on that decadent missionary again, and this time I would give him something to cry about,' said the boyish Rosemary, remembering the often painful treatment she had suffered and the buggery she had endured.

The three women laughed and settled down to sleep.

Afterwards, she lay still, as if asleep, her head swimming with the effects of the champagne and sex, and her thoughts were again on Olensky and escape. She had needed this outpouring of sexuality and intensity of lust, but her heart was with her lion lover. She yearned for him. It was such an awful thing to have come so close to escape in Zanzibar – to have heard his voice, to have called to him. She felt like a trapped beast taken from her mate. Her tears fell on the slumbering head and slender neck of Rosemary McKinnon. Perhaps, she thought, I can devise a plan of escape, with Rosie's help, and Janet McKinnon's.

Meanwhile, she would try to enjoy her new status as the sultan's latest, favourite concubine.

'Mathilde, you seem to be settling in quite well, am I correct?' The sultan lay on his back in the large alabaster bathtub with Mathilde bathing his feet and massaging his muscular calves. He had made sure, so far, that his greedy brother had not been told of this new concubine. He wanted her all to himself. He loved her long blonde hair falling over his face or sweeping across his balls as she caressed him. He thought her hair was the colour of yoghurt mixed with honey, and in certain lights it was like moonlight on the dunes. She was a fine figure of a woman, and she bruised easily, which he liked. He whipped her buttocks only once a week, so as not to ruin her skin. He leant forward to stroke the triangle of soft pink flesh which opened and closed tantalisingly between her legs as she massaged him.

'Of course, my lord Sultan, it is a very beautiful, tranquil existence . . . only . . .'

'Only what? Do not stop your administrations, please, my dear.'

'I am used to outdoor exercise, my lord. This lazy life is ruining my health. You do realise it is very bad for women not to get regular exercise? I will lose my muscle tone.' She squeezed her upper arm as if to demonstrate her reduced muscles.

He laughed indulgently. She leant forward and sucked his cock in the most slow and sensual way. He groaned and writhed. She stopped her sucking.

'Sultan, take me out riding with you. I love horseback riding. It would be the best exercise possible for my thighs and buttocks.' She sat, her hand idly rubbing his large, soapy cock, admiring its thickness. She kissed it and licked it lightly.

He groaned again.

'Yes, yes, all right, Mathilde, you hussy. You may ride with me.'

She bent her head over his thighs, took his cock in both her hands and lowered her mouth over it, taking it right in as far as it would go, until she felt she would gag. She sucked hard and held his balls and the root of his sex. He moaned and cried out loud and she swallowed the foaming sperm.

The three white women were usually given no more freedom than the other concubines. None of the members of the harem were ever let out of the building, which included the courtyard garden and pools. Their only exercise was in the form of swimming in the pools of the main hall. Their only recreation apart from that was playing games. Many of the women played card games, gambling their diamonds and gold chains with wild abandon. Many played backgammon, sometimes fighting over the results. Some played Mah-jong. Nearly all indulged in a little love-making with each other.

'Janet, I hope you do not think that I have usurped your position in the harem,' said Mathilde one morning while they played board games.

'Good God, no. What do I care if he fucks you instead of me for a while anyway? I get no extra benefits from being his most used concubine. You won't either, you know.' Janet puffed on her cigarette and moved a checkers piece to take two of Mathilde's.

'Are you happy here? Don't you want to get out?' whispered Mathilde, so the hovering slave-girls would not hear.

'Well, it's all right, but I miss shopping, I suppose, and dressing up, and playing bridge.'

'Come now, woman, you are more intelligent than that! Surely you want your freedom?'

'Ah well, I suppose I do really, but what is there to do? We are trapped. This is it, and we must make the most of it.' Janet took all the rest of Mathilde's pieces with a satisfied smile.

'I disagree. We can get out, if we use our feminine wiles to trick the sultan.' Mathilde pretended to kiss the ear of Janet in order to whisper this possibility of treachery.

'What are you saying? How?' Janet caressed Mathilde's heavy breasts, enjoying the weight of them in her hands.

'I will tell you later, when Rosie returns from her fun with old Jerry.'

Poor Rosemary McKinnon was still the favourite plaything of the obscene brother of the sultan. It was her misfortune to look so like a boy from certain angles that the Sultan of Jerah was moved to enjoy her charms very often.

The Sultan of Abizir had so far kept his new concubine from his brother's grasp. He found it very frustrating that he wasn't able to enjoy the three white concubines all at once just whenever he wanted them because Rosemary was usually in his brother's chamber.

His brother was older, and therefore had more status, so he had to allow him the use of all and any of his harem until he chose to go home.

The island where the Sultan of Abizir had his kingdom was to the south of Arabia, off the coast of Somalia. His harem was mostly made up of the beautiful women and girls from Ethiopia, the Yemen, the Atlas Mountains and Persia.

His brother's kingdom was far to the north on the mainland of Arabia.

The sultan wished he would go back there.

Mathilde was dressed like an Arab Sheikh. Her abundant hair was hidden under a veil of white cotton and her face had a red and white patterned scarf over it. Only her eyes remained unhidden. She was dressed from head to foot in the robes of an Arab horseman. Her steed was a grey Arab mare, tall and sturdy of limb but with delicate grace.

'You sit well on my mare,' said the sultan.

'She is beautiful. What is she called?' said Mathilde.

'Abia. It means "great" in Arabic,' the Sultan told her. He looked magnificent, and Mathilde couldn't keep her eyes off his straight stance, the broad shoulders, the muscular legs, and the fine head with the curved nose and wicked mouth.

'Thank you for this, my darling Sultan,' Mathilde shouted and galloped off among the red hills.

He laughed indulgently and let her go. There was no escape from his kingdom. The island was only about the size of the Isle of Wight and he owned it all and the people on it. Not one of his people would take a woman off the island, under pain of death. Someone had attempted to escape, once, many years ago. She had been caught trying to swim away from a capsized dugout canoe. The fisherman who had let her have his craft, in return for sexual favours, was beheaded. No-one had offered to help any unhappy concubines since.

He let Mathilde ride away.

Back at the harem Bonnita and Sissy were enveloped in shrouds of water vapour, but the fog of steam did not completely hide their activities. Sissy was on the marble floor, kneeling at the feet of the Jamaican beauty. Sissy's tight-curled head was buried in the open groin of Bonnita.

'Sssssssissy . . .! Oh, Sissy, that is so wonderful! Kiss me some more, just there. Mmm!'

Bonnita leant back, her legs wide apart, her bottom on the edge of the divan, so her pubis tilted upward and her sex lips were spread open. Sissy licked the inner lips and stuck her tongue inside the red tunnel of flesh. She rolled her tongue around the bud of the erect clitoris. Bonnita writhed on Sissy's mouth, opening and closing her vaginal muscles to draw the soft lips and tongue further in. She loved Sissy. Sissy had been her friend ever since they had found themselves together on a slave ship from the West Indies. She and Sissy shared their misfortunes and pasts. But now, Bonnita was a concubine and Sissy a slave-girl to the Sultan of Abizir. Bonnita's looks were unusual. She was tall and slender and her almond eyes were almost black. Her long hair was tightly plaited in strands. Her bottom was high and rounded and her waist was very small. She and Sissy stole every moment they could together, kissing and caressing in the steamy pool. As one of the sultan's practising concubines, Bonnita had certain privileges. She could choose her slave-girl. But Sissy was already the slave-girl of Janet.

Sissy lapped the juices that ran from Bonnita's dark triangle and Bonnita drew her up and kissed her lips, tasting her own salty flavour on her mouth and tongue.

Sissy, a small, dark-skinned Granadian, stocky and taut muscled, sat on Bonnita's lap. Bonnita slipped her hands in front and behind her pubis and rubbed the tender flesh. Sissy moaned softly and kissed Bonnita. She took both Bonnita's breasts in her hands and trapped the nipples between her fingers. Bonnita lifted Sissy a little, shifting her weight so she could tuck her fingers into her dark red folds of delicate flesh. Sissy smiled and drew her breath in between her teeth. Bonnita's fingers pressed further in, deeper and deeper, feeling the fleshy muscles holding on. Sissy's strong internal muscles sucked on the pleasure-giving fingers as if there was a cock inside her.

'Put something more inside me, Bonny, please, Bonny,' pleaded Sissy.

'Do you want the aubergine I stole from the kitchen? It is rather large, my darling. It might hurt you.'

'Yes, yes, the aubergine. Put it in me!'

Bonnita reached into Sissy's basket of oils, herbs and unguents and pulled out a seven-inch long purple vegetable, shiny skinned and phallic. It was not the length that was so formidable, but the width. It was about five inches in diameter.

'Lie down so I can insert it more easily,' ordered Bonnita.

Sissy stretched out on the divan, her knees raised and her legs apart. Bonnita licked the end of the aubergine and put it into her mouth to see how far she could get it.

'It's very thick, just like a huge cock!' Bonnita giggled.

'Go on, try and put it in me,' pleaded Sissy.

Bonnita pressed the thinner end, denuded of its prickly stem and leaves, against the wide open sex lips. She watched closely as her lover swallowed the vegetable. She pushed gently, watching Sissy's eyes narrow in enjoyment and desire. Bonnita licked her fingers and moistened Sissy's sex around the obscene swollen vegetable, and Sissy sucked it in further and further, her eyes closed in bliss. Bonnita kept up the gentle caressing as she pushed and pulled on the aubergine, seeing the creamy white juices which came from Sissy's sex smeared over the bulbous fruit.

Sissy moved her hips faster and faster, shoving herself on to the false cock, making it touch all of her sex, and vibrate her clitoris. She cried out suddenly and Bonnita held tight to the 'cock' held in deep inside Sissy's sex, then pulled it out, pushed in hard, pulled out, then carried on pushing and pulling until the dark-skinned slave fell back in a swoon of delicious collapse. Bonnita slowly and carefully slipped the aubergine out.

'Was that good, my darling?' she whispered.

'Slave stuffed with aubergine,' giggled Sissy. 'A delicious combination, don't you think!'

Chapter Twenty-Two

*B*aron Olensky had been in a state of deep gloom and despondency since the debacle at Chukwani. He and his men had found the waiting house, but had lost Mathilde.

Olensky went to the Sultan of Zanzibar and made an official complaint about the existence of such a place, and accused him of being a part of the conspiracy to kidnap a European woman. The sultan laughed and asked for the proof. He also suggested that Olensky would be charged for the murder of the soldier at the fortress unless he left Zanzibar immediately.

The frustrated baron did as he was told, together with his little band of faithful sailors, who had enjoyed the fight at least.

They headed north towards Arabia, sailing close to the sandy shore but outside the danger of the sharp reef rocks. They fished for sailfish and tuna, and put ashore for fresh fruit and water. It was while they were on one of these trips for fresh provisions that they came across a clue as to where the harem might be. There was a group of about eight women, subdued and exhausted, and chained together at the ankles, sitting in a disconsolate group on the wharf of a Portuguese-African harbour. They were all young, beautiful Somalis. Their proud eyes were sad and their whole demeanour was of beaten, miserable slavery.

'Who are these women? What have they done to deserve this bondage?' Olensky demanded of the men who guarded them.

'They are prisoners. They have done wrong,' said one large, armed guard.

'Oh, I see, and where are they being taken?'

'They await a boat to take them northwards – it will come soon. We will get paid when it comes.'

The baron, still in the clothes of an Arab trader, showed an interest in the shipment of the women. The men waited in the harbour bar, a scruffy little room with sand on the floor. They drank slowly, so as not to get inebriated. Olensky knew they were on to something. These women were not criminals. It was probable they were slaves on their way to the harem where Mathilde Valentine was being held.

The boat arrived in the harbour and the sailors disembarked. They were a motley crew – mostly Portuguese, although some were Greek and some African. The captain was a low-browed Greek, overweight and already red-eyed and puffy faced with drink. He and his men went straight to the bar to get drunk. Olensky made a point of buying the captain several bottles of a strong banana-based liquid that soon brought a staring gaze to his eyes. He talked to him at length and got the information he wanted. Meanwhile, the guards sat with the group of slaves, angry that they had not yet been paid and had the women taken from them.

The baron left the slumped captain and his crew in the bar, then took the head guard to one side and made him an offer of money. The guard agreed readily to hand the women over to Olensky.

Once on the boat, the women were set free of their

chains and bonds and given fresh water and food. When they were clear of the harbour they set sail for a large, safe beach twenty miles north, where there was a fishing village, and the women were released. When they arrived, some of the women were so grateful that they gave their bodies to the sailors, though the sailors had not demanded it. One of the women, a proud example of her race, beckoned to Sabah Madaan from the shallows as he stood leaning over the deck. She smiled and beckoned again, jumping up and down to show him her charms. He could not resist. He removed his clothes and jumped overboard into the clear blue sea, his erection standing up proudly. He swam to her and held her tight. Other women beckoned to the crew and they too joined the salty orgy. Olensky alone stayed on the dhow, amused and aroused by the sight of the thrashing limbs, the naked flesh, the flash of a hand between legs, a penis waving in the water. The crew enjoyed the women and the freed women enjoyed the lusty crew. Eventually they tired and the crew returned to the boat and the women waded ashore and lay on the sand, recovering, before they began their trek back to their villages.

Olensky was energised. He was on the right track. He now knew he would find Mathilde again.

Mathilde, meanwhile, was finding out more about life on the island of Abizir. Her solitary horse rides took her all over. She took note of the little harbours, two of them, where small dugout canoes carried provisions from village to village, and saw that shallow draught steamers went from Abizir to the Somali coast and further north to Arabia. There was, as she had thought there must be, another palace, in the cool hills, where the sultan's wives were kept in purdah. The palace was made of pink marble and gleamed as if the sun's rays shone permanently on its towers and minarets.

She rode to its high walls, traversed its perimeters and

saw children playing in the shady green-boughed court-yards through the golden gates. She rode back to the sultan. He was in the green hills with his falcons. She leapt from her horse and stood close by him, her hands on his crotch. He turned to kiss her, pleased at her warmth and affection towards him.

'Who looks after your wives' health care?' she said lightly, her arms wrapped around his waist. He called his falcon back to him and it landed on his arm. Mathilde watched in awe and sadness. The golden feathered bird, with its proud hooked beak and its yellow eyes, looked free but was as much a prisoner to this powerful man as she was.

'My wives and children go to the mainland when they are very sick. There is no medical care here, apart from one or two old midwives who have special skills.'

'I see. Would you like me to take over the care of your wives and children?'

'No, I want you here with me, at all times.' He gave his falcon to his man-servant, picked Mathilde up in his arms, lifted her as if she was a child and pressed his lips on her belly. He sat her on her horse and mounted his own grey stallion. Then he rode with her to a tented encampment in the hills, where he made love to her, violently, as usual. He pressed his hard cock on her belly, drew it over her breasts and put it into her soft mouth.

'Your mouth is as soft as your mare's,' he said. 'I could put a bit in your mouth and ride you.' He fucked with ferocity, getting his pleasure from her helplessness against his superior strength. He tied her wrists above her head so her breasts stretched flat. He turned her over and spanked the pink buttocks until she yelled for mercy, then he took her from behind. He used her without regard to her own pleasure, but she took it anyway, pressing her thighs together to feel his balls kick on her perineum so she had her orgasm too.

It was about a week after Mathilde had asked to be doctor to his family that one of the sultan's babies became seriously ill. It was his latest child, a few weeks old, and it was failing to thrive. The sultan had a weakness for babies. This baby was a dark-haired boy, the child of his second wife. She was tired of childbirth, having given the sultan seven children in as many years. Five of them, all boys, had died in infancy. The child and the wife were too ill to endure the short sea journey to the mainland and medical assistance.

The sultan held the baby in his arms and realised that he looked like him. He rode back to the harem and asked Mathilde to help.

Mathilde and the two Mrs McKinnons rode out with the sultan most days. It was a marvellous new freedom, brought about by Mathilde's successful care of his sick wife and baby. The sultan enjoyed the company of his white concubines and had learnt the new pleasures of making love out in the desert with them all. His brother was not an athletic man and the Sultan of Abizir found that it was a good way to keep his favourites out of his way. Mathilde was still his own secret.

The two Mrs McKinnons had both learnt horse riding in their childhood and Rosemary had been a member of the Sutherland Hunt, so they enjoyed this opportunity to get out on a good horse.

The three horsewomen and the sultan rode side by side, galloping and racing over the hills. They let him win, of course, though Rosemary could easily have beaten him, had she chosen. His stallion wanted to win too. He showed off to Mathilde's mare, who whinnied and pawed the ground in praise. The women laughed. The geldings were unimpressed.

The sultan had set up a tented camp at an oasis for these outings. Eunuchs waited there with fresh fruit juice and alcohol, Turkish cigarettes for Janet McKinnon, and delicate morsels of roast meats and aubergine stuffed with pine nuts and apricots. The riding party dismounted and left the horses in the care of the servants. They stripped off their dusty clothes and plunged into the small freshwater pool. The sultan stood naked in the shade of a palm tree and watched the concubines. He was very proud of his possessions, the white females. He was probably the only sultan he knew of with European concubines. His private kingdom was inviolate, his secret safe. He held his cock loosely in one hand and stroked it to erection. He watched Janet's breasts float on the limpid surface of the water. Rosemary swam to her and held her close. They bobbed up and down together, playing with each other's breasts. Mathilde swam alone, her arms slicing the water determinedly. Janet grabbed her as she passed close by, and she spluttered and ducked and resurfaced. They all laughed together and hugged each other.

'Oh, it's so cool and lovely here,' said Janet on one of their outings. She kissed Mathilde on the lips and Mathilde, one eye on the sultan, returned the kiss. He stroked his erection while he watched. Rosemary joined the delicate embrace, and their hands were under the water, stroking each other's thighs and bottom cheeks. Their breasts, Rosemary's small, high apples and the other's more luscious fruit, floated and sank, bobbed about and invited each other's tongues to lick the erect nipples. The women pleased each other, and the sultan watched and enjoyed the gentle spectacle. At last he plunged into the pool and swam to them, and they took him into their circle and touched him. He was surrounded by feminine flesh rubbing up against him; their softness on his hardness, their soft fingers on his hard cock. He kissed them in an orgy of lust. His cock was held by all three women and his balls were delicately clasped and fondled. Fingers slyly invaded his anus. His firm, tight buttocks were slapped and he spanked their soft globes.

His fingers and theirs explored every orifice. He closed his eyes as his penis was enclosed in warm flesh and the semen was pumped out of him by willing thighs.

And so the weeks passed.

The sultan still thought Mathilde a delightful novelty. He gave her whatever she wanted. He made her presents of pearls and diamonds, gold and rubies. She refused them at first but then accepted them, placing them together in her quarters, separate from the other women of the harem. He found Mathilde was an exciting companion, not least because she was clever and sure of herself. She now ran a weekly clinic at the palace. She had to remain veiled during these clinics, but her self-confidence had returned with the use of her skills. She also suggested that he ought to have his concubines medically examined regularly. The sultan was in a mood to give her anything she desired. His baby boy was putting on weight, and his wife was looking better and feeding the child successfully.

The sultan's half-brother was still a thorn in his side, but reverence for family kept the Sultan of Abizir from throwing him out.

The Sultan of Jerah still used his brother's concubines. His sexual tastes were bizarre and the concubines always had to give themselves satisfaction after bringing him to his solitary expulsions.

Rosemary, the Sultan of Jerah's favourite, had been sworn to secrecy over the existence of Mathilde, but on one occasion she couldn't stop herself from telling him.

She had been called in by the obese sultan, who had lifted his voluminous skirts and let his balls fall into the hands of several small concubines. They handled his precious plums gently, their little fingers playing his scrotum as if it were a harp. He could only watch his gentle lovers in the looking glass that lay the length of the bedchamber. He lay on his side and the girls were strewn around him like kittens on their mother's belly.

171

He was a beached whale, being prodded, poked and tickled.

'That's enough, now, my little dears. Do up my suspenders and tighten my corset. I want to play with my little white friend's bottom.'

The concubines did as they were told, tightening the old man's corset and lifting his skirts to do up his stockings.

Rosemary tried not to laugh. It did not do to laugh at the odd antics of this man. He was apt to get angry and beat her at any excuse.

'Oh, Sultan, you are very pretty with your pink stockings and frilly suspenders,' she lied.

He stroked her cropped dark hair. She was naked as usual, except for the compulsory neck collar and chains around her ankles and wrists.

He clapped his hands and a eunuch appeared carrying her riding outfit.

'Put it on, my precious little boy,' he said to Rosemary, and she did as he said.

Then, to her surprise, she discovered that there was a hole cut in her breeches, under her crotch and bottom, so her shaved sex and anus were exposed. The sultan took her riding crop and gave it to her, begging her to cut his buttocks with it. She smilingly complied, but didn't have the strength to really hurt the obscene transvestite. He bent over a low stool and she thrashed him until he ordered her to stop. She felt like carrying on with the punishment. After all, he had given her much worse in the previous months. But she stopped as soon as he demanded it.

'Now you bend over, you naughty boy,' he said, and took the leather crop from her.

Rosemary took up the required position and braced herself for the whipping. But first he bent his gross form on the floor and licked her visible private parts. She lay still, thinking of his fat cheeks pressed against her bottom. Her sex grew hot and wet at his insistent tongue. She squirmed to get more of his fat tongue. He stood.

'You naughty boy, you like that, don't you?' he said, lifting the crop, and brought it down hard on Rosemary's little bottom. He gave her twelve sharp cracks with the crop she had used on her chestnut gelding the day before. It was then, with tears in her eyes, that she told Jerry about Mathilde.

Why shouldn't Mathilde suffer a bit too? she thought. It's not fair.

'Oh beautiful one, oh owner of the world's most wonderful balls, oh holder of a most precious cock, like a giant carrot. Oh! Please stop, Jerry! I have some news for you,' she sobbed.

'What news? Is it gossip? I love gossip, what is it?' He slobbered his lips over her anus and poked a finger inside.

'We have a new white woman in the harem. Your brother has been hiding her from you. She is very white and very beautiful, and has a lovely posterior.' Rosemary had great difficulty keeping calm while Jerry had his fingers inside her anus. She had learnt, during her brief 'marriage' to Charles McKinnon, to enjoy buggery. His hands had held her pubis and pressed into her vagina while his cock was inside her back passage. She had taken her satisfaction where she could, pressing against his hands. His penis had pushed the walls of her anus and pressed against his fingers in her vagina. The sensations had not been wholly unpleasant. Now she used her experience with the handsome Scottish bigamist and white slave trader, as he had been proved to be, with the poor, sad old man who knelt behind her. He was supported by his eunuchs so he did not slip while he positioned himself to slide his small but needy cock into the smooth cleft of Rosemary's boyish buttocks. He slid in with a sigh and let her do all the work, pushing and pulling herself along the length of his rod.

'Oh, you naughty, naughty boy,' he said, sighing loudly. Then he slid off her on to the floor, where his eunuchs covered him after first ordering two little slave-girls to wash his genitals.

Rosemary stood to leave and just as she left his chamber, he called out to her, 'I will have you – all three of you – soon.'

Chapter Twenty-Three

Mathilde was riding her mare early one morning. She became aware of a faint drumming on the earth. Then she saw, in the far distance, a cloud of dust rising into the still, pale sky. She rode towards the cloud, curious as to its reason. Her horse struggled to climb a high dune and as she reached the crest she saw a caravan of camels galloping towards the harem. There were a dozen laden beasts, some with men riding them, some with boxes and parcels strapped to their saddles. The Arabs did not see Mathilde as they rode close. She watched them fly by, and her gaze was drawn to the handsome features of a young man. He sat proudly in the saddle, his broad shoulders obvious through his white flowing garments. His lower face was covered from the sand, but his eyes and brow were royal.

The sultan welcomed his eldest son, seventeen-year-old Omah, to his harem.

'My own precious boy, you look well! How are you?' He hugged and embraced his favourite, with joy and satisfaction. This son was at college in England, and this was the beginning of his long holiday, which he had chosen to spend with his father and mother, the sultan's first wife. His mother lived in the palace with the other wives and children. He would go to see her later, but his base was to be at the harem with his father.

Eunuchs brought trays of food and the sultan, his brother and the sultan's son lounged on silk cushions. They laughed and talked of the boy's education, the gossip of the harem, and the health of the extended family.

'I hear there is a new white concubine,' the Sultan of Jerah interjected casually.

His brother was angry that his secret was out but could not show it.

'Yes, that's right. She won't be to your taste, though, brother. Her hips and buttocks are too feminine and her breasts are luscious little pomegranates.'

'Oh, I think I must be the judge of that, brother,' said the Sultan of Jerah.

'Father, I am tired from the journey,' Omah interrupted. 'Will you allow me to retire to my room until later?' He rose, bowed to his father and uncle, and was then taken to his room by a eunuch servant.

There, in the silk-covered chamber, which had cool marble walls and tiled floor, waited three slave-girls. They were dressed in thongs of gold chains which circled their narrow waists, divided their bottom cheeks and came up between their legs, cutting into the brown sex lips, which were clean shaven. Their ankles had fine chains around them, as did their wrists. Their glossy black hair was dressed in tight curls. Their sand-coloured skin shone and gleamed with scented oils.

He allowed them to undress him, as his father's slave-girls always did when he was at home for the holidays.

Since he was a boy, perhaps fourteen, he had been given this special treatment from his father's slaves. He had looked forward to it during the long, cold term times. He had been sent away to school in southern

England at the tender age of seven and knew only the harshness of community life with a lot of boys and men.

He was still technically innocent, having failed to lose his virginity in England. English girls were too cold, he thought. He thought all young white women were desirable, with their transparent skin and their blue veins pulsing beneath. He loved the violet eyelids, the downy cheeks, the blush on white skin. But he had had no success with English girls of his own age. But the case was that he was so beautiful that the English female students he had met were either intimidated by his looks or assumed he was homosexual.

His robes were taken from him, and the slave-girls stood and stared in admiration at his young body. They were used to the fat old Sultan of Jerah and the more attractive but middle-aged Sultan of Abizir. This splendid youth was all they could desire. His face was a younger version of his father's, with the proud, hooked nose and fleshy lips, but he had not yet acquired the cruelty of manner or the ruthless expression that marred his father's face. His body was firm, athletic and had no spare flesh. They tenderly touched his smooth chest and flat belly, the young hip bones sticking out. His buttocks were tight cushions of velvet. They stroked and sighed and admired. His long, curly black hair was washed of sand and the tangles of the desert were combed out. His back was scrubbed and his thighs and calves massaged. They fought to wash his genitals, each girl striving to please him with gentle caresses. His penis grew straight and thick from an almost hairless groin and sat neatly on two perfect plums. As he was very young, his erection was touching his stomach, and didn't have the habitual droop of his father's. It was a fine upstanding cock and they recognised its worth and royalty. First one kissed the swelling cock, then another would take over the licking, soft caress. The third concentrated on his anus, slipping her soapy fingers between his buttocks and tenderly stroking the little brown opening. Omah sighed and strained against the touch of the three slave-girls. It was a short-lived pleasure: the excitement was too much for the young man and he soon spurted his white foam into the mouth of a slave.

Later, his father introduced him to his new concubines.

'This is my son, Omah, my first born. You will do whatever he wants, and make sure he enjoys his vacation, please, ladies.'

'Well, all right then, if you say so.' The languid Janet McKinnon blew her cigarette smoke out of her nose and gave Omah a smouldering look of pure lust.

'How long are you staying here?' asked Rosemary. She too thought she had never seen such a lovely youth. His chin was smooth as a peach. He cannot even be shaving yet, she thought.

Mathilde had similar thoughts. Does the father expect us to fuck his son? she thought. Well, if it must be, so be it!

'What are you studying?' asked Mathilde.

'Art and Arabic literature,' said the youth, who was feeling the effects of the alcohol they were consuming. He admired this voluptuous, blonde woman with her heavy fall of hair and wide mouth that promised kisses like the ones he had earlier enjoyed from the slave-girls. His mind was full of sex, as was only normal. He leant forward to see better the curve and rise of Mathilde's breasts under her gown. All three women were veiled and relatively modestly attired in gauzy muslin robes, draped and arranged to show off their bosoms, buttocks and the cleft of their pubis. Not a great deal was left to the imagination.

Omah's head fell forward and he slumped on to Mathilde's bosom.

'Your son is drunk, Sultan,' said Mathilde.

'I'll put him to bed, shall I?' Janet McKinnon was on

her feet, trying to wrest the youth from Mathilde's reluctant embrace.

'No, let the eunuchs take him. I want him intact for his eighteenth birthday in two days' time. Come and look after *my* needs, Janet. My son's will be satisfied all in good time.'

She laughed and shrugged her shoulders.

'Oh! All right, Sultan, I suppose he will have to wait for my expert tuition,' she sighed.

Mathilde and Rosemary laughed and poured Janet another drink, but she pushed it to one side and sat on her master's lap. The boy was removed by the eunuchs and put to bed on his own.

The Sultan of Jerah tapped his lap and nodded at the boyish Rosemary, who obediently rose and went to him. Mathilde lounged on her cushion, leaning on one elbow, and she casually watched the love-making, if it could be called that. Both men were only after their own immediate satisfaction with no thought for the enjoyment of their partner, so the act was quick, abrupt and animal-like. The huge mass of flesh that was the Sultan of Jerah shook and trembled like a jelly as the slender, tiny Rosemary rode him, her back to his belly and his cock locked inside her anus. Mathilde was moved by the sight of Rosemary's shaved sex opening like a flower on the lap of the sultan. She wanted to touch the pink, smooth sex lips. The sultan lifted Rosemary's little legs and folded them up so her feet were touching her sex. He pushed her legs open and pressed his fat hand on her sex. Mathilde's own sex felt slippery and moist and her fingers automatically went to fill the hole that was there and needed filling. She sighed and moaned quietly and moved her fingers and hands around her sex to press and caress and pinch her clitoris. The Sultan of Abizir noticed her discomfort and clicked his fingers to her. She went to him and kissed his cruel mouth. He was lying back with Janet sitting on his cock. He pulled himself up and made Janet lie down. He mounted her, and bade Mathilde to get behind him and touch him from behind. She saw the thick cock slither in and out of Janet's gaping sex, their juices mingling. Mathilde's hands went down between his buttocks and took the root of his cock in her capable hands. Janet's buttocks slammed down on to him and Mathilde's hands stroked his balls and pumped his root. He came loudly, his cries sending Janet over the edge of desire. Her moans were loud and animal.

Mathilde was unsatisfied, as was Rosemary. The Sultan of Jerah lay like a huge dead sea-lion, exhausted and sweaty.

Rosemary, Mathilde and Janet went off to the washing pool to be cleaned by slave-girls while both sultans were cleaned and undressed and put to bed by their servants.

The three women plunged into the pool. The slave-girls knew what their duties were. They had soon soaped the white women, and were using their fingers, hands, breasts and bellies as sponges to rub the concubines all over. Rosemary wanted her slave-girl to put fingers into her anus as well as her vagina. Janet was delighted at whatever anyone did to her. Mathilde enjoyed watching the others' excitement. The slave-girls were soon enjoying the caresses of the concubines; their gentle kisses, their passionate mouths, their pummelling hands. Tongues and fingers, thighs and breasts – all were used to please each other. Bellies pressed on bellies, breasts were flattened by breasts, tongues were entwined with tongues, and pink petals opened and closed over darker flowers. Black buttocks slapped on white bellies, pale bosoms and brown breasts were fondled and squeezed and dark long nipples and pale pink nipples were stretched by slender fingers. The sighs and whimpers of the six females filled the pool, like seal pups calling for their mothers.

180

Chapter Twenty-Four

Young Omah, favourite son of the Sultan of Abizir, had recovered from the previous night's overindulgence. He was at the age when a hangover is an unknown experience. He woke feeling alive and well, with no sign of a headache or a stomach upset. As usual, he woke with a stiff cock. In England, he would have had to relieve himself, in his lonely room at the college, perhaps with the help of his vivid imagination. Here, in his father's harem, there was no need for that.

He rang a little silver bell and three slave-girls appeared. They wore veils over their faces and silver chains around their breasts, hips and ankles, from which hung tiny silver bells. Silver and silk G-strings divided their bottom cheeks and their sex slits. They sat on his bed, giggling and playing with the chains around their slender bodies. They tinkled like tree decorations as they moved. Omah lay back with his hands behind his head and they did their morning duty.

The tallest girl, whose breasts were like little pyramids set on their side, their rosy peaks capped with silver rings, sat by his side and stretched her long brown arm across his chest. She leant forward and put her soft

181

mouth on his. The kiss was long and sensuous, and he felt his prick quiver. The other two girls were intimately entwined, positioned so he could watch them. They stroked each other's bottom cheeks and touched between each other's legs. They stretched the silk strings to expose their sexes to him. They drew the silk tighter into their slits so their sex lips bulged obscenely either side. They put out their tongues and waggled them at him. They wiggled their hips at him and shook their little bellies. His cock grew harder, and the slender slave who had draped herself over him casually stroked the brown stretched skin. He groaned as she pressed her fingernails down its length, marking the sensitive skin with white lines. She dug in her fingers under the scrotum and squeezed gently. He squirmed and shifted. She kissed him again, but he pushed her face away so he could watch the erotic dance. The two performers slid their young bodies up against each other, pressing pelvises together. Their jutting hips met, their bellies squashed together. They clasped each other's buttocks and swayed in a sensuous dance, grinding their hips and sex parts together. The tall slave-girl licked Omah's fine, upstand- ing cock and fondled his balls, tickling the root of his cock at the same time. He called out in a moan and spurted his prolific foam into the girl's face and over her bosom.

He was not pleased. She should have taken his cock deep into her mouth so he could come in her throat. He knew his rights. His father would never have stood for it.

Omah leapt out of bed, sat on the edge and told the two dancing girls to place the other slave over his lap. They giggled and ran about the room after her, while she squealed and tumbled, showing her well-oiled pri- vate parts to them all. They grabbed her eventually and dragged her to him. They put her over his knees and held her head down. Her pert bottom was up high and he placed a hand over it, feeling the fine texture of her dark skin. He spanked her hard and his cock grew under the pressure of her body. She squeaked every time a blow fell on her round bottom cheeks. The other two held her there, close to Omah. He could smell their musk, their perspiration and their perfumed bodies. He licked their breasts and grabbed at their little cunts, pulling the strings that separated their sex lips. He spanked the girl over his knees and felt his erection pressing into her. The slaves were not allowed sexual intercourse with the sultan or his retinue, but everything else was allowed. The heavy foreplay was probably more exciting than the real thing, he thought. He was, of course, still a virgin and knew no better. He felt between the open buttocks and thighs of the girl he was spanking, slapping at her sex parts. He watched the flesh redden and swell. He slipped fingers inside her and heard the slurping of her juices. The other two slaves rubbed their sexes against his face and he licked them. They held his head and pressed against his mouth. He made them all come, and he came again, holding his cock against the squirming slave on his lap.

Later that morning, he rode off on his father's steed, the white stallion. He loved to ride alone in his father's country, breathing in the scents of the desert, the herbs and flowers. He stopped and dismounted to pick a yellow thistle flower. He lay back, his head on his hands, and contemplated his present and his future. Not one of his fellow students would have believed that this place existed in the twentieth century. He was, of course, sworn to secrecy over the existence of the harem. It would have angered his emancipated girlfriends to learn that his father owned concubines. His male friends would probably have pretended to disapprove but he knew they would be jealous really. But of course Omah was only too aware that his father's concubines were soon to be his to use too, as from his eighteenth birthday

– and he could certainly reconcile his modernism to that ancient tradition.

He heard a cantering horse approach and stood to see Mathilde riding towards him, her veil covering her nose and mouth and her white flowing garment flying in the wind.

She reached him and slid off her mare.

'Good morning, Omah, are you refreshed after your gallop?' she asked.

He was surprised at her lack of subservience.

'Do you always ride alone?' he asked her, aware, as he had been last night, of her exotic beauty.

'Sometimes. I am going to see your father's wives and children this morning. I am their medic, did you know?'

'No, I did not.' Omah was surprised. He had been shocked to see white women in his father's harem, but knew better than to ask questions. That there was a qualified doctor among the concubines was even more strange.

'I will ride with you,' he said, and thrust his foot into the stallion's stirrup.

She eased her mare away quietly while the stallion reared and fought the bit between his teeth. He was showing off for the mare.

Mathilde smiled understandingly.

The boy was embarrassed and kicked the stallion. It reared again and threw the sultan's son from its back, before kicking its legs like a mustang and careering off into the desert in the direction of the harem.

Omah was only stunned. He had banged his head on a rock and was bleeding from over his right ear. He was more humiliated than injured. Mathilde lifted his head gently and opened his eyelids. He would be all right. With difficulty she got him on to her mare's saddle and mounted behind him and rode slowly to the wives' palace, which was half a mile away and closer than the harem. She held him as he swayed in the saddle, his wound bleeding into the sand.

His mother was expecting him but not like this. She took him into her arms and cried over him as if he was a baby. He smiled at her alarm.

'I am fine, little Mother. Do not panic! See – it is only a cut.'

'Yes, he's right, it is superficial,' said Mathilde. 'Let me clean it and cover it with a gauze.'

His mother had met Mathilde several times on her clinic visits and admired the young Englishwoman.

'You see, Mathilde,' she said, 'he is my first born and his father's favourite. He can do no wrong.' She smiled proudly at her son and patted him on the cheek. Mathilde admired his beauty, silently. He looks like a young Valentino, she thought.

'So, Mother darling, are you well?' he said to the Sultana of Abizir, who was a good-looking woman in her fifties.

'Better since Dr Valentine has been looking after us,' she said.

'Mother, I am sure Dr Valentine deserves your admiration, but she is only a concubine, and you mustn't make so much of her. Father will not like it,' he whispered, as Mathilde was busy examining the ear of one of the sultan's grandchildren. The baby was crying loudly, and his mother, a girl of fifteen, was hiding behind a marble pillar while her sister held it. The young mother was totally veiled and spoke no English. Omah's mother spoke English well. She was a self-educated woman, as many of the sultan's wives were. They had a vast library of books and a fine collection of paintings in the palace. She was an artist too, which is how her son had acquired a taste and feeling for art.

'Hush, boy, what do you know? You are not living here any more. You have foreign ways now. Look at you! Nearly a man!'

'I am a man, Mother, but I know that to you I will always be your little boy.' He smiled and kissed her affectionately on the cheek.

Mathilde saw the kiss and thought how charming the lad was. He looked up and smiled at her. She looked so clever in her white coat. What a shame she wore the veil covering her lovely mouth. He thought of the slave-girl's mouth on his sex, and he imagined Mathilde's mouth on him.

They rode back to the harem together, Omah borrowing a horse from the palace. Mathilde always felt more confident of herself after these clinics. After all, she was not a helpless concubine, she told herself. She could not believe she had been here for months. How had it happened? She had been so happy with Olensky in his beloved East Africa. Her heart was a stone in her chest.

'Omah,' she said, 'do you approve of your father's harem?'

'Approve? It is not my place to approve or disapprove of the way my father lives.'

'But how can you, a modern youth, with a college education, accept this archaic system of bondage? It's outrageous to incarcerate all those women for the sake of one man's desire.' She looked angrily at him.

'I am my father's son. His ways are mine,' he said with tight lips, and whipped his horse to move it on faster. The horse whinnied and shied and Omah had great difficulty in keeping his seat.

'You should know better,' she said, and he did not know if she meant his treatment of the horse or the acceptance of his father's way of life.

He cantered on, embarrassed, and did not speak to her again.

Olensky was still sailing along the coast of Somalia, stopping at every port for news and provisions, but it hadn't been trouble-free. There was a storm and the dhow was damaged. He had to pay for the repairs, and time was lost. But he felt sure he was on the right track and he would come to the place where his beloved Mathilde was a prisoner. But it was taking so much time. Then a sailor became very ill with denghi fever and they had to put him ashore and leave him to be nursed. Other members of the crew caught the infectious disease and the dhow had to anchor for two weeks while they rested and made their recoveries. Two of the crew died from the disease, while many others were very weakened by it and lost weight. The voyage was becoming a nightmare.

It was the opportunity the Sultan of Jerah had been looking for. He badly wanted to try out the new concubine, but in his haste to make the most of his brother's absence, he thought he had better use all the white concubines at once.

He gave orders for all three to be prepared for him.

The slave-girls at once dropped all their other duties to attend to the white concubines' toilet. Mathilde, Rosemary and Janet were first bathed in the cleansing pool with fragrant soaps. The foamy water slid off their breasts and buttocks and ran down the channels of their thighs. They were depilated with sharp razors, and the long blades rasped their underarms and their legs and slid smoothly over their sex mounds. Then the white concubines lay with their legs apart, watching the steady hennaed hands ease the blade through the slight fuzz. Mathilde loved this procedure. The soapy fingers found their sly way into the folds of flesh to arouse her, and the intimate places were pummelled and rubbed to swell and throb. The women were then washed with fresh water to remove the fuzz and the soap before the oiling of their bodies. Little hands smoothed the delicately scented oil behind the knees, over the calves, into the curve of the instep. The oil slid with the delicate touch of the slaves under aching breasts and around thighs. The white female buttocks were slapped and pummelled, the oil melting into the white skin. The slaves also rouged the women's nipples, sex lips and mouths. They watched each other change from natural female animals into strange exotic, fetishist images. Their eyes were painted with kohl to make them look larger and their bodies were anointed with perfumes. Their hair was brushed and dressed and they were attired in the way the sultan had ordered.

They went to his chamber. Rosemary wore her very revealing jodhpurs, a white shirt and riding boots. Janet wore nothing but her gold and diamond bondage chains and collar with the addition of a wide belt of a silver metal. This was tightly fastened and drew in her already narrow waist, so that her movements were constricted. Her buttocks were pushed out and her ribcage held in. Her heavy breasts rose above the hard edge of the metal belt. Her hair was tied back in a high-plaited tail. Mathilde was also in her everyday concubine uniform of heavy gold collar and anklets and bangles. Her belly and pubis felt very naked. A narrow chain encircled her waist and from there threaded through her pubic slit dividing her inner labia. It pressed into her clitoris and kept her in a state of readiness. From behind, the chain disappeared into her bottom cleft. She stood before the very large Sultan of Jerah and looked with horror at him. He was dressed in a red corset, laced tight about his waist and belly, but it could not hide the immensity of his flesh. Under his belly, hardly visible, was his little cock, sadly propped up by a thong that went between his fat thighs and up between his sagging buttocks. His breasts bulged over the bodice and his nipples were rouged. He wore high-heeled red sandals but did not attempt to stand or walk in them. He carried a long whip.

Oh my God, what have we got here? thought Mathilde.

'How nice to meet you, my dear Dr Valentine. Do sit down.' The sultan pointed to his lap.

She thought of refusing outright but she had heard of his cruelty and knew she could expect a thorough whipping if she didn't do as he asked.

'I am pleased to meet you, Sultan. I would rather stand if you don't mind.' She tried to imagine that she had her white coat on and a stethoscope around her neck.

'But I do mind. I do mind.' He patted his lap again. 'Come!'

She sighed and sat on his lap. His fat little arms went around her and he pawed her breasts and belly and put a thumb between her legs.

'Yes, you are a fine figure of a woman. I see what my brother likes about you, but he is right – I prefer a smaller figure.' He shoved her off his knees with no ceremony and said, 'Rosemary, come here, my boyish little darling.'

Rosemary was furious. She had hoped that the pressure on her to please the obese sultan would be lessened by the novelty of Mathilde. But it was not to be. However, the sultan could see the interest it would cause his tired sex drive if he whipped the new concubine – or rather, if someone else whipped her while he was otherwise occupied. He gave the whip to Janet, and told her to put on high-heeled black boots which came to her thighs. He told the eunuchs to tie Mathilde to wall chains and he lay down with the slender, boy-like Rosemary to watch the flagellation.

Mathilde could not believe this was happening to her. She sobbed as the whip cut into her buttocks. Janet was an expert, getting the fine leather thong to snap in the air with a dreadful crack, which terrified her before it hit her flesh on just the spot Janet chose.

Janet seemed to quite enjoy her role as chastiser. She relished the sound the whip made as it licked the pale flesh and turned it red. Janet's waist and ribcage were held in tight by the wide corset-like belt and her belly bulged below and her large bottom cheeks shook with each whip lash.

Mathilde cried out at each blow.

Rosemary was delighted that at least she wasn't getting the rough end of things this time. She played with the sultan's prick and made it stand up straight and then she sat on it, so that it went into her tight little anus. He grew redder in the face as she rose and fell on his erection, while Mathilde's bottom and thighs went the same colour as the whip fell on her.

The rasping chain between Mathilde's legs rubbed and chafed at her clitoris. She was torn between hatred for the sultan and a desire to orgasm.

Janet's breasts rose and fell in time with the whip cracks and her rouged nipples grew long and hard. Her sex lips were rubbed by the top of the boots and she was getting very excited at the sight of Mathilde's flaring hips and round, reddened buttocks.

'Touch her between the legs,' ordered the sultan, and Janet was happy to do as she was bid. She kept the whip wrapped around the breasts of Mathilde and she caressed her firmly.

Mathilde was grateful that the pain had stopped and she welcomed the firm fingers between her aching thighs. Her vagina was so moist, it surprised her. She was ashamed the whipping had excited and aroused her so much. The feminine caresses were like balm on her flesh. She moaned and drew back to meet the embrace.

Janet's damp, perspiring breasts pressed hard against Mathilde's back while her fingers explored deep the secret tunnel. Mathilde felt the waves of desire and overwhelming need for release overcome her. She went with the feeling, letting herself go deep into the abyss.

She did not know which was her body and which was Janet McKinnon's. Their flesh was one. She exploded, her spasms carrying her into a place she had never been before. Her head fell forward in supplication, and Janet's kisses covered her neck and back.

Chapter Twenty-Five

*T*he Sultan of Abizir cut the engine of his powerful boat and let it drift into the little wooden pier.

'A fine craft, is it not, my son?' he said. He was showing Omah his new motorboat.

'A wonderful toy, father. May I take it out on my own sometime?'

'Yes, of course, my boy, you don't have to ask. What is mine is yours, always.' He tied up the boat to a bollard and let his servants take charge of it.

The handsome pair, both tall and good-looking, walked together, hand in hand, as was the tradition in Abizir.

'And does that apply to your concubines, Father?'

'Of course,' said the sultan.

'Even your favourites?'

'It is the anniversary of your birth, my boy. You may take any one of my concubines as your own.'

'For just my birthday, or for always?'

'Yours to keep. Your first concubine.' The Sultan of Abizir was feeling very generous today.

Omah was silent. They walked along the little harbour, quiet apart from a few fishermen mending nets on the wide stone wharf. The sultan slapped him on the back.

'Come, Omah, it is an important decision, but you mustn't take it so seriously. You may try out as many as you like before you make up your mind which you want. You have three months in which to come to a decision.'

That night in the harem there was to be a celebration for Omah's eighteenth birthday. He was nervous at the thought that he had to perform sexually. His virgin state was an embarrassment to him.

He spent the rest of the day sketching. It had long been in his mind to do a series of drawings and perhaps later some paintings based on scenes in the harem. The fountains and the frond of ferns, the flowers hanging from the tiled balconies, the marble pillars and the alabaster pool – all these were a stunning backdrop to the main scene of slaves and concubines. He had only been allowed in the harem since he was sixteen years old, but he had been drawing since he was a child. His mother encouraged him, admiring his work and showing it to the other wives and their families. He drew portraits of his mother, brothers and sisters. He drew pictures of the palace horses. He drew desert landscapes. She showed him art books and bought him oil paints, and he went out into the desert and set up his easel to paint the sunrises and sunsets.

So today, on his eighteenth birthday, he set up his drawing easel in the harem. He was surrounded by so many beautiful women it was difficult to know where to begin. Instead, he sketched the pillars, the overhanging balconies, the ornate lamps and the fountains. He could not bring himself to study the bodies of the women. It was too much for him. Every time he began to look at the women they drew near him, brushed up against him and left their erotic scent hovering. They tormented him, touching his knees as they walked past or sweeping their diaphanous robes so they caressed his legs and arms. Their clicking tongues spoke of his beauty, and they sighed over his curly hair, proud nose, soft lips and his broad shoulders.

In the end, his erection hurt him so much he had to leave the harem and go to his room to cool down.

He wondered if life was like this for everyone: the longing and desire, the eventual satisfaction – or release, anyway – and then again the build-up of lust. Would there ever be time for anything else?

He thought of what Mathilde had said to him. Was it right for his father to have so much power over all those concubines? The world was changing. When he ruled Abizir, how would he behave? Would he be a copy of his father? He felt a certain resentment that Mathilde had made him question his destiny. How dare she? She was, after all, only a concubine. But he knew this was not true. She was an educated woman. A valuable member of society. What was she doing here? How had his father obtained the three European concubines?

Omah lay on his low couch, sipping cool water to refresh himself. He felt the sudden need to unburden himself to Mathilde. His conscience was pricking. He had been discourteous to her.

He called a eunuch and asked him to see if Mathilde would see him. Five minutes later the eunuch came back and said that Dr Valentine sent her regards but could not make herself available at the moment. Omah dismissed the eunuch and went back to his couch, sulking.

His father had arranged for the harem virgin population to dress up in finery for the evening's celebrations. The others – the ones who had slept with the sultan at least once – wore only the gold collar and other insignia of submission. But they had covered their hands and faces with henna decorations and hennaed their hair so it shone with chestnut tints. They twittered among themselves like a flock of little brown birds. The virgins were dressed to show off their erogenous zones. Gowns fell from smooth shoulders and draped over pert breasts, allowing rouged nipples to peep over the bodices. Loose robes were cut on the cross to accentuate a round belly or a thrusting hip. Buttocks were exposed and strapped with thongs between the cleft. The sight of all these beauties, exposed for his gaze, filled Omah with a general desire for female flesh. His eyes fell on rising bosoms, bosoms that fell like melons from silk garments into his waiting hands. His cock swelled and rose under his traditional robes, which he wore at all times while he was in his father's country. He felt like his skin was melting. He felt that if anyone touched him, even on the palm of his hand, he would explode.

His father plied him with drink.

'A little will relax you, but do not drink too much or your performance will suffer, my boy,' he laughed.

Omah stuffed almond bread and roast lamb into his mouth and tried not to think of the coming ritual.

The Sultan of Jerah was dressed in conventional Arab robes for once. But he had a whip with him and kept cracking it and looking lustfully at slender slaves and pert, adolescent concubines.

'Who is that little one?' he asked his brother. 'Is it really a girl? It looks like a boy with his cock hidden under his legs.' The concubine was wearing a little loincloth of silk which hid her sex parts. Her pert buttocks rose from her dipped back, dimpling prettily.

The Sultan of Jerah licked his lips thoughtfully. His eyes were glazed.

Dance was performed in the central area of the harem, while the feast went on all around. Bonnita squeezed under a framework of bamboo, only moving her feet and hips. She leant backward, her head almost touching the ground behind her, her pubis thrust forward and her sex lips open like a red, smiling mouth. She gave an arousing performance. She was dressed in woven silk strands that threaded between her pointed breasts, around her narrow waist and draped around her hips and down

195

between her high, round buttocks. Her long, straight legs were bare apart from silk and silver straps that surrounded her thighs, cutting into the soft flesh. Her feet were decorated with silver rings on her toes and anklets of silver and silk. Her belly button was bright with a diamond stud, and her nose was also studded on each side of the bridge.

Her hair was plaited tight into strands tied close to her head. Her almond eyes glowed and glittered with an intensity brought about from the erotic nature of her dance. She wove a pattern around the floor with her slinky movements. She gyrated and thrust her belly forward, her legs apart, so her sex was offered to the watching royalty. Her sex lips were rouged with the same dark red as her other lips and the buttons of her breasts. She held long ribbons of silk which made patterns in the air as she moved, echoing the dance movements of her body. Her hips thrust forward, her belly almost touching Omah's face, and she leant backward, her long brown neck and soft throat exposed. He wanted to kiss the belly that was so close to him. He could smell her musky scent. Her sex lips were within touch of his lips. He restrained himself. All the women here were lovely. He wanted them all. He placed his hands under his armpits. Bonnita curled her body and unwound it like a spring. She wound the ribbons around Omah playfully and he sat, unsmiling, trying to control his animal urge to grab her breasts and her hips. His father laughed loud and smacked the girl on her bare buttocks. She smiled and moved away, bowing low to them both.

The two European concubines, Janet and Rosemary, were veiled for the occasion but only their faces were covered. Their breasts, bellies and buttocks were oiled and scented and placed on display for the boy's sake.

'I feel like a pig in a market,' said Janet. Her large breasts were held high in a sort of sling arrangement of silk straps. Her belly was also erotically displayed, and the curves of her hips and buttocks were shown off to best effect by the cunning arrangement of straps, which intertwined and surrounded her genitals. Her hair was dressed elaborately and little flowers scented her neck and head. Her lips were a scarlet colour and when she parted her legs, the gathered royalty could admire the red of her other hungry mouth.

Rosemary was wearing a little G-string of flimsy satin, which hid her sex only a little. If she moved it swung and exposed her to the gaze of all. Her little breasts were oiled and hung with silver chains, the pink nipples peeping through the strings of silver in a tantalising manner.

Omah did not know where to look first. His eyes fed hungrily on all he saw. The scents of the warm flesh surrounding him almost made him faint. Slave-girls sang high piercing songs, that made his blood go cold. Dancing girls writhed and swayed, revealing flesh in many shades and hues. They threw off their veils one by one and showed themselves to him. The youth was hot and bothered. He drank the fresh juices that were handed to him and gratefully took the cool cloths to wipe his brow.

'Where is the doctor?' he asked his father.

'I don't know!' The sultan looked around in surprise. 'She should be here. Where is she, Janet?'

'She is indisposed, my lord,' said Janet.

'She must be here for my son's birthday celebrations,' said the sultan. 'Go and fetch her,' he ordered a eunuch.

Mathilde was so sore from the whipping she had endured the night before at the command of the Sultan of Jerah that she was finding it difficult to move. Her back and thighs and buttocks were covered in stripes and she was stiff all over. She couldn't wear the garment – a strappy gown – that had been allotted her for the occasion, so she decided to miss the celebrations. She was humiliated by her injuries at the sadistic sultan's hands – or rather at Janet's hands, but by his command. Janet had helped the slave-girl bathe Mathilde's wounds afterwards and put salve on them.

'You'll soon heal, don't worry,' she had said. 'I am awfully sorry, my dear, but I did enjoy it rather, didn't you?' she had asked, quite seriously.

'Well, I don't know that I enjoyed all of it. Only some parts of the procedure,' Mathilde had said, pointedly.

When the eunuch went to fetch Mathilde, she was bathing in a hot bath of oily water, trying to mend the damage.

He dragged her out of the bath with little or no ceremony and made her dress and do her hair. She was furious.

'How dare you treat me in this manner!' she shouted. 'Wait until your master hears of this.'

She strode into the marble hall and up to the sullen figure of the Sultan of Abizir and said, 'I am not well enough to attend your celebration.'

But the sultan was not pleased with Mathilde.

'I said I wanted you here. You must remember, you are mine, Mathilde. You have no choice here – no free will. You are mine.' He slapped her hard across her face and she felt tears fill her eyes. Then he saw the marks through her diaphanous robe, and became even more angry.

'And who did this to you?' She lowered her eyes to the ground. 'Tell me!'

'I did it, Sultan, at the orders of your brother,' said Janet, frightened at his frowning features and the fire in his eyes.

The throng of concubines and slaves were silent. It was as if a low cloud full of thunder sat on their heads. They waited.

The Sultan of Abizir stood and leant over the prone, obese form of his brother.

'Enough is enough, brother. You have outstayed your welcome. You will leave tomorrow,' he said.

His brother laughed in fear and shock. 'But I am welcome always in my brother's house, am I not?'

'No longer! Leave me.' The sultan raised an imperious arm and his brother's mouth stayed open wide in disbelief.

'You cannot do this to me. All I did was thrash a concubine. I have done so a hundred times before and you have not complained. Be reasonable, brother.' He tried to smile and laugh it off as a joke, but the Sultan of Abizir was deadly serious.

'You will leave tomorrow,' he repeated. 'Now leave us, please.'

The gathering was silent as the humiliated Sultan of Jerah was hauled to his feet by several strong eunuchs and escorted to his chamber.

Mathilde was embarrassed at the scene her arrival had instigated, and still smarting on the cheek from the hand that had struck her.

'Play!' commanded the sultan to his musicians. 'Dance!' he ordered his dancing girls. The ceremony continued, in a more subdued atmosphere.

'Mathilde, you will go to your chamber,' said the sultan quietly. She left, grateful to leave the staring company.

She went to her couch and lay on the cool cotton sheet and cried herself to sleep.

Omah had been shocked at the scene his father had made, shocked at Mathilde's whipmarks; and amazed that the sultan had sent his uncle away.

He must be very fond of Mathilde to do that, he thought.

'Father, was that wise?' he asked, quietly.

'I will not have my favourite damaged in that manner. He is a brute and a fool. I wanted to give you the

199

opportunity of choosing her for your bed tonight.' His black eyes flashed with anger.

'I will have the other blonde please, Father; the older Mrs McKinnon,' said Omah. 'For tonight, anyway.' He had been drawn by her arrogance, her proud bearing and her large breasts. He could see that she lusted after him and he knew that her experience would stand him in good stead in the long night ahead.

'A good choice, my boy!' The sultan smiled at last and the surrounding court breathed a communal sigh of relief.

Chapter Twenty-Six

*J*anet McKinnon smiled beguilingly at the lad, pleased he had chosen her. She had assumed she would have him, sometime, but she was especially delighted that she would have the awesome task of his deflowering.

She remembered another student a long time ago. As they had both been virgins the whole experience had been a disappointment for them. Their fumbling hands had not known how to please each other, though their bodies had cried out to be joined. And they had had sexual intercourse, but it was a let-down for her. He had come as soon as he had entered her and she had had no orgasm.

It was a long time before she slept with another inexperienced boy. Instead, she had made sure her sexual partners were older men, experienced in love-making. It was a well thought-out campaign. She had chosen the men. They were often friends of her father. Unfortunately, they were usually married, but this had not stopped her from enjoying the affairs. These men had been only too pleased to give the buxom and pretty girl her first lessons in love. They had taught her how to please a man; how to lie; how to arrange her limbs for penetration; how to press their genitals in just the right way. One had introduced her to the pleasures of spanking. He was a schoolmaster and enjoyed a little extra erotic flagellation after work. She remembered the pleasure she had always felt at the pressure of his hands on her bottom. He had made her pretend to be a schoolgirl – she had hardly been more than that! She had had to hitch up her skirts and bend over a chair. He would pull down her knickers to her ankles and push her firmly, head down, bottom up. His hands would stroke the smooth young flesh, admiring the unflawed skin, the rise of her cheeks, the narrow, dark cleft. Then he would suddenly smack her hard, several times on each buttock, and the stings on her flesh made her cry out, her eyes watering.

'You are a naughty, naughty girl!' he had said, his mouth dry with desire. She would turn her head to see him with his large erection in his hand, rubbing it vigorously. He had often come all over her buttocks, too excited to get his penis into her. Not only *young* men had this problem, she realised. But she enjoyed the erotic quality of these punishment sessions. Sometimes he left without satisfying her, and she wandered around in a state of hot need, her legs rubbing together, her sex lips swollen and her knickers wet. She had lusted after all men. She wanted to hold all men's cocks between her legs.

She had taken several lovers during her affair with the schoolteacher. She enjoyed the notion of going from one cock to another. They were each different and each gave her much pleasure. Her cunt could adapt itself to any size or shape. She had found that size was no problem, though she had had more satisfying orgasms from a large cock than a small one. But men with smaller members had seemed to make more of an effort with their caressing and pleasing her.

On one particular day she had accommodated four

men and had eight orgasms. She had always been a sensual woman and she took great pleasure in her sexuality. In recent years, before she had become involved with and married the charming and decadent Charles McKinnon, she had introduced several very young men to the joys of sex. Virgins had become her forte, and as she grew older she increasingly enjoyed the adoration of youths and their appreciation of her skills. How foolish she had been to be seduced by the dark and mysterious Scot, who looked like the devil himself but pretended to be a man of God! Who knows where she would be now if she hadn't married Charles. But, she remembered, Charles had had the most enormous prick she had ever had the pleasure of accommodating. That was the real reason she had married him.

It was a strange life, she thought. Here she was in a sultan's harem, about to begin the awesome task of showing a boy how to be a man. However, Janet McKinnon was sure she could make the ritual pleasurable for Omah.

She sat by him, the satin basque-brassière pushing her bosoms into high, proffered, ripe fruit. She pushed a breast towards Omah's mouth, but he turned instead to her lips, kissing them deliberately and pushing his tongue inside her rouged mouth to find hers.

She reciprocated, closing her eyes and swooning in a bliss of contact with young flesh. His hard chest, covered still in the white robe, was pressed up against her naked breast. Her nipples tingled. He left off kissing and sat with his hand in hers. They watched the dancing girls, ate, drank and touched each other intimately, but they did not make love there and then. His erection was hurting him. He needed release. He thought of the slave-girl kissing his cock, sucking it hard. He took Janet's hand and stood. He said his goodnights to his father and Rosemary McKinnon. He and Janet left the assembly to the loud sounds of ululation – a hundred voices raised in a blood-curdling cry of jubilation. His moment of truth had come.

They were surrounded by slave-girls and accompanied by eunuchs as far as Omah's bedchamber. Janet's own slave-girl and another, a Persian girl, went in with them to help with their undressing and washing.

However, Omah dismissed them, saying he wanted to do these things himself. They departed sorrowfully, having looked forward to the disrobing of the beautiful youth. They had wanted to touch his fresh young skin, feel the hardness of his hairless chest, massage the muscular legs and see the young erection pressed against his belly.

Janet was feeling blissfully aware of her charms. Her breasts tingled and glowed. Her belly was firm and round and her face had a natural charm and grace. Her buttocks were luscious and full, and she knew her bottom was her best attribute, or so she had been told by many men. Champagne was brought in to them in a silver bucket of ice, as if they were a honeymoon couple in a hotel room. He opened the bottle with expertise – at least he knew about champagne, he thought – and they drank to love.

'May I undress you, my lord?' Janet asked quietly, kissing him lightly on his mouth edges and licking the upturned corners of his delicious lips.

'Yes please, Janet. May I call you Janet?' he asked, shy suddenly.

'Of course, my sweet lord. What shall I call you?'

'Omah is fine.'

Janet McKinnon, 35 years old last birthday, was in a swoon of delicious anticipation. She had not drunk very much wine, and her flesh and spirit were ready for love. She unhooked his buttons and lifted the white robe over his head. He stood, naked except for his sandals, which he shook off his straight, well-defined feet.

'Yes, you are very like your father,' she noted. 'The

shape of your legs and feet, the muscles. Your hips are like his only narrower.' She stroked the youth's smooth body while he stood and shivered, though not from cold. His cock was slack now, lying elegantly on his thigh. It had been erect all evening, and now it had let him down. He was mortified.

Janet led him to the low couch covered in layers of lion skins. He sat on the edge, looking down in nervousness and humiliation.

'What is it? Are you scared of me?' she asked. He shook his head of black curls. 'Kiss me on my lips again. You kiss so well,' she said, deliberately flattering him.

He looked up at her as she knelt in front of him. Her skin was like a peach, her lips full and welcoming and her breasts breasts soft and full. He fell on to her breasts, kissing them hard and squeezing them tight between his fingers.

'Now, now, not so fast please, Omah.' She drew his hands and mouth away and kissed him gently. 'You want to remember this first time, don't you?' He nodded. 'Then we will do things properly. Let me make love to you first and allow you your royal release, then we can get down to the real love-making.'

She knelt before him and took his swollen cock, which rose from a hairless groin, in her generous mouth. He moaned as his cock was surrounded by her mouth and her tongue licked and sucked at the tip and the stem. He felt as if she would swallow him. He closed his eyes and thought of the slave-girl who had done this to him, and then he thought of Mathilde's mouth. The red rouge from Janet's lips was smeared over his cock and belly and thighs. He pressed his hands on her head. Her hair had fallen from its intricate arrangement, and the dark blonde, heavy curtain fell on his cock and stroked his balls and thighs. It felt like there were wings of birds caressing him.

He pressed his hands on her breasts and held them

higher than their corset of straps, squeezing them together. He sat, his knees apart, as this beautiful woman sucked his cock. He came into her mouth and she swallowed his white foam, which spurted in several floods down her throat.

'There,' she said, wiping her mouth with a napkin. 'Doesn't that feel better?'

'Oh God, it feels wonderful. You are wonderful!' the boy said.

'Now for the fun,' she said.

She led him to the shower room and disrobed. She wore only her gold and diamond collar and her anklets and bracelets of bondage. He allowed her to soap him all over and she rubbed her voluptuous body against his slender form. His erection grew easily in her soapy hands. She turned her back to him and he put his hands on her belly and breasts. She rubbed her bottom against his cock and felt the hardness develop. She put her arms behind to clutch his buttocks and press him to her. He kissed her neck, her ears and her shoulders. She writhed her bottom and hips harder on his sex and felt his cock swell and throb.

She turned and kissed his lips slowly and luxuriously, holding his narrow hips in her capable, knowing hands. He could have been her son he was so young. The thought excited her terribly, and she wound her legs around him. He lifted her so she was wrapped around him, her sex open and wet. Standing in the shower, his back against the marble wall, he penetrated her. She helped keep him in by holding his cock at the base with one hand. He was strong and held her easily, but his legs began to sag as the excitement became too much. He sank to his knees, and she sat on him, rising and falling on his upstanding cock, which tingled with the delightful friction. He sighed and moaned and she licked his lips and kissed his face. He turned suddenly and pushed her on to the wet floor. The water still fell on them, cooling their hot bodies. Their hair was soaking wet, tangled and streaked across their faces. He watched her chest, neck and face flush and heard the sighs get faster. He felt his own excitement rise and fill him. He pressed his penis deep into her, feeling the extent of her fleshy sex as it ate him. This feeling was not like the sucking he had experienced; it was like a swallowing of his sex but he felt that he had the power. He controlled her with his fleshy rod, and he could see from her expression that he was giving her supreme pleasure. Her eyes had glazed and her throat was exposed to his teeth. He pushed harder and harder, his penis becoming part of her. He felt it become part of her flesh. He came, violently, suddenly, shockingly. His cries were long and loud, like a tortured beast. Janet McKinnon came for the third time. Her juices flowed easily for this lovely youth. She felt young again.

'Oh, oh, Omah!'

The rest of the night was a night to remember, as Janet McKinnon had promised the innocent youth. He made love to her in every position he could think of and several that had not occurred to him. At last she lay exhausted, her lust fulfilled, she thought, and gazed at the sleeping boy.

He is very pretty, almost like a girl, she thought, and she thought of the slave-girl Bonnita and her bouncing breasts. She gathered her own full globes into her hands and stroked them thoughtfully, then pressed her fingers into her open vagina.

In the morning she had gone and in her place were two pretty dark-skinned concubines from the Atlas Mountains, and he was miraculously clean and refreshed. They fed him with freshly squeezed orange juice from their dark, juicy mouths, and held him down and kissed his body all over. They sucked him and licked his scrotum from in front and behind, and put sly fingers into his anus and around his proud cock. They sat on his

207

face and showed him their private parts, opening their sex lips wide with hennaed hands. They drew their hair across his belly and stroked him with their little bottoms, then fell on his fleshy rod with cries of delight. He penetrated them one after the other in an orgy of youthful joy, and they all laughed and leapt on each other like the children they still were at heart. His mouth found their little breasts and bit their pert nipples, while his cock rubbed their bellies and pressed their anuses. His hands were on them, in them, over their genitals. He spanked one and the other held his cock. He liked this game very much. He liked the power he felt at the smack of his hands on the dark flesh, and the feeling of helplessness with his cock trapped in the girl's hands. He felt conflicting emotions of power and submission, and he enjoyed this dichotomy. He could see the point of slavery, he felt. He could see the point of being in someone else's power. He suggested they tie him down and use him as they wanted. The girls giggled but complied happily. They found silk ropes and tied the youth to the couch, attaching the ropes to his arms and legs and tying them to the four corner posts of sandal-wood. He lay stretched out for them to play with. His cock stood upright like a little flagpole. They licked it and played with it, flicking it with their fingers. They tickled him under the arms and he screamed for mercy, which sent them into streams of laughter and hysterical tears. They decided to gag him with a silk scarf to stop his cries. They kissed his nipples, his chest, his flat belly, his thighs, his knees, his feet, his arms, his shoulders and his neck. They pretended to ignore his cock, which throbbed and stretched for attention. It rose and fell on his belly and at last they deigned to notice his sobbing distress and they kissed it lovingly and sucked the length of its proud, straight stem. He moaned in happiness and lust.

They played with each other, touching each little

breast and nipple, kissing each bouncing buttock, licking each other's bare-shaved sex and pushing their tongues inside the sweet purse of flesh. He was helpless; he could only watch. His penis throbbed and flickered without their touch. He desperately wanted his cock enfolded in flesh; he needed the pressure and the lovely friction of flesh.

As if knowing what he was thinking, they turned from each other's body and took his penis into their hands and mouth and pressed it into their secret orifices. He came in a volcanic eruption of sperm. Which orifice or whose, he did not care; he only wanted release. His virginity had gone. He was a man.

Chapter Twenty-Seven

*O*n the night of his son's birthday, the Sultan of Abizir was in the arms of Mathilde Valentine. The sight of her back, sore and red from the beating at his brother's hands, had excited him and he had to have her. He had not called her to him but had waited until the harem was quiet after the celebrations. Then he went to her. He tapped at her door, a courtesy that was not usual to him. She was curled up in bed, trying to sleep, but her tears had blocked her nose and she was having trouble breathing, so she lay there in some discomfort, trying not to think of her present situation but remembering her past. A past which seemed irretrievable; another world, another century. She felt as if she had moved back in time to a world where women were treated as chattels. The twentieth century might never have existed. How would anyone ever find her? She was in a time warp. She would never find her way back to her own time.

The sultan quietly opened the door and went to her, gathering her in his powerful arms. He kissed her face and neck, smoothing the tear-dampened hair from her eyes. Her lips were swollen and he kissed them hard.

He turned her around so he could see her criss-crossed back.

'Did Janet really do this?' he said.

'Yes, but only because your brother commanded,' she whispered. His smell was of almonds and lemons. His hair was curly and swept his neck and fell over his proud brow. She smiled. 'It does not hurt too much.'

'Come here,' he said, and swept her into his arms and lifted her high so her legs were around his waist. She was not a small woman and he needed all his strength to keep her up while he stood, supporting her. His robes were discarded, his erection exposed. She felt it hard against her belly. She reached down to it and held it firmly in one hand, rubbing up and down. His hands were on her hips and she winced at his touch. He became more excited and pushed his penis into her. He held her with both hands, pulling her on to him close so his penis was tightly enclosed by her. She felt his passion overtake him, and he came in quick, short spurts, filling her with his fluids. She had not had an orgasm, but she felt that she had given him something valuable, and she was happy enough. This man, who lived in utter luxury and had everything he wanted and everyone he wanted, was a paradox in the modern world. But he was powerful, and she felt the excitement of that power. His body was hard and attractive and even his cruel face had a charm that aroused her senses.

She still thought of escape, and she was determined, but the beating had left her demoralised and she wondered if she would ever escape from this archaic existence. The other two white women seemed almost resigned to their fate, especially Janet. But Mathilde pined for her lion lover and her life as a woman of some importance. She ought to be able to make use of her own sexual power to get more freedom and the possibility of escape from the island.

Meanwhile, her only thought was of sexual release.

His sudden, quick fucking had aroused her. She wanted him to give her pleasure now.

He had collapsed on to the low couch and she called her slave-girl to bathe them both. The slender creature entered the room and washed their genitals, thighs, hips and buttocks with a wet silk cloth. They lay there, relaxed, while she dried them gently, rubbing her hands between Mathilde's legs and then the sultan's. Mathilde watched his cock rise and fill at the touch. The slave-girl left. They both drank the wine she had brought and leant on their arms facing each other.

'My lord, do I please you?' said Mathilde.

'You know you do.' He was holding his penis in one hand and rubbing it over her belly.

'Will you lick my sex?' she asked tentatively.

'If you wish,' he said, his eyes on her breasts, watching the pulse of her heart tick on the white skin.

'Only if it will please you, my lord.'

He slid down the bed so his face was between her closed legs. He licked gently around her thighs and dipped his tongue into the dark slit between her plump sex lips. He tasted the sea-scent of her cunt and sucked the fleshy cushions. Her legs opened and his tongue went deeper into her. She lay back, her arms over her head, her neck stretched back and her belly pressed upward to meet his sensual touch. Her sighs were quiet and she grabbed the end posts of the bed to brace herself. His tongue was exploring her perineum, the delicate area of sensitive flesh between the vagina and the anus. She opened wide to the caress. He sucked on her and lapped the juices. His hands were on her belly and behind her vagina, holding her bottom, his thumb on her sex lips, so she did not know which was his tongue and which his fingers. Her breathing became laboured. She felt her skin flush and the pain of her beating had disappeared. She imagined she was one huge vagina; she felt she was melting into his mouth. She was an oyster about to be swallowed. He moved to draw his tongue up across her belly and waist and on to her breasts. His hands were all over her sex, rubbing and slapping the swollen pouch and slipping into the moist slit.

'Put my cock into you,' he ordered.

She reached down to his enormous erection and felt the breadth of it, around which her fingers would not meet. She gasped at its massive size. It felt bigger than it had before. She placed the round head into her vagina and pushed down on to it, watching as her body swallowed the huge cock. He moved deep into her, right to the hilt of his cock, so she felt his balls bang on her buttocks. Her legs were held high now, and he put them over his shoulders and lifted her harder on to his stem, so she felt she was growing from his cock. Her breasts grew pink and sore and the nipples sang with tenderness. He stared into her eyes with his alien gaze, knowing his power over her. She was his slave, his concubine; she was only there for his sexual use. She gave in to the feeling of helplessness. Her orgasm was severe and her cries were loud. He bit her nipple and came into her again, his white rain filling her.

Olensky's hired dhow was afloat at last, with the captain Sabah Madaan and his depleted crew. The coast moved quickly past the boat, or so it seemed because the sea was so calm. They had had many delays through sickness and accident, but at last they were underway and heading towards the Island of Abizir, where the baron felt sure he would find Mathilde.

Omah awoke to the sounds of the desert. A hawk screeched and dropped suddenly on to a succulent lizard. The wind was fierce and warm already at 7 a.m. The wind blew from the north, from Arabia, where his uncle, the Sultan of Jerah, had his palace. He thought of the scene that had taken place last night, before he had been taken to bed by the white concubine, and he wondered if his father would have reason to regret his angry words to his brother. Omah stretched his young, straight limbs, luxuriating in his own beauty. He smiled as he thought of the night's events – the love-making and this morning's erotic awakening. He had slept again after the slave-girls had bathed him.

The Sultan of Jerah had slept badly, more from over-eating and dyspepsia than from anger, but he felt angry this morning. He did not want to leave this very comfortable and lazy existence in his brother's harem. He would have to fetch his wives from the palace and listen to their complaints and nagging. He really ought to make his brother change his mind. Perhaps he should apologise for spoiling the white concubine? No, he could not possibly admit he was wrong. He would have breakfast first and then decide what to do.

Omah remembered that his father had said he could have any of his concubines, and he wanted Mathilde. There was something about her face that attracted him – the intelligence, he supposed. Her body was lovely, of course – that was only to be expected of one of his father's concubines – but she was unusual. He would probably never have the opportunity of such a prize again. He knew his own mental limitations. He was creative but not terribly talented, and he knew by comparing himself with fellow students that he did not have a first-class brain – even if his mother thought he was a genius!

He liked Mathilde's spirit, and her smile, and he imagined her lips around his cock. He realised he had thought of her mouth all night. He breakfasted alone on his balcony, which was protected from the prevailing wind. Between low yellow and brown hills, where there grew tall date palms, there was a distant view of the coast, shimmering in the early sun. The sea was a pale jade.

He arranged to take his father's boat out for a spin. He would have Mathilde at his side.

When Mathilde found out, she was annoyed that he wanted her to accompany him.

'But it is my clinic day with the concubines, my lord,' she said to the sultan. 'It is important to check on their health regularly, as you know.'

'You will go with Omah.'

There was no arguing with the Sultan of Abizir.

He was full of conflicting emotions that morning. He was on the verge of falling in love with Mathilde. He realised this was a foolish emotion and he knew she would never agree to be his wife. He could continue to fuck her if she remained in the harem, but only if she was his wife could she accompany him on his trips abroad, and only if they were married could she have his children. The wives had certain privileges that the concubines were denied.

He also had the problem of his recalcitrant brother. He determined that he *would* leave today as he had ordered. He went to see him, and was surprised to find him still in his night robes.

'Oh, brother, you didn't really mean that, last evening, did you?' he wheedled with his honey tones.

'Indeed I did. I want you to go. You have outstayed your welcome, you sadistic pervert.' The sultan stood, looking marvellous in jodhpurs and boots. He flicked his crop on the side of his leather boots.

'You are a handsome devil, you know, little brother. Can't you be kind to your fat old sibling?' He scratched his belly through his robe, and yawned, showing a mouth full of almond bread.

'Just leave, this morning, before I thrash you,' the younger brother said and left the room.

Rosemary was delighted that the sad old Sultan of Jerah was leaving.

'Thank goodness! I could not have stood to have him bugger me ever again. Why can't I have a fuck with the son instead of the brother?' She said the shocking words in her upper-class Edinburgh accent and Janet laughed.

'Well, I dare say you will have a chance to feel that young flesh. He will go through us all in good time. He is a delightful young lover, and is so willing to learn. I cannot wait to have him to myself again,' she crowed.

'Oh, poo, you will not have him before I do. It is not fair!' The boyish Rosemary flicked her shorn locks behind her ears and swam away from the smug Janet McKinnon.

Janet admired the young woman's svelte form as she sped through the water, her arms knifing the water.

That morning, Mathilde had 'endured' her ritual depilation, as always. She could not remember a time when she had not been smoothly shaved between her legs. It was a harem tradition that she always enjoyed – the smoothing on of the creamy soap by soft hands, the swift flick of the razor, the cleaning off with rosemary-scented water, the drying with warm towels, and then the soothing oils that were fragrant and cool on her nakedness. She always felt desire for more delicate embraces with her slave during this procedure. This morning her vagina throbbed and her sex lips opened like a flower's petals as the morning sun touched them. Her heartbeat grew fast, and her mouth was dry with desire.

She kissed her little slave-girl and held her lovingly in her arms.

'Kiss my breasts,' she ordered, and the slave did so, and gave every sign of enjoying herself. Mathilde touched the slave-girl's bottom and felt the smooth, peach-like bloom of her youth. She caressed the girl's bare cunt and pushed fingers inside. They came out wet with juice. The slave-girl's G-string was pressed into her slit, and Mathilde's fingers went either side of it, into her vagina. She urged the slave-girl to do the same to her, and they lay, erotically entwined, about to have their first orgasm together, when the door flew open and the Sultan of Abizir marched in, his riding crop in his hands.

'Leave,' he ordered the slave-girl and Mathilde also rose, embarrassed at being caught *in flagrante* with her slave.

He took Mathilde in his arms and kissed her passionately. She was astonished at this show of emotion, but allowed him his ardent caresses. Her blood was hot from the foreplay he had interrupted. She returned his embrace and felt his erection through his robes, pressing into her. Her nakedness was beautiful. She was newly shaved and her juices flowed. Her breasts were heavy with sexual desire. Her lips grew swollen and soft, and her skin was on fire. She lifted his robe and took his cock in her hands. She went down on her knees and took it into her wide, soft mouth. She held it there with her tongue and lips, her teeth grazing his stem. She held his loins and pulled his cock further into her mouth, almost swallowing the head. She opened her throat to take the thick rod of flesh. He held her head close to his thighs. He moaned and looked down at her. She crouched, her legs wide, her head grinding in his groin. He thought how very beautiful she was. He closed his eyes and spurted his sperm into her welcoming throat.

She knew she had him in her thrall. He was in love with her, she was almost sure. He would be at his most vulnerable while he was in this state of grace. She must make the most of this opportunity to escape, but how? Her immediate thought was for sexual release.

There was a knock at the door. The sultan was recovering from his orgasm. He stood, leaning against the wall. Mathilde covered his nakedness with his robe again and wrapped a robe around herself. She answered the door.

217

A worried eunuch stood there, unsure whether he should have disturbed his master.

'What is it?' said the sultan.

'Your greatness, it is your brother. He is in the chamber of the young white concubine. There is much noise coming from there.'

Mathilde and the Sultan of Abizir went immediately to the room that Rosemary and Janet shared. There was a piercing scream. The sultan ordered the eunuchs to force the locked door. They had it open in a moment.

The scene was one of unmitigated orgiastic sadism. Two slave-girls were tied to a wall, slumped in exhaustion from buggery and thrashing. Janet McKinnon was dressed in high leather boots, had a long, thin dildo strapped to her pelvis and held a riding crop. She stood behind the Sultan of Jerah, and had been tickling his many folds of buttock flesh and sagging thighs with the leather crop, as was obvious from the marks that crossed his flesh.

Rosemary was naked, strapped over a low leather stool. Her bottom was raised high. Her back, thighs and buttocks were covered in red weals. She was sobbing. The Sultan of Jerah, also naked except for a red satin corset and high-heeled shoes, was wielding a long paddle with a fearsome leather strap. He had it raised to strike the young woman again. His penis was flaccid and had shrunk to the size of an acorn. Rosemary's anus had a large dildo inserted in it, and the opening was stretched wide. Mathilde stared.

She instinctively grabbed the whip from the hands of the naked sultan. His rouged face leered at her and he laughed.

His brother came to life and took the whip from Mathilde. He began to thrash his brother with it, not gently or erotically, but with a fury that would not abate. The paddle struck his back, his legs, his sagging elephantine buttocks and his calves. The Sultan of Jerah fell off his high heels on to the sides of his ankles and moaned in pain. His brother continued to whip him, striking him wherever he could – his face, his shoulders, his genitals. The fat sadist curled up on the floor and sobbed for mercy.

Mathilde removed the dildo gently from Rosemary's bottom, horrified at the length her friend had been made to take in her anus. She untied the sobbing woman and took her in her arms, comforting her.

'He is an animal, a filthy animal,' sobbed Rosemary.

'Come with me, my dear, I will take care of your injuries,' said Mathilde, taking her from the room, where the sultan, out of his mind with anger, was still beating his now unconscious brother. Janet stood, stupefied, her mouth sagging open and her breasts dripping with sweat.

Chapter Twenty-Eight

*T*he harem was in turmoil. The word had flown around that the Sultan of Jerah was dead, killed by his brother's hand. And two of the slave-girls were injured, but no-one knew how. The bathing pool was empty. Armed eunuchs stood by the locked doors of the concubines' quarters. They were herded together, twittering like anxious sparrows. A contrite Janet was helping Mathilde care for Rosemary and the two slave-girls. Their injuries were not serious but they needed immediate attention and medical care. Mathilde had set up a small rest room within the harem for sick concubines and this was where the three victims of the mad Sultan of Jerah were resting.

Omah, thwarted of his desire for fun for the moment, had helped his father see to the laying out of the body of their relation. His wives had been collected from the palace to view the heavy but somehow diminished body of their husband. His children were crying over him, and his wives were keening. The Sultan of Abizir was unrepentant of the severe and fatal punishment he had dealt his brother. He was only glad his mother was not alive to witness the death of her son. In the foolish way of many mothers, she had loved this ridiculous, gross son more than her other children. His little foibles had always been overlooked. Indeed, she had lent him her clothes before he had acquired his own female garments. She had dressed him in her corsets when he was still a boy, and had allowed him to take sexual advantage of her slaves at an early age.

Mathilde dressed the wounds.

'Get more dressings please, Janet,' she said, unsmilingly, to the repentant woman.

'I didn't want to help him. He made me, you realise?' Janet said defensively.

'I'm sure,' said Mathilde, her lips tight.

'What will happen to the sultan?' said Janet, as much to change the subject as any desire to know.

'Who knows about the death except us? He is hardly likely to telegraph the event to the civilised world, is he?'

'You mean he will get away with it?' said Janet.

'Yes, I expect he will,' said Mathilde, wrapping the gauze around the thighs of one of the injured slave-girls.

Over the next couple of days, the concubines were kept quiet in their quarters while the funeral arrangements were made. They were bored by inactivity. They had been expecting some fun and games since the arrival of Omah, and were disappointed at the lack of sexual activity.

However, they passed their time as they always did, playing games of chess or dominoes and making delicate love to each other.

Omah was in a turmoil of emotions. He was shocked that his father could have killed his own brother in a fit of rage. His father had told him what had happened and he had no reason to disbelieve him. There were several witnesses, after all. In Abizir, the sultan was the law, the judge and the executioner.

A few days after the burial ceremony, which only the

males attended, the widows and children were sent home to Arabia, and Omah came out of mourning to return to his new-found aim and purpose. He meant to have Mathilde.

He asked again if he might take his father's boat out.

'Of course, my boy. Here are the keys.' The sultan threw the gold keyring to his son and thought again how handsome he was.

'And may I take your white concubine, Mathilde?' Omah asked hesitantly.

'But of course, Omah, my son. Use her as you wish. I think you will find she is very accommodating. Try her mouth,' he added, as Omah left the room.

Omah blushed. He had been thinking only of her mouth for days.

The wind blew through their hair, the sea air fresh and cool.

'Oh, this is wonderful! Why don't we do this all the time?' Mathilde cried in delight. She stood in the bow of the little speedboat, holding on to a metal handle set in the prow, while the handsome son of the sultan stood at the wheel and steered. Mathilde, wearing a loose blue robe, looked perfect. Her nipples stood out stiff in the cool breeze. She was naked under the robe, and her thighs tingled in anticipation of the sexual embrace she knew would take place later with this lovely youth.

'Mathilde, remove your face veil,' said Omah. She did as he said, relieved to be rid of the archaic covering. 'Come here,' he said, and kissed her mouth. She pressed her body to his, feeling the hardness develop under his robe. He kissed her passionately, and his mouth reminded her of his father.

Their bodies curved together. He steered the boat into a little cove, where the sand was dark and coarse and small palms grew in a crescent around the shore. He anchored and let the boat rock gently. Then he took off his robe and stood in front of her, his legs apart. She stared admiringly at his body. It was like Michelangelo's David, perfect in shape and form, the muscles defined but not grossly so and the line of his neck and head just right. He was so well proportioned, she wished she could draw. He was a work of art. He stood on the edge of the boat and dived overboard into the turquoise water. She removed her clothes and followed him. They swam to the little shore and he found a smooth, flat rock where they lay, naked, close together, the sun's rays drying them quickly. He leant over her and looked into her eyes.

'Kiss me,' he said.

She kissed his mouth, and his neck and shoulders. She tasted the salt on his skin and drank his youth. Her lips followed his ribs and his stomach. She kissed his hips and he shivered. Her lips and tongue licked at his belly button, sucking on the little cave. Her mouth nuzzled and caressed his thighs, leaving his insistent cock and the nudging balls alone for the moment, but admiring them on the way past to his legs. Her tongue was finding his instep, kissing the delicate indentation. She took his foot in her hands and licked like a dog might adore his master. He lay, his cock sticking up straight from his groin, his balls tight and firm. She moved up him and nudged the balls with her nose, nuzzling into his thighs. Her mouth was on him at last. He felt her tongue wrapping around his throbbing stem. Her lips held him. She had him in her beautiful mouth. He moaned and held her head to his groin.

It does not fail to work, she thought, and sucked firmly, all the while holding his balls. He stretched away from her and put his hands over his head. He was hers to use. He wanted her to fuck him, to show him what to do. He pushed her from his mouth and she moved closer to him, her belly against his. Her nipples were raised to

223

his mouth and he sucked. She almost swooned in gratitude. The youth's mouth on her nipples – such bliss!

His penis grew to its full length, not as big as his father's but younger, straighter and harder. She cleaved to him, drawing up her knees to expose her sex parts to his cock and hands. His hands were all over her. He grabbed her naked sex lips and pulled at them, opening them to expose the inner lips and the bud that bloomed red. She showed him how to rub the bud gently; how to cover it with her sex lips and rub on to it; how to slap the pubic mound with a flat hand; how to rub the perineum with several fingers. She guided him through the ritual of love so that she was satisfied before he was. When he came, he cried real tears in joyful satisfaction. The last few days had been a trial and his nerves were tight. He felt as if he was being nursed by this woman; shown how to make love by a nurse who knew exactly which part of his body to touch at any time to give him satisfaction. He felt complete.

He held her by her full buttocks and turned her over so her back was on his belly. She raised herself and sat on his cock, which was happily erect again. She lay back against his chest and let him lift her and lower her on to his penis. Her juices moistened her and she felt like silk. She was a silk tunnel and he filled her. The strong thrusts were ramming into her, making her cry out with desire for more of his cock. She wanted the biggest cock in the world to fill her. She came, and her spasms made him come too.

They made love all morning until the sun became too high. Then they swam lazily back to the boat and made their way back to the waiting horses at the harbour.

Before they reached the walls of the harem, Mathilde replaced her face veil.

'You look even more lovely without your veil than with it,' he said.

'It is another ridiculous humiliation we have to endure under your father's rule,' she said.

'Mathilde, tell me how you came to be here,' said Omah tentatively. He had not meant to ask her, but now he had made love with her, he needed to know her story.

'Do you really want to know?' she asked.

He nodded. She thought again how like his father he looked, especially in profile.

'I was kidnapped by the same slave trader who acquired the two Mrs McKinnons for the sultan. I was taken from the man I love, and from my work as a doctor in Kenya.'

She sounded bitter and he was shocked. He had not thought of her having a past or a life of her own. And she loved a man. How lucky he was, to be made love to by this lovely woman! Omah was suddenly jealous of this unknown man.

'I am sorry!' he said, and he really was.

Mathilde looked at the sultan's son. She had made passionate love with him just an hour ago, and now she had forgotten him in her longing for Olensky.

'Omah, what are you going to do with your life?'

'I shall take over my father's oil wells and his other businesses, eventually, when he retires or dies.'

'And until then?'

'Enjoy life!' said the callow youth.

'And your art? Your mother tells me you are talented.'

'Oh, my mother would say the sun shines from my behind!' he said, smiling. She laughed. 'Do you think I am talented?' he asked.

'What do I know about art? I have seen some of your drawings at the palace. I thought they were good. You should carry on at art school and keep practising until you are good. You can't expect to be a genius just yet.'

'Do you think I am immature, Mathilde?' He looked longingly at her.

'You are a very lovely young man, Omah. One day

you will be a fine man, I am sure.' Mathilde smiled softly at him, her heart softening as she saw his nervousness and innocence. He was, after all, only a boy, and he could not be expected to put the world to rights. It was not his fault that his father was an out-of-date tyrant and a powerful potentate.

The Sultan of Abizir was finding comfort in the plump, rounded arms of Janet McKinnon. He was still in a state of shock after his frenzied attack on his brother, and he was trying to forget his lack of control. He had always prided himself on his self-control. He had killed many times before, but always to a preconceived plan. His kingdom was a closed society and no-one outside would hear of the manner of his brother's death. The Sultan of Jerah's wives had been told that their husband had died as a result of his own excesses, and they accepted this explanation. They knew his nature.

The Sultan of Abizir knew he could trust the silence of his servants, slaves and concubines. What chance had they to report to anyone outside the kingdom? His son, Omah, he knew, would never tell a soul of the bloody events.

He tried to relax and concentrate on the matter in hand – the breast in his mouth and the fleshy sex lips under his hand. His penis had not let him down. It reared, powerful and rampant, and Janet held it in a soft, plump hand, rubbing it firmly. He slapped her buttocks to indicate his desire for her to turn over and present her bottom to him. She leant over the end of the leather couch so her bottom was high and her head and feet low. She parted her legs and her pouting sex lips and the red slit of her vagina were exposed, as was the brown blossom of her anus. Her breasts pressed against her ribcage, hurting her a little. Her hands clasped a ring on the couch. The sultan leant over her to fasten her bracelets to this ring so that she was helpless to move.

Then he slapped her large buttocks, watching the white flesh turn red with each blow. She flinched at each stroke, but her sex grew wet and slippery with excitement. Her belly slid on the leather. Her bosoms rubbed and chafed. He stood behind her, his cock in one hand, the other hand smacking her abundant flesh. He loved the sound of the contact of his palm on her fatty tissue. He rubbed his cock rhythmically and his eyes narrowed. He watched her juicy lips open and close. His hand moved closer to the dark lips, slapping her genitals. He saw them swell to his touch. His cock hurt. He moved closer to her and slammed his cock down on her buttocks. She stretched up her bottom to try and reach it with her vagina. She wanted it inside her. The leather rubbed her pubis and caused her clitoris to swell, while his hand still slapped her sex, arousing her unbearably. She calmed herself, waiting for his cue. He slapped her with his hard, silky penis, rubbing the anus and perineum tantalisingly. She opened her legs wide, opening her sex to him. He saw the red inside walls of her vagina and pressed his cock into it, the muscles enclosing him. He slammed into her, his balls heavy and firm on her pubis. She moaned in delight. She held him deep inside, right at the top of her fleshy tunnel, then let him slide out slowly, right to the mouth of her sex, rubbing the tender flesh of her naked lips. The deep thrusting and exquisite pressure that followed overwhelmed her. The leather under her belly, the cock deep inside her, his strong hands on her, the balls banging against her – she exploded again and again..

Chapter Twenty-Nine

M athilde's time in the harem was dream-like. She was easily seduced and accepted the lazy life, the erotic clothes, the beauty of the slaves and concubines and the love-making that went on everywhere.

The amount of exposed flesh was hypnotic. Slave-girls danced, showing their undulating bellies and their bouncing breasts. Their buttocks quivered. Mathilde's mind wandered often. She remembered the times she had indulged in a little voyeurism on the beach at the mission, watching Joseph and Grace make love in the warm waters of the Indian Ocean. She remembered the time she had spent in the waiting place in Zanzibar – with the seductive Serena and the two naughty slave-girls, Qitura and Parveneh, who had deliberately offered themselves to her.

In the harem she had many opportunities for love-making and voyeurism.

Her slave – a Somali girl – was very delicately made, like all Somalis, and her features were fine. She had long, straight hair, a slim build, long legs and delicate hands and feet. Her name was Zara. She had always been a quiet slave, not pushing herself forward as some did.

She was proud and modest and had a sad quality, Mathilde noticed. But her hands had a magic in them. Her massage talents were renowned throughout the harem. Mathilde was very appreciative of her slave's nightly attentions. But the sultana had heard of her and wanted her as her own slave. She could have ordered the masseuse sent to the palace without a word to Mathilde, but her respect for the doctor meant that she actually asked her if she could have Zara. Mathilde was loath to be without this paragon, but she knew she could not refuse the sultana.

Instead of Zara, Mathilde had to chose another slave-girl as her own. She looked carefully at the gathered females. She had not always been at ease in the superior presence of the Somali girl, so she thought she had better choose a girl with an easy, open nature. One who laughed a lot. She wished she could have the luscious Bonnita, but she was a concubine, not a slave. Mathilde wondered at the difference.

She had watched Bonnita one day in the swimming pool. Her muscular, athletic shape sped through the water. She was very fit. Two slaves helped her out of the water. Water ran down her flanks and dripped on to the marble floor. Her sex sat high and to the front of her pubis, so it was very visible. Most of the women, it was very obvious (to a doctor at least), had their vaginal openings immediately under their legs, even towards the back, so their slits disappeared between their legs and their sex lips were not visible unless they sat and opened their legs. Bonnita was shaved under her arms and between her legs. The tight, curly hair on her head was cut very short. Her mouth was a pouting bee-stung echo of her other lips. Mathilde watched the two slaves dry her. One of the slave-girls was Bonnita's – a small, sullen Persian. The other she had not seen before. She was a Samburu, from Africa. Mathilde had seen women of this tribe in Kenya. Her straight nose and high

229

cheekbones were lovely, and her mouth was soft and smiling. Her brown plaited hair was stranded and lay flat on her head with a silver chain around her brow.

Mathilde went over to the group and asked Bonnita if the slave belonged to any of the concubines.

'No, she is no-one's yet. She has just arrived. Do you want her?'

'Yes, I think so. I have just lost my slave to the sultana.'

'Well, shall we play with her and see if she is to your liking?'

'... I er ... that would be a good idea.' She had watched the lovely Bonnita and lusted after her many times. This was an opportunity too good to miss.

Bonnita led the other three over to a double couch that happened to be free. The slaves fetched clean cotton sheets and lay them under the two concubines. Bonnita lay down and patted the bed next to her.

'Come, Mathilde, I have long wanted to touch your white skin.'

Mathilde drew close to the musk-scented Caribbean dancer and allowed her to kiss her on the lips. Mathilde felt moisture gather between her legs immediately. Bonnita grabbed the new slave-girl and told her own slave to go away and get them drinks and oils.

The slave smiled hesitantly and sat down on the edge of the bed. Bonnita kissed her and told her not to be scared.

'We are all friends here and our only job is to please our sultan and your job is to please us and the sultan.' Bonnita pulled her into the bed between her and Mathilde.

'Now, show us your little pussy, my sweet,' said Bonnita, drawing the girl's legs apart. Her dark slit opened like a ruby rose and Mathilde and Bonnita slipped their fingers between the petals, admiring the firmness of her flesh, the softness of her tunnel and the tightness of her internal muscles. The slave swooned and moaned as they brought her to orgasm together. Then it was her turn to please them. She licked Mathilde's white thighs, unable to believe that anyone could be so white and pink. Bonnita slipped behind Mathilde and held her buttocks in both hands as the slave licked her private parts. Mathilde was melting with desire. She wanted Bonnita's mouth on hers and her sex pressed close to hers. The Samburu girl swung her breasts so they slapped on Mathilde's sex. She sucked Mathilde's breasts. Bonnita had insinuated her way down Mathilde's body and had her legs wrapped around Mathilde's neck. Her tongue was inside Mathilde, lapping. The slave-girl stroked Mathilde's breasts, and then her oily fingers found her anus. Mathilde exploded in an orgy of lust. She did not know which girl was invading her, and she did not care. She cried out, and they stopped their efforts at pleasing her and turned to please each other.

Mathilde watched the slave press her slender body to Bonnita. She saw their bouncing breasts flatten and heard their bellies squeak together with smeared sweat. She saw the scissored legs of Bonnita and the flash of red flesh between her legs. She watched her wide mouth close over the small breasts of the Samburu slave. Mathilde leant forward and put her hand over the Caribbean's offered pubis. Bonnita writhed her hips and Mathilde's fingers slipped inside. She stroked and pinched the bud of Bonnita's erect clitoris. Bonnita moaned and moved her legs further apart. Mathilde put her lips to the girl's thighs and began to lick and suck. The slave-girl kissed Mathilde and stroked her bottom, slipping her fingers beneath her buttocks and slapping her swollen sex parts. The two concubines moaned in unison.

Afterwards, Mathilde asked the slave, 'What is your name, my dear?'

'Iva,' said the girl, smiling broadly.

'Iva, you will attend me from now on,' said the contented Mathilde.

Dr Valentine was in her white coat, attending to the palace clinic. The wives waited with their small children. The girls were kept quiet while the boys were noisy and allowed to behave badly. They threw almond bread at each other and shouted and pulled each other's hair. They leapt around and jumped up and down on the sofas. Their mothers smiled and patted them as if they were naughty puppies.

Mathilde enjoyed these clinics. It was the only time she felt whole. She was proud of her body and the power of her sexuality over the sultan, but she was in peril of losing her identity. She had been thinking more about Olensky these last few days than she had for a quite a while. When she was first captured it was as if she had been bereaved – her life, her family and her lover had all been taken from her. She had tried not to think about it because it hurt too much. Lately, though, she seemed to have a little power of her own. As a medic, she was needed by the palace inhabitants. She hadn't yet thought about how to bring about an escape from the sultan, but it was always in the back of her mind.

She knew the sultana liked and admired her. She persuaded the sultan to get the medical supplies Mathilde told her they needed. Things were changing in the harem too, and the concubines enjoyed far better medical care than they had ever had. The problem was, Mathilde reasoned, the sultana liked her too much and would not be eager to help her achieve her freedom.

The sultan was practically in love with her, she thought, but he would have to be tricked if she was to get away from his omnipotence. He was no fool. And the handsome young Omah .... could she persuade Omah to help?

One morning, as she rode her mare back to the harem,

she saw Omah galloping towards her across the hills. His face was covered but she could not fail to recognise the masculine beauty of his shape and his proud bearing. He had matured physically in the few weeks since his birthday and the flowering of his sexuality. She was proud that she had helped to bring about this maturity. They had made love daily since the first time.

He rode up to her and reined in his horse.

'Mathilde! Have you finished your clinic?'

'Yes, just finished. Did you want me?'

'You know I always want you.' He leant over and kissed her.

They turned their horses and rode away from the direction of the harem, making love in a tented camp under a billowing white cotton roof. The youth wanted her to show him how to please a woman. He learnt quickly and eagerly. She held his fingers and helped him to explore her soft flesh, showing him her erogenous zones. She bade him kiss the inside of her arm, the back of her knee, the sole of her foot. She told him to part her buttocks and lick her dark, hidden hole. She held open her sex for him to lick and kiss her there. Her breasts were caressed gently and her sex was penetrated deeply. He was an ideal student of love. She drew patterns of nail marks on his dark, honey-coloured skin. His back was etched with the marks of her admiration. He gripped her thighs and left bruises.

'Feel me there, behind my sex. Slap my bottom and touch my sex at the same time. Yes, like that, yes!' She kissed him passionately when he did it right. She ignored him if he did not try hard enough.

They made love until the sun began to sink and then they went back to the harem.

The sultan was waiting for Omah. He stood, imperious and rather sinister-looking, his mouth covered against the blowing sand. He nodded curtly at Mathilde. She nodded back and dismounted, then gave her mare to a servant and went back to the harem.

'Did you want me, Father?'

'No, I wanted Mathilde, but she did not return at the usual time from the clinic.' He tried to lighten his voice but his heart was heavy.

'Sorry, father, it won't happen again,' said Omah.

Next day, Omah woke with an erection. He called for slave-girls to relieve him. Two little Nubians leapt on to his bed and grabbed his cock. One kissed it and the other rubbed his belly and stroked his balls. He rubbed their bare little bottoms and made them squirm. They played happily with his cock and balls and kissed his pretty mouth. They were not allowed to fuck him, only to relieve his stress. It was a strangely erotic duty. He did give them some enjoyment too, but only in a desultory manner, lazily caressing them. His main concern was for his own satisfaction – and that was their one aim too. Their little breasts tingled as he touched their brown, swollen areolae. He liked to hear their giggles as his penis throbbed in their fingers. They were sprayed with his snowy foam, and they rubbed it over themselves in glee. They washed him and left him to doze again before his breakfast.

His father was jealous of his success with his favourite white concubine. The sultan had changed since the murder of his brother. He had become twitchy and easily alarmed, and he was suddenly aware of his own mortality. He was scared of getting old. He had offered his concubines to his son as a matter of course, but now he found he was resentful. He was shocked at his own feelings of inadequacy. He could only get an erection these days while he was hurting a woman. He had always gained satisfaction from whipping and spanking but now he could not achieve an erection until he had caused a woman to scream.

Janet and Rosemary McKinnon were frightened at this

234

development. Their master was becoming as sadistic as his late brother. They spoke together about his change of character and thought to mention it to Mathilde, who had not had much experience of his cruelty lately because she was spending most days in the arms of Omah.

They showed her their recently acquired bruises. She was alarmed.

'How did he do this to you?' she asked.

'He tied us up and beat us with a cat-o'-nine-tails and masturbated over us,' said Rosemary, sobbing. 'It is intolerable!'

'He is suffering some form of paranoia, I think,' Mathilde said. 'You must be careful not to be alone with him.'

'Ha! And how are we supposed to do that?' said Rosemary. 'He has total control of us all. How are we to protect ourselves if he chooses to be brutal?'

'I think the time has come for us to try and escape,' said Mathilde quietly.

'Oh yes?' Janet McKinnon laughed. 'And how are we to do that?'

'Leave it to me. I'll work something out,' said a pensive Mathilde, rubbing arnica into their backs.

Omah had no idea that his father was jealous of him. He carried on in the way of all callow youth, looking only for pleasure and sexual release. He rode hard and swam each day. He took the boat out, usually with Mathilde, and swam and made love.

One day, she asked if she might learn to steer the boat. He stood behind her as she held the brass wheel.

'What's that for?' she asked.

'That's the throttle.'

'And what is that?'

'That's the radio.'

'A radio?'

'Yes, my father's boat has all the modern conveniences.'

'And what is that?' She reached behind her to press his semi-erection through his robe.

'That is my secret weapon. I will show you in a minute,' he laughed.

That day he had insisted that she wear her doctor's white coat. He cut the engine. They kissed. He felt up her legs and under the coat. She wore nothing underneath. He pushed his fingers between her legs and felt them slip into the moist, warm purse. He undid the top buttons of her coat, revealing her breasts. He nibbled the pink nipples, stretching them and making them hard.

'Pretend you are my doctor and you are examining me,' he ordered her.

'Where does it hurt?' she asked, smiling.

'Oh, between my legs, Doctor. I have a small pain in my groin.'

'Remove your robe,' she ordered.

He stripped without modesty. He knew he was beautiful. She placed her cool hands on his flat stomach.

'There?' she said.

'No, further down, Doctor, between my legs.'

Her hands slid down across the smooth belly and pelvis to the hollow of his groin. She pressed it.

'Do you feel anything there?'

His penis, which had been lying half-erect, stirred.

'Not there, further down.'

'There?' She held his scrotum sac in her soft hands, gently stroking the puckered flesh, feeling the hard balls within.

He squirmed and drew in his breath between his white teeth.

'Yes, I feel something there,' he whispered.

'Yes, I'm sure you do,' she said.

His penis rose from his thigh and stood proud, as only

a very young prick can do, straight up so it pressed his stomach. She could not help but admire the beauty of its form. She stroked it. It quivered. She held the stalk between her fingers and pushed to the base. She held his cock under his scrotum at the root and squeezed gently, while stretching the skin of his penis up to the helmet with her other hand.

'Is that better?' she asked playfully. 'Does it hurt?'

'Oh, it hurts, it hurts, but it is wonderful! Your healing touch is just what I need, Doctor,' he groaned.

She renewed the pressure of her hands, watching his face contort in pleasure.

'This is a new experimental cure for your unhappy condition,' she said, and leant forward to take his silky rod into her mouth. She first licked her lips and then opened her mouth wide to take the cock slowly into it. He moaned as she sucked firmly. She still held him at the root and stroked his scrotum. He pushed on her head. He came into her mouth almost immediately and she swallowed the musky, salty emissions.

They lay in the bottom of the boat under a blue canvas canopy. His arms were around her. She shifted and half sat, looking at his lovely face. Yes, he was like his father, especially the hooked nose and the fleshy lips. But Omah's lips had an upward curl and were humorous. His father looked more cruel than ever at the moment.

'Omah, it is my turn. You must seduce me now,' she told him.

'All right! What do you wish me to do?' He toyed with one of her breasts, squeezing the nipple between his fingers.

'Oh, pretend to be the young son of a sultan and in love with me. Pretend to rescue me from your cruel father. Pretend – ' She stopped. Omah was sitting up, his face thunderous. 'Omah, what is it?' she asked.

'Nothing! Nothing!' He pressed her to him violently and tore at her white coat, ripping it open and exposing

237

her full breasts and firm belly. He pressed hard on her flaring hips and pulled her legs apart. His penis was erect again. He pushed it into her with no foreplay. He held her tight and fucked her violently. Aggressive thrusts pressed her back into the bottom of the boat. He kissed her lips and drew blood. She swooned under his hard embrace, welcoming the pressure of his strong hands on her arms and the bruising of her lips.

Her juices ran. Her mouth was dry. He rammed his fleshy rod into her again and again. He wanted to despoil her, fuck her, make her come violently. She cried out as her whole body became inflamed. Her orgasm flooded her and her neck curved back, her throat offered to his mouth. His spasms lasted a long time. He pulled out of her immediately and it was as if she had had a leg removed, or an arm. She was bereft.

He drove the boat back to the harbour, not answering her casual questions. She realised she had gone too far in her cloaked suggestions. She had hoped to plant the idea of her escape in his head and encourage him to see the folly of this unnatural existence. She pretended not to notice his discomfiture. She joked about her medical coat, and the tears and stains on it.

When they reached the harbour, he dismissed her with a tentative kiss on one cheek and she went back into the concubines' quarters.

Chapter Thirty

*T*he sultan rode out into the desert with his son. The day was hazy. A cloud of dust hung heavily and they wore their protective scarves over their mouths and noses.

It was difficult to speak.

'Have you chosen your concubine, my son?' asked the sultan.

'Yes, Father, I thought you realised ... I have chosen the doctor,' Omah said apologetically.

'I see!' The sultan's mouth was a straight line under the cloth.

'I hope you do not mind?' Omah asked, with a worried tone to his voice.

'No, of course not. But you realise that you cannot take her with you when you go back to college?'

'Oh, of course I realise that, Father. I will of course leave her in your tender care.'

'Hmm!' This was the sultan's last comment on the subject.

They cantered easily, their steeds sweating in the heat.

'Your other birthday gift should have arrived by now. It was ordered for you some time ago.'

'Another gift, Father?'

'Yes, Omah, I have bought you a new Arab stallion. He is coming from the mainland. The boat should have been here by now.'

'A stallion? Thank you, Father!' The boy looked delighted and his father was pleased. The sultan tried to dismiss the stab of jealousy which had recently marred his relationship with his son. He stabbed his horse in the flanks with his spurs and cantered on ahead.

Baron Olensky was tanned dark as leather from the sea air. He looked more like an Arab trader than ever. He was losing money on this search for the kidnapped doctor but his safari business and his duties as game warden in Tsavo would have to wait. Mathilde Valentine was more important than anything else. He had thought that maybe the hurt of the loss of her would fade, but he still felt the pain of her disappearance as if it were yesterday. He felt he had failed her. He had made it his business to look after her, had insisted on taking her into the bush, and had left her on her own at his *shamba*. It was his fault she had been kidnapped.

Olensky wanted her desperately. He could only think of her soft lips on his and her breasts squashed to his chest. He remembered the firelight at *Nyumba ya Simba* dancing on her hair. He felt the pressure of her strong legs wrapped around his neck. He tasted her salty juices on his tongue.

They sailed with the prevailing wind, northward towards the Arabian coast. They passed other dhow, taking fruit and vegetables along the coastal strip. Coir, ivory, animal skins and spices were carried, and Sabah Madaan had decided to trade a little along the way to help with the cost of the journey.

The dhow called in at a small port in Somalia to unload a cargo of coconut husks for the coir industry. Olensky, with Sabah Madaan and his men, went to a harbourside bar for refreshment. The small bar was busy with traders making deals. The baron fitted in well with the other Arabs. His robes were spotless and his face dark. He had lost a little weight since Mathilde had been kidnapped, but his extraordinary eyes still glittered with an orange-brown light. Madaan was talking to a thin man with a short beard. He called Olensky over to them.

'This man has a horse to deliver to an island sultan. His dhow has sprung a serious leak and he must let someone else do the job. What do you think?'

'Where is this island?'

'Not too far. Abizir, just off the north Somali coast, between here and Arabia,' said the Arab. 'This horse is costing me money. I have to feed it and stable it, and it is an unbroken stallion, very difficult to handle.'

'Cash on delivery?' asked the baron, pretending to be uninterested in the deal.

'Yes, cash on delivery to the Sultan of Abizir,' said the swarthy little character.

'All right, we'll do it.'

They shook hands on the deal and Madaan made arrangements to pick up the horse from the stable where it was being temporarily housed on the dock.

The baron felt a surge of excitement. They were nearly there. He would have his lover in his arms again before long.

They collected the horse, which reared and fought as they took him from his stall and led him, screaming and foaming, to the dhow. They had to fix a special ramp and blindfold the beast before they could lead it up on to the boat.

The horse took some corn from Olensky, who stroked his nose and flanks and soothed his nerves with soft whistling and a calming humming. He took off its blindfold and saw the frightened eyes regard him with interest. The baron missed wild creatures, and he felt an affinity with this unbroken horse. His soothing hands quieted the creature. It whinnied and snickered. Olensky gave it more food from his hands. The stallion stopped jerking his head and stayed quiet at last.

They set off on the evening tide, pulling up all their wide sail to catch the prevailing breeze.

Omah thought of what Mathilde had said to him the day before. He knew she had not been joking. He had it in his power to set her free from the harem. He could marry her, if she would have him. Or he could take her away from Abizir and let her go back to her other life. If he let her go, there was the risk that she would tell of the murder of his uncle. He would be implicated. He must marry her, then she could not give evidence against him. She could travel with him outside of Abizir. She would still be veiled, of course, but she would have more freedom than she had at present.

He knew he would have to have his father's permission before he told Mathilde of his plan.

That evening, there was the usual dinner party. Sumptuous food was prepared each evening and several concubines were invited to share the feast and the lovemaking that usually followed the meal. On this particular evening there were two pretty concubines from Egypt present.

'Father, may I talk to you?' Omah asked nervously.

'Go ahead.' The sultan clapped his hands to dismiss the slave-girls and concubines. Omah cleared his throat. 'What is it, my son? Spit it out.'

'I wondered what you would think about me marrying the doctor,' he blurted.

'Marry her? Marry my favourite concubine? How dare you suggest such a thing!' The sultan stood and strode up and down the dining room, furious. He could feel his blood boil. 'You young idiot!' he snarled.

Omah swallowed hard. He had not expected absolute, unmitigated approval of his plan but he was not prepared for this angry outburst. He had not realised that Mathilde was such a favourite. He bit his tongue. What a fool he had been not to see that!

'Father, I . . . I take it back. It was a foolish idea. I am infatuated; you know how it is?' He laughed and shrugged his handsome shoulders as if he had been joking.

The sultan was appeased.

'Yes, I know how it is,' he said, pleased that his son realised that he had been stupid. 'Now, no more of this tomfoolery, Omah. Let us get back to the entertainment of the evening.'

He clapped his hands again and his audience reappeared. The eunuchs poured wine while the dancing girls and musicians moved into position. The two Egyptian virgins sat on the royal laps and kissed father and son. They were attired in transparent gowns, with thighs and pubis exposed. Their high, round breasts peeped over the top of their garments like little rosy apples with the stalks still connected. Wine had been imbibed in great quantities, and father and son were sleepy and amorous. The Egyptian concubines were oiled, shaved and rouged, and flower-scented perfume rose from their pores. Their breath was sweet and fresh. Omah's concubine got his cock out and licked its head. He enjoyed this homage more than any other. He held her head down and she slipped the erect young cock into her round mouth. He groaned. His father was having trouble with his erection. It would not harden even though his virgin concubine was rubbing it between her legs. She looked to the sultan.

'What shall I do with it, my lord?' she asked.

'Suck me, you idiot,' he bellowed. 'No, wait, let me mark you for your insolence and stupidity.' He clapped his hands and a eunuch placed a riding crop into his hand.

He pulled the girl on to her stomach over his lap, but

he could not hit her properly in this position. He pushed her off and told the eunuchs to strap her to the wall. They did this, though the girl whimpered and begged for mercy.

Omah had come into his concubine's mouth and was watching his father in trepidation. The girl who had given him relief had scuttled off to a corner and was crouched there, watching in terror as her companion felt the first blow from the riding crop.

The sultan wore a smile of fury on his handsome face. He raised the crop again and hit her. She screamed. His cock remained slumbering on his thigh. It had shrivelled to a purple plum. He raised the crop again and again.

Omah called out. 'Father! Father! Stop!'

The concubine screamed and then slumped at her bonds, quiet.

Omah did not know what to do. His father was foaming at the mouth, still wielding the crop. His eyes had glazed. Omah stepped forward.

'Father, that's enough!' He took the crop from the sultan's trembling hands. His father sat down on the floor, as if he was hypnotised. He sat, slobbering from his mouth. Sweat poured down his face.

Omah cut the concubine free and told the eunuchs to fetch Mathilde. The other concubine ran to her friend and held her in her arms.

'What has he done?' she sobbed.

'Leave us,' Omah ordered, and the girl ran from the room.

Mathilde arrived at the scene and took in the situation immediately.

'Get your father to the couch,' she told Omah. 'Fetch water and dressings,' she ordered the eunuchs.

'And what has he done now?' she asked Omah, as she saw the wreck he had made of the concubine.

The sultan was moaning quietly to himself, but his words were unintelligible. Omah was very concerned.

'Has he had a breakdown of some sort?' he asked Mathilde.

'I'm not qualified to say, really,' she said, 'but he is probably suffering from some form of shock. I think he should be taken to his room and kept quiet for a while.'

She attended to the concubine's cuts and had her transferred to the harem sick room.

Next day, the sultan's condition had not changed. He was quiet, but acted as if he was alone, talking to himself. He could not react to any other person. Omah tried to speak to him but it was as if he was invisible. The sultan looked straight through him. Mathilde had given him a sedative, made up from herbs by the old herbalist at the palace. Omah's mother had been called to the harem by Mathilde. She was shocked at her husband's condition.

'Will he recover?' she asked Mathilde.

'I don't know. Probably. He has had a shock and I think he is trying to shut it out; pretend it hasn't happened. I have seen this happen before. He must be kept quiet. He might well recover.'

But the sultana thought her husband looked old for the first time ever. He had shrunk. His eyes looked empty. He was diminished. She sobbed silently and held him tight. He didn't seem to know she was there.

Chapter Thirty-One

*O*mah was in the white concubines' quarters. Mathilde, Rosemary and Janet were dressed in masculine
Arab robes, completely covering their features and their
female shape. They each carried small cotton drawstring
bags containing all the precious stones that had ever
been given to them by the sultan.

Omah walked with them to the horses and they all
mounted. They rode away from the harem and the
Sultan of Abizir. They passed the palace of the Sultana
of Abizir, and heard the tinkling laughter of children
behind the high walls. They reached the small harbour
and Omah gave Mathilde the gold keyring. On it were
two keys. One was to start the boat's engine.

'What is the other key for?' Mathilde asked.

'To release you from your bondage collars,' he said.

'Will you do it please?' she asked, turning her face to
his.

Omah turned the key on all three bondage collars.

'Oh, that feels so good,' said Rosemary, rubbing her
white neck.

'Thank you for everything you have done for us,' said
Mathilde, and kissed him on the mouth.

The three women clambered into the motorboat, tripping in their long garments.

'Are you sure you will be all right?' Mathilde asked the youth.

'He is my father. I must stay with him and look after him. You know that.' He looked suddenly older, and his black eyes glinted with a sort of pride.

'Yes, I realise that. You are very brave. You will be a good leader of your people,' Mathilde told him.

He stood and watched as the craft drew further from the shore. He waved his arm once and then took the bridles of the three horses and rode back towards the harem, not looking back.

The women were quiet but excited. The escape had been arranged very hurriedly by Omah. The boat was full of fuel and there was extra in cans. They had enough food and water to last them two days. Omah had given Mathilde a map of the coastline. He had told them to keep close to the shore. They were to head south towards Kenya. No doubt they would have to abandon the boat, which was hardly seaworthy, and hire a dhow to take them most of the way, but the motorboat would get them part of the way and hopefully far enough from the island.

'He is very brave, you know. He should have killed us really,' said Mathilde.

'Why do you say that?' asked Rosemary.

'She's right,' said Janet. 'We could tell the authorities about the murder of old Jerry and implicate Omah.'

'But we won't, will we?' said Mathilde. 'We won't!'

They cruised along for one day and one night with no problems. They were heading in the right direction, according to the compass. But on the second day they had to go outside the reef because of unexpectedly shallow water and jagged rocks which threatened to hole the fragile craft. The sea on the inside of the reef was turquoise, clear and calm. Outside the reef were huge waves and a strong current. Steering was difficult and so was keeping a straight course. They had rationed their water and still had some left, but on the third day they had nearly run out of fuel. They would have to go ashore and get fresh supplies, though that was debatable in a small settlement, and they were worried that they were not yet far enough from the influence of the Sultan of Abizir. He could have recovered from his state of shock and sent men after the escaped concubines. Omah would not be able to protect them from his wrath if they were taken back. If they could not get any more fuel, they would have to try and hire a sailing boat.

Mathilde steered the boat towards the land and looked for a gap in the reef. She negotiated it successfully and made for a crescent beach which looked depressingly void of life, trying to hide her anxiety from the others. Suddenly the engine failed. She drew out the throttle and flooded the engine. It would not start. The boat rocked gently on the waves. Even worse, they were not floating towards the coast but out to sea again. Mathilde tried again to start the motor. She suddenly remembered the radio and tried to work that, but she could hear only a faint hiss. She flicked switches and talked into the microphone. Nothing! She tried again. The two Mrs McKinnons were beginning to panic.

'Oh, for goodness sake! We should have stayed in the harem,' said Janet.

'And be beaten to death?' said Rosemary. 'There must be oars on this wee boat, aren't there?' she asked, and started looking around.

They found a pair tucked into the narrow space under the bow deck. They found rowlocks too. They fixed the unwieldy oars into them and began to pull. Mathilde steered the boat along the coast. If they could reach a harbour they could perhaps get their boat mended and buy fuel. They had plenty of money in the form of jewels. But the boat, in spite of their best efforts, was drifting away from the shore instead of towards it. The outgoing tide was dragging them inexorably out over the now well-covered reef into rough waters.

A cry came from Olensky's dhow.

'Boat ahead!' called the sailor at the mast-head.

'Ignore it,' said Madaan. 'The island we are looking for can't be too far away.'

'But it is drifting. It is in trouble,' said the sailor, looking through his telescope.

'All right, let's go and see,' said Madaan.

The small boat drifted out with the current. The women were utterly exhausted from the rowing. They saw the dhow ahead, and as they drew closer, they could see the crew – black-skinned, swarthy men. They could also see a horse, tied up in the bow.

'It is the birthday stallion for Omah,' said Mathilde. 'Oh my God, we are going to be discovered.'

The three women awaited their fate. They held each other tight, sobbing quietly.

'It is no use,' said Rosemary. 'They'll realise we are women and that this boat is obviously not ours.'

'Don't give up hope just like that. We've come this far,' said Mathilde. 'Let me do the talking.'

The dhow drew close to the motorboat.

'What have we here?' said Madaan as he and Olensky boarded the craft.

Mathilde held her scarf over her face and said gruffly, in broken Arabic, 'We have broken down and cannot restart the motor.'

Madaan and Olensky looked hard at the three 'Arabs'. Mathilde stared at the 'Arab' trader. The trader looked strangely familiar. He smiled disbelievingly and looked into her eyes. His eyes were golden and fiery. In them she could see the red earth of his beloved bush, the mammoth baobab trees and the yellow lions.

Her heart jumped in her bosom. She threw off the cloth that hid her face.

'Jorge! Is it you?' she cried in disbelief.

'Mathilde!' he said, unable to say anything more.

Mathilde threw herself into Olensky's arms. They had found each other. Her lion lover was in her arms again. They held each other tightly, as if someone was trying to separate them. She felt herself bruised by his strong arms.

'My God, Mathilde, we were on our way to find you, and you find us!' he laughed.

The three women laughed hysterically, joyous at their rescue. At Madaan's suggestion, they let the sultan's boat drift away and left the bags of jewels in it, to give any finders of the small craft the idea that the women had perished. They did remove most of the better diamonds, though, at Janet McKinnon's suggestion.

'We earned these,' she said, fondling the glittering gems.

Janet McKinnon was pleased to see the baron again and kissed him in delight. Rosemary was belatedly introduced to him and the women were given water. Madaan and his crew grinned in delight at the sight of the three white women, touching their white skin in wonder.

'Leave them be,' barked Madaan. 'They have had enough of men for a while, no doubt.'

Janet and Rosemary smiled cheerfully at the captain and thanked him for his thoughtfulness.

'May we go below and wash?' said Janet.

'Of course. Please make yourselves at home,' said the baron.

The women washed, then ate the food offered to them by the cook. Rosemary and Janet found a pile of blankets in the cabin and lay down together. Mathilde went on deck to be with Olensky again.

'What shall we do with the stallion?' said Madaan to

the baron. They had changed direction and were heading south, back to their homeland.

'Well, we could sell him at the nearest town. But the animal might be recognised and we would run the risk of being accused of stealing it. We'd better take him back with us to Kenya.'

'Or we could turn around and deliver it to the island of Abizir and collect the money,' said Madaan.

'No!' said Mathilde firmly. 'I don't want to go back to the island of Abizir ever again. Knowing the sultan's son, as I do, I feel sure he would be only too pleased to know that the animal will be cared for properly.'

'How well do you know the sultan's son?' the baron asked her, smiling.

'I'll tell you all about it another time, my darling.' Mathilde kissed him reassuringly and held him tight around his waist. 'Did I tell you how handsome you look dressed as an Arab?'

'Did I tell you how delicious you look in those masculine clothes?' he replied.

She turned her face to his and bathed in the glow of love that came from his gaze.

'Let's go home,' said the baron. He took off his gold chain and went to place it around Mathilde's neck.

'Oh no!' she said. 'Please, no! I shall *never* wear chains again.'

Later, they lay in each other's arms, naked in the dark night.

'And what do you want, when we get back to Kenya?' her lover asked.

'I want to tell my family I am safe, and then – '

'Then would you ... would you do me the honour of becoming my wife?' He touched her cheek delicately and felt the tears which came with his words.

'Oh yes, Jorge, I will be your wife – if I can carry on working also.'

'My home will be yours, whenever you want to be

there,' he said, imagining that she wanted to work away from him, in the city.

'Could I set up a hospital in the bush, do you think?'

'You could do anything you set your mind to, my darling,' he said, and kissed her.

LOOK OUT FOR THE ALL-NEW BLACK LACE BOOKS – AVAILABLE NOW!

All books priced £6.99 in the UK. Please note publication dates apply to the UK only. For other territories, please contact your retailer.

DRIVEN BY DESIRE
Savannah Smythe
ISBN 0 352 33799 0

When Rachel's husband abandons both her and his taxi-cab business and flees the country, she is left to pick up the pieces. However, this is a blessing in disguise as Rachel, along with her friend Sharma, transforms his business into an exclusive chauffeur service for discerning gentlemen. What Rachel doesn't know is that two of her regular clients are jewel thieves with exotic tastes in sexual experimentation. As Rachel is lured into an underworld lifestyle she finds a familiar face is involved in some very shady activity! **Another cracking story of strong women and sexy double dealing from Savannah Smythe.**

FIGHTING OVER YOU
Laura Hamilton
ISBN 0 352 33795 8

Yasmin and U seem like the perfect couple. She's a scriptwriter and he's a magazine editor who has a knack for tapping into the latest trends. One evening, however, U confesses to Yasmin that he's 'having a thing' with a nineteen-year-old violinist. Amelia, the violinist, turns out to be a catalyst for a series of erotic experiments that even Yasmin finds intriguing. In a haze of absinthe and wild abandon, all parties find answers to questions about their sexuality they were once too afraid to ask. **Contemporary erotica at its best from the author of the bestselling *Fire and Ice*.**

Coming in July

COUNTRY PLEASURES
Primula Bond
ISBN 0 352 33810 5

Janie and Sally escape to the countryside hoping to get some sun and relaxation. When the weather turns nasty, the two women find themselves confined to their remote cottage with little to do except eat, drink and talk about men. They soon become the focus of attention for the lusty farmers in the area who are well built, down-to-earth and very different from the boys they have been dating in town. **Lust-filled pursuits in the English countryside.**

THE RELUCTANT PRINCESS
Patty Glenn
ISBN 0 532 33809 1

Martha's a rich valley girl who's living on the wrong side of the tracks and hanging out with Hollywood hustlers. Things were OK when her bodyguard Gus was looking after her, but now he's in hospital Martha's gone back to her bad old ways. When she meets mean, moody and magnificent private investigator Joaquin Lee, the sexual attraction between them is instant and intense. If Martha can keep herself on the straight and narrow for a year, her family will let her have access to her inheritance. Lee reckons he can help out while pocketing a cut for himself. **A dynamic battle of wills between two very stubborn, very sexy characters.**

ARIA APPASSIONATA
Juliet Hastings
ISBN 0 352 33056 2

Tess Challoner has made it. She is going to play Carmen in a new production of the opera that promises to be as raunchy and explicit as it is intelligent. But Tess needs to learn a lot about passion and desire before the opening night. Tony Varguez, the handsome but jealous Spanish tenor, takes on the task of her education. When Tess finds herself drawn to a desirable new member of the cast, she knows she's playing with fire. **Life imitating art – with dramatically sexual consequences.**

Coming in August

WILD IN THE COUNTRY
Monica Belle
ISBN 0 352 33824 5

When Juliet Eden is sacked for having sex with a sous-chef, she leaves the prestigious London kitchen where she's been working and heads for the country. Alone in her inherited cottage, boredom soon sets in – until she discovers the rural delights of poaching, and of the muscular young gamekeeper who works the estate. When the local landowner falls for her, things are looking better still, but threaten to turn sour when her ex-boss, Gabriel, makes an unexpected appearance. **City vs country in Monica Belle's latest story of rustic retreats and sumptuous feasts!**

THE TUTOR
Portia Da Costa
ISBN 0 352 32946 7

When Rosalind Howard becomes Julian Hadey's private librarian, she soon finds herself attracted by his persuasive charms and distinguished appearance. He is an unashamed sensualist who, together with his wife, Celeste, has hatched an intriguing challenge for their new employee. As well as cataloguing their collection of erotica, Rosie is expected to educate Celeste's young and beautiful cousin David in the arts of erotic love. **A long-overdue reprint of this arousing tale of erotic initiation written by a pioneer of women's sex fiction.**

Black Lace Booklist

Information is correct at time of printing. To avoid disappointment
check availability before ordering. Go to www.blacklace-books.co.uk.
All books are priced £6.99 unless another price is given.

BLACK LACE BOOKS WITH A CONTEMPORARY SETTING

☐ IN THE FLESH Emma Holly	ISBN 0 352 33498 3	£5.99
☐ A PRIVATE VIEW Crystalle Valentino	ISBN 0 352 33308 1	£5.99
☐ SHAMELESS Stella Black	ISBN 0 352 33485 1	£5.99
☐ INTENSE BLUE Lyn Wood	ISBN 0 352 33496 7	£5.99
☐ THE NAKED TRUTH Natasha Rostova	ISBN 0 352 33497 5	£5.99
☐ A SPORTING CHANCE Susie Raymond	ISBN 0 352 33501 7	£5.99
☐ TAKING LIBERTIES Susie Raymond	ISBN 0 352 33357 X	£5.99
☐ A SCANDALOUS AFFAIR Holly Graham	ISBN 0 352 33523 8	£5.99
☐ THE NAKED FLAME Crystalle Valentino	ISBN 0 352 33528 9	£5.99
☐ ON THE EDGE Laura Hamilton	ISBN 0 352 33534 3	£5.99
☐ LURED BY LUST Tania Picarda	ISBN 0 352 33533 5	£5.99
☐ THE HOTTEST PLACE Tabitha Flyte	ISBN 0 352 33536 X	£5.99
☐ THE NINETY DAYS OF GENEVIEVE Lucinda Carrington	ISBN 0 352 33070 8	£5.99
☐ DREAMING SPIRES Juliet Hastings	ISBN 0 352 33584 X	
☐ THE TRANSFORMATION Natasha Rostova	ISBN 0 352 33311 1	
☐ SIN.NET Helena Ravenscroft	ISBN 0 352 33598 X	
☐ TWO WEEKS IN TANGIER Annabel Lee	ISBN 0 352 33599 8	
☐ HIGHLAND FLING Jane Justine	ISBN 0 352 33616 1	
☐ PLAYING HARD Tina Troy	ISBN 0 352 33617 X	
☐ SYMPHONY X Jasmine Stone	ISBN 0 352 33629 3	
☐ STRICTLY CONFIDENTIAL Alison Tyler	ISBN 0 352 33624 2	
☐ SUMMER FEVER Anna Ricci	ISBN 0 352 33625 0	
☐ CONTINUUM Portia Da Costa	ISBN 0 352 33120 8	
☐ OPENING ACTS Suki Cunningham	ISBN 0 352 33630 7	
☐ FULL STEAM AHEAD Tabitha Flyte	ISBN 0 352 33637 4	
☐ A SECRET PLACE Ella Broussard	ISBN 0 352 33307 3	
☐ GAME FOR ANYTHING Lyn Wood	ISBN 0 352 33639 0	

| ☐ VELVET GLOVE Emma Holly | ISBN 0 352 33448 7 |
| ☐ VIRTUOSO Katrina Vincenzi-Thyre | ISBN 0 352 32907 6 |

BLACK LACE BOOKS WITH AN HISTORICAL SETTING

☐ PRIMAL SKIN Leona Benkt Rhys	ISBN 0 352 33500 9 £5.99
☐ DEVIL'S FIRE Melissa MacNeal	ISBN 0 352 33527 0 £5.99
☐ DARKER THAN LOVE Kristina Lloyd	ISBN 0 352 33279 4
☐ STAND AND DELIVER Helena Ravenscroft	ISBN 0 352 33340 5 £5.99
☐ THE CAPTIVATION Natasha Rostova	ISBN 0 352 33234 4
☐ MINX Megan Blythe	ISBN 0 352 33638 2
☐ JULIET RISING Cleo Cordell	ISBN 0 352 32938 6
☐ DEMON'S DARE Melissa MacNeal	ISBN 0 352 33683 8
☐ DIVINE TORMENT Janine Ashbless	ISBN 0 352 33719 2
☐ SATAN'S ANGEL Melissa MacNeal	ISBN 0 352 33726 5
☐ THE INTIMATE EYE Georgia Angelis	ISBN 0 352 33004 X
☐ OPAL DARKNESS Cleo Cordell	ISBN 0 352 33033 3
☐ SILKEN CHAINS Jodi Nicol	ISBN 0 352 33143 7
☐ EVIL'S NIECE Melissa MacNeal	ISBN 0 352 33781 8
☐ ACE OF HEARTS Lisette Allen	ISBN 0 352 33059 7
☐ A GENTLEMAN'S WAGER Madelynne Ellis	ISBN 0 352 33800 8

BLACK LACE ANTHOLOGIES

☐ WICKED WORDS 5 Various	ISBN 0 352 33642 0
☐ WICKED WORDS 6 Various	ISBN 0 352 33590 0
☐ WICKED WORDS 7 Various	ISBN 0 352 33743 5
☐ WICKED WORDS 8 Various	ISBN 0 352 33787 7
☐ THE BEST OF BLACK LACE 2 Various	ISBN 0 352 33718 4

BLACK LACE NON-FICTION

| ☐ THE BLACK LACE BOOK OF WOMEN'S SEXUAL FANTASIES Ed. Kerri Sharp | ISBN 0 352 33793 1 £6.99 |

To find out the latest information about Black Lace titles, check out the website: www.blacklace-books.co.uk or send for a booklist with complete synopses by writing to:

Black Lace Booklist, Virgin Books Ltd
Thames Wharf Studios
Rainville Road
London W6 9HA

Please include an SAE of decent size. Please note only British stamps are valid.

Our privacy policy
We will not disclose information you supply us to any other parties. We will not disclose any information which identifies you personally to any person without your express consent.

From time to time we may send out information about Black Lace books and special offers. Please tick here if you do not wish to receive Black Lace information. ❏

Please send me the books I have ticked above.

Name ....

Address ....

....

....

....

Post Code ....

Send to: Cash Sales, Black Lace Books, Thames Wharf Studios, Rainville Road, London W6 9HA.

US customers: for prices and details of how to order books for delivery by mail, call 1-800-343-4499.

Please enclose a cheque or postal order, made payable to Virgin Books Ltd, to the value of the books you have ordered plus postage and packing costs as follows:

UK and BFPO – £1.00 for the first book, 50p for each subsequent book.

Overseas (including Republic of Ireland) – £2.00 for the first book, £1.00 for each subsequent book.

If you would prefer to pay by VISA, ACCESS/MASTERCARD, DINERS CLUB, AMEX or SWITCH, please write your card number and expiry date here:

....

Signature ....

Please allow up to 28 days for delivery.